THE MAN THAT
GOT AWAY

THE MAN THAT GOT AWAY

A Constable Twitten Mystery

LYNNE TRUSS

R A V E N BOOKS

LONDON • OXFORD • NEW YORK • NEW DELHI • SYDNEY

RAVEN BOOKS
Bloomsbury Publishing Plc
50 Bedford Square, London, WC1B 3DP, UK

BLOOMSBURY, RAVEN BOOKS and the Raven Books logo are trademarks of
Bloomsbury Publishing Plc

First published in Great Britain 2019

A catalogue record for this book is available from the British Library

ISBN: HB: 978-1-4088-9054-7; TPB: 978-1-4088-9053-0; EBOOK: 978-1-4088-9056-1

2 4 6 8 10 9 7 5 3 1

Typeset by Integra Software Services Pvt. Ltd.
Printed and bound in Great Britain by CPI Group (UK) Ltd, Croydon CR0 4YY

MIX
Paper from
responsible sources
FSC® C020471

To find out more about our authors and books visit www.bloomsbury.com
and sign up for our newsletters

For Anthony Goff

Today, in 1956, the English class system is
essentially tripartite – there exist an upper,
a middle, and a lower class. It is solely by its
language that the upper class is clearly marked off
from the others.

> Alan Ross, 'U and Non-U: An Essay in
> Sociological Linguistics', from *Noblesse Oblige*,
> edited by Nancy Mitford (1956)

Every Saturday night at 8
We want to drown our sorrows
So off we goes to the Waxworks
To look at the Chamber of Horrors.
There's a lovely statue of mother there
We like to see it rather –
It's nice to see her as she was
The night she strangled father.

> Hilaire Belloc

'It's my belief,' Constable Twitten announced,
'that the person who's been in charge of all things
criminal in Brighton since 1951 is in fact you,
Mrs Groynes! ... And you have been operating
from the very heart of the police station, where
bally well no one takes any notice of you!'

> From *A Shot in the Dark* (2018), concerning the
> management of crime in Brighton in 1957

One

It was a blazing day in July. The threepenny deck-chairs on Brighton seafront were in high demand; ice cream was melting fast; the aroma of cockles in vinegar wafted on the breeze, mixed with the distinctive smell of unprotected human flesh being slowly and painfully cooked on the bone. What a day to be at the seaside! If you closed your eyes, you could faintly hear – beyond the fluttering of the overhead bunting – a romantic medley from *The King and I* played by the brass band of the Grenadier Guards. Holiday-making parents watched proudly from their deck-chairs on the shingle as their pasty, knobbly offspring cavorted in ill-fitting swimsuits under the scorching sun. If they considered the issue of infant catastrophic sunburn at all, it was only to make a (small) mental note to buy calamine lotion before the end of the day.

'You look like a ruddy lobster, Charlie!' mothers called, cheerfully. 'I shall have to pop into Timothy White's, the way you're going!'

Or, 'You mark my words, Dawn! You'll bleeding well suffer tonight!'

This being 1957, of course, attitudes to tanning were not sophisticated. You exposed pale city skin to solar rays for the first time in twelve months; some of it went a nice colour while some of it burned; the burned stuff could ultimately be peeled off by a skilled relative, with the larger sheets preserved for a while as souvenir curiosities. As for sun*stroke*, the same blithe unconcern applied. A child screaming and delirious in the night was just the price you paid for a day at the seaside, like Nan breaking her last molar on a stick of rock, or having to beat your carpets outdoors for the next fortnight to get rid of all the sand.

Along the Prom, two young women immaculately dressed like flying-boat hostesses – in white high heels, buttoned blue jackets, mid-calf skirts and smart little brimless hats – smiled regally at the tourists as they walked.

'Good morning,' they said, in a general kind of greeting. 'What a lovely morning! Welcome to Brighton. Good morning. Good morning. What a charming day!'

'Cor!' was the main response, and rightly so. These two elegant figures represented a body known as the Brighton Belles, attractive women hired by the council to make themselves useful to tourists during the summer.

'Enquire of a Brighton Belle!' ran the slogan on the posters on the wall outside the station, on hoardings and even on the sides of the buses. No one arriving in Brighton could miss the advertising, which depicted nicely dressed holiday-makers (small children holding multi-coloured beachballs aloft, mothers in headscarves and fathers in hats), all with happy cartoon question marks over their heads as they approached the blue-suited beauties.

> **Whatever you want to know,**
> **Wherever you want to go,**
> **Enquire of a Brighton Belle!**

Incidentally, it had taken a small committee of men in suits around two hours to come up with that slogan. It was the grammar that worried them. Did you enquire *of*? Or enquire *from*? Opinion was divided equally, and there was an awkward *impasse* until the young clerk employed to take the minutes piped up unexpectedly that he couldn't listen to this any longer, and that 'enquire from' was technically illiterate, so at last they had their answer.

But the members of the committee were not embarrassed. They were pleased to have undertaken such a lengthy deliberation in the public interest. At this time in Brighton's iffy town-planning history, when great swathes of venerable Regency architecture were being demolished on a say-so to oblige the interests of dodgy developers, it was important that other matters municipal should appear to be above board.

Anyway, the slogan worked. Whatever they wanted to know and wherever they wanted to go, holiday-makers did enquire of a Brighton Belle. The whole scheme was a massive success. People asked the Belles everything they could think of: the quickest way to the station, how many pebbles were on the beach, which horse to back in the three-forty-five at Doncaster, where was the nearest place to spend a penny, how to tell the difference between heat rash and smallpox, and (most frequently) what time they got off work, and did they favour a Babycham, 'the genuine champagne perry'?

It wasn't easy to become a Brighton Belle: the prerequisites eliminated 99 per cent of the female population at a stroke. You had to be tall, shapely and fair of face, with excellent posture; also well-spoken, courteous, blind to class difference and fluent in at least three foreign languages. You must be helpful and kind – and a total pro at brushing off sexual advances without causing offence. Basically, you had to be Grace Kelly, only without the recent romantic attachment to a member of the House of Grimaldi (because you also had to be single).

And sometimes you didn't even wait to be enquired of.

'Good morning, madam, I see you've written some post-cards!' said one of the Brighton Belles now, stopping to speak to a slightly startled pensioner, seated in a blue-and-white-striped deck-chair. 'I can post those for you if you like.'

The pensioner – a Mrs Tucker from Bow in East London, wearing a warm coat with a fur collar despite the temperature – instinctively gripped her postcards tightly. She couldn't imagine why this uniformed glamour-puss with the cut-glass accent was bending over her with white-gloved hand outstretched.

'Mavis?' she said, uncertainly. 'Woss appnin? Woss she want?'

'She's offering to post them, Mum,' explained the buxom red-haired woman in yellow gingham, sitting beside her. In this woman's hand was an open paperback book with a drawing of a Regency buck on the cover; she'd chosen it randomly from the stall beside the Palace Pier, and the edges of its pages were browned and crisp from being displayed for weeks in the sun.

'I expect posting other people's cards is her job, poor thing,' she said, looking up at the two Belles. '*Is* it your job, dearie?' she asked, sympathetically.

'Well, yes,' said the Belle, whose name on a little gold lapel-badge was given as Phyllis. 'It's *part* of my job, anyway. I could also direct you to the Pavilion in Italian, if you wished. My colleague Adelaide here could point you to the public library in Serbo-Croat!'

Phyllis smiled and continued to hold out her hand, but the old cockney woman refused to surrender her postcards. This was the trouble with dealing with the public, Phyllis was beginning to realise: they never quite followed the script. You imagined they would be thrilled when someone who sounded like a lady-in-waiting offered them menial services; instead, you got awkward scenes like this.

'Let the poor girl do her job, then, Mum,' sighed the gingham woman, wresting the postcards from her mother, and checking they had stamps on. She handed them over quite grandly.

'There you are, dear. With our compliments. And I hope you won't mind my saying it, but I do hope you get a proper job soon.'

Luckily for Phyllis, the woman's attention was then caught elsewhere.

'Charlie!' she shrieked (with laughter) at a passing child. 'Bloody hell, you're so red now, you're blue!'

On such a bright day, it was a shame to find yourself inside a gloomy, airless wax museum, but such was young Constable Twitten's fate this morning. The great Inspector Steine, famous as a wireless personality and star of the Brighton Constabulary, had last week received an invitation from the historic 'Maison du Wax' in Russell Place, begging in very flowery language that he agree to the creation of an Inspector Steine mannequin. Hence the unusual visit.

All that was required of him (the letter had said) was his gracious consent, plus a short hour of his time sitting for the Maison du Wax's legendary blind model-maker Pierre Tussard (never for legal reasons to be confused with Tuss*aud*, the similarity of the name being a mere unfortunate coincidence); it would also be appreciated if Inspector Steine would provide without charge a spare uniform and a pair of shoes, and the standard donation of thirty-five pounds ten shillings for unavoidable expenses such as wax, human hair, rent of building, fire insurance and so on.

The generosity of this 'invitation' had of course caused general hilarity at the station.

Sergeant Brunswick, a down-to-earth man, chuckled, 'Thirty-five pounds ten! That's more than most people earn in a month! And I bet the inspector still falls for it!'

Mrs Groynes (the amusing charlady) had wholeheartedly agreed, saying that she would bet her entire – and famously comprehensive – collection of scouring powders on a positive outcome.

Only young Constable Twitten had loyally chosen to believe that vanity would not always prevail with Inspector Steine in the face of an obvious scam. Which was why, when Steine of course accepted the invitation without a second thought, Twitten had felt morally obliged to go with him to his first sitting, on this bright July day when the world outside was sizzling with life and ozone, and the world inside was airless and quiet, creepy and murky, and full of weakly spot-lit livid-coloured effigies helpfully labelled 'Winston Churchill' or 'Shirley Temple'.

Directed up the echoing stairs, Steine and Twitten passed through a room of such exhibits – the constable horrified by the general tawdriness, the inspector making enthusiastic remarks such as, 'Over here, Twitten! I had no idea Queen Mary looked like this! It turns out she's got a face like a bun!'

This particular wax museum had been part of the Brighton entertainment landscape for many years, and for this reason alone it demanded to be admired: for the way it had managed to survive despite its sheer and utter terrible-ness. To be fair, it owed its continued existence mainly to factors beyond its control, such as the regularity of sudden coastal squalls driving holiday-makers indoors, the system of landladies strictly locking out their guests until half-past four, and above all, the British seaside visitor's heroic determination to enjoy him- or herself, even when nothing remotely enjoyable was on offer.

Based loosely on the lines of the famous Madame Tussaud's, Brighton's Maison du Wax featured grisly execution tableaux (Mary Queen of Scots, complete with little dog under her skirts), effigies of notorious murderers (Dr Crippen, Neville Heath) and figures from modern-day entertainment (Gloria Swanson, Mr Pastry) – all bearing scant resemblance to the people concerned, although Robert Newton's peg-leg and threadbare parrot gave the onlooker a sporting chance of identifying him as Long John Silver. When you looked round in the gloom, you saw everywhere the same illuminated staring eyes and preoccupied (somehow constipated) expressions, the same wiry hair springing at unnatural intervals out of visible pocks in the scalp.

On the plus side, however, the museum charged only tuppence for admission, which made it the cheapest attraction on the entire South Coast.

Inspector Steine and Constable Twitten were greeted at the top of the stairs by Angélique, the middle-aged daughter of Pierre Tussard – and there was no mistaking her for someone unconnected to this dusty, moribund, phoney business. She was dressed in a high wig of ribboned brown curls and a full-length, short-sleeved frilly frock of acid green, like a revolutionary Parisian at the time of the Terror.

'Ah, *Inspecteur!*' she trilled, in a laboured French accent. 'We are *honaired* by your *press-ance.* Did you *remembair* ze thirty-five-pounds-ten?'

'I did, yes.'

'Excellent! *Zut alors.* Step zis way.'

Upstairs, in the special 'measuring room', Twitten sat in a corner, taking the whole thing in. For a keen amateur social anthropologist (and incorrigible know-all) such as he, it was all bally fascinating.

'You will meet *mon père* very soon, *monsieur*,' this bizarre figure twittered, encircling Steine's cranium with her tape measure.

'I see,' said Steine, keeping still.

'You have a fine as-we-say-in-*ze*-world-of-waxworks *bonce*, *monsieur*.'

'Well, thank you very much.'

'The making of the *statue de cire* is a combination of science and art, as you will *discovair*. Of measurement most precise, and of art most *accompli*.' She giggled in a theatrical manner and then added, 'It does not 'urt one *beet*.'

The inspector, who had seemed a little tense until now, was visibly relieved.

'It doesn't hurt, you say?'

'*Non, non, non.*'

'So you won't be turning me upside down and dipping me in hot wax like a toffee apple?'

Twitten started.

The woman shrieked with laughter. '*Non, non, non!*' she said.

This was good news for Steine. He'd been seriously wondering where they would put the stick.

'I think someone has been to see *Monsieur* Vincent Price in *ze* film *House of Wax, peut-être?*' trilled the woman.

'Well, yes,' Steine admitted. 'But not me, I assure you. I rarely visit the cinema. No, it was my sergeant. He went to see *House of Wax* several times, and said it was terrifying. He also said that if I spotted a boiling vat in here, I should exit the premises at once, the extorted thirty-five-pounds-ten notwithstanding.'

8

Twitten, from his corner, watched Angélique's reaction. Had she noticed the word 'extorted'? Apparently not. She worked on with her pretty tape measure, unperturbed. But she did explain that whereas the Vincent Price film *House of Wax* had been quite a shot in the arm to the entire wax-model business (admissions had more than doubled the year of its release), it had also engendered some very misleading and unhelpful ideas about how the models were made. In the film, Vincent Price basically killed people and then coated them in wax (like, indeed, a toffee apple). Here at the Maison du Wax, by contrast, sitters could remain alive throughout. They merely had to submit to an examination by touch – a touch so light and gentle! – from Angélique's dear blind papa.

At this point Angélique was called away to the telephone, leaving Steine and Twitten alone with a wall of hand-tinted photographs of famous people gamely posing alongside their Maison du Wax figures and looking understandably uncomfortable. Some of the figures weren't even the right height, and the celebrities were obliged to crouch slightly, or raise themselves on the balls of their feet. If you hadn't known the old model-maker was blind to begin with, you would certainly be able to deduce it from the results.

'Sir,' said Twitten, carefully. Should he mention how dreadful the wax models were here? Should he point out that '*remembair*' and '*discovair*' were not proper French words, and that 'bonce' was not a specialist term?

'What now?' snapped Steine.

Twitten decided against it. 'Nothing, sir,' he said. And, on balance, he was probably wise to do so.

Things were still uneasy between Inspector Steine and his clever new recruit. In general terms, the twenty-two-year-old Twitten's quickness of mind combined with his inability to shut up about anything – *ever* – was simply irksome to the inspector, who valued a sense of ordered calm. Moreover, Twitten's zeal for raking up old cases that had been – quite satisfactorily, in Steine's view – filed away under 'unsolved' was both unnecessary and intolerable.

However, something in particular had caused a greater strain between them. Within days of joining the Brighton Constabulary, young Constable Twitten had publicly denounced Mrs Groynes the station charlady – and this bears repetition: he had denounced *Mrs Groynes the charlady* – as a criminal mastermind responsible for a massive network of underworld operators in Brighton as well as for cold-blooded murder!

Under pressure from all directions, Twitten had now formally retracted his absurd allegations, and pledged never to repeat them, on pain of being dismissed from the force. But seeing as Mrs Groynes had happily admitted to him in private that she *was* a criminal mastermind responsible for a massive network *et cetera* (and had been getting away with it for years), this wasn't easy. In fact, it had brought him close to tears of frustration.

'Don't cry, Constable dear,' Mrs Groynes had told him, quite kindly, when they had discussed his unusual predicament. 'You have to accept defeat graciously, that's what. Everyone believes your insane idea about me was planted in your brain in front of hundreds of witnesses by a hypnotist, who was then unfortunately shot dead in a bloody fracas before he could de-hypnotise you. I beat you, dear; just admit it. I'm a genius who destroyed your credibility in a single stroke.'

'You *are* a bally genius, Mrs Groynes,' he had conceded, 'and I take my hat off to you. The hypnotism ruse was brilliant.

No one will ever believe me now when I point the finger at you. They'll say it's all in my mind.'

'That's right, dear.'

'But you forget that you're still an enormous criminal, with a vast underworld network of ruffians, and as an officer of the law, I have to do something about you.'

'But you *don't* have to, dear!' she had expostulated. 'Because you've been stitched up like a kipper, dear! So now, in a way, you're off the bleeding hook, do you see?'

And after a day or two to think about it, Twitten had reluctantly (and miserably) accepted her argument, because remaining a police officer was more important to him than anything else, and because plotting the eventual downfall of Mrs Groynes could be better done from inside than outside the force. And so here he was, accompanying the famous Inspector Steine in his public duties, and being careful not to say anything contentious. He was determined to fit in. Just two days ago, he had been issued with a brand-new white helmet, the traditional, exotic headgear of the Brighton policeman. Putting it on for the first time had been quite an emotional moment – until Mrs G privately pointed out that the introduction of white helmets had actually been her own idea. ('It means we can spot a bleeding rozzer a mile off, dear!')

'I've never spent much time in a wax museum before, sir, have you?' he said now.

'No, none,' said Steine.

'Actually, my parents did take me to Madame Tussaud's once, when I was nine, but we didn't stay long because I started pointing out what was wrong with the exhibits.'

'Why does that not surprise me, Twitten?'

'Well, I believe you'll sympathise, sir. I don't know if you've heard of the famous model of a policeman on the stairs that's supposed to be so lifelike people ask him what time it is?'

'Yes, thank you. I *have* heard of that wax policeman. Everyone has.'

'Well, sir, naturally I rushed to see him, and people were crowding round, saying, "Ooh, isn't he lifelike?" and "I keep expecting him to speak!" and also, of course, "Up yours, you filth! Your lot stitched up our Jimmy!" And what do you think, sir? *The buttons on his tunic didn't match with the style of his helmet!*'

'What?'

'That's how bally un-lifelike he was, sir.'

Steine was shocked. 'Are you sure?' he said. 'In Madame Tussaud's?'

'Yes, sir. The buttons were Metropolitan; the helmet was City of London! What a blunder! Any schoolboy knows the difference! You would think they'd be interested, but when I pointed it out, they asked Father to take me away at once!'

———

At Luigi's, the inspector's favourite ice-cream parlour, where the jukebox was playing Perry Como's 'Papa Loves Mambo', and all the top windows were open, a distinguished-looking middle-aged man in a homburg hat and light raincoat plonked a holdall on to one of the shiny brown tables, with his frothy coffee beside it.

It was a glorious day to be at the seaside, and Luigi's was buzzing with youthful customers (quiffs, bobby socks, pony-tails) ordering banana splits and Knickerbocker glories, and also respectable couples in their twenties drinking coffee from stylish Pyrex cups and saucers.

One such young couple smiled across to the man, who introduced himself with the single word 'Melamine', and warmly shook their hands. Fifteen minutes later, the couple left, hysterical with laughter. As they told their friends back in Palmers Green afterwards, 'Lord Melamine' had really taken them in to begin with. He sounded so very posh!

———

At the police station, they were having a quiet day. Mrs Groynes poured Sergeant Brunswick a cup of tea and offered him a slice of gala pie, complete with a segment of hard-boiled egg. He sat down to receive both at his desk.

'Lovely, Mrs G,' he said, appreciatively. 'That's lovely, that is.'

Mrs Groynes smiled. She knew how to keep her boys happy. As it happened, their needs were absurdly simple, but she had genuine affection for them anyway, especially Sergeant Brunswick. She liked to think of herself as a sort of substitute mother to the well-meaning sergeant – a substitute mother with just a bit of a dark side. On the one hand, she brought in tasty things for him to eat because she knew he liked them; on the other, she might arrange for him to be shot in the leg if it served a wider purpose.

It was a beautiful relationship, and the sergeant certainly cherished it, and never got impatient with Mrs Groynes when (say) important bits of criminal evidence, left in his desk drawer for safe-keeping, were accidentally thrown away with the tea leaves.

'I've got some of those so-called London cheesecakes for later, dear,' she said now, her eyes twinkling. 'With that nasty shredded coconut on the top.'

'I'd be as fat as butter if you had your way, Mrs G.'

'You deserve it, dear,' she said. 'Now … how's the leg?'

Sergeant Brunswick winced at the reminder. He had indeed recently been shot in the leg at close range, as part of a classic criminal master-plan that climaxed at the Hippodrome in Middle Street. This master-plan had, of course, been entirely conceived by the dowdy woman in a paisley overall now swabbing the lino with a mop.

'The funny thing is, it's quite itchy,' he said.

'You're right, dear,' said Mrs Groynes, thoughtfully. 'That *is* funny.'

Brunswick sighed, and sat munching his pie and sipping his tea in contented silence for a little while, while Mrs Groynes mopped. He was such a nice-looking man, she thought, it was a shame he never had a girlfriend. The trouble was, women seemed to sense his desperation.

'Did young Clever Clogs Twitten show you that book he's reading, Mrs G?' the sergeant asked at last, the gala pie now reduced to a few pastry crumbs.

Mrs Groynes stopped mopping. 'What book's that, then?'

'Blimey, you're lucky!' said Brunswick. 'He's flaming obsessed with it. It's called *Noblesse Oblige*, if you please.'

'Never heard of it, dear.'

'Well, it's written by this la-di-da woman, and it's about how the so-called "upper class" have got different names for things from the rest of us.'

'Have they?'

'Well, so this book says. So if you say a word like *radio* or *serviette*, people can tell, just like that – ' Brunswick clicked his fingers ' – you're not upper class.'

'But everyone says *radio* and *serviette*, dear.'

'I know!'

'And who wants to sound upper class, anyway? That's daft.'

'I know. Young Twitten asked me what I'd call *that*, for instance.' He indicated a mirror on the wall.

Mrs Groynes was confused. 'What you'd call what, dear? The mirror?'

'Exactly. I said, "What would I call that mirror? What would I call it? I'd call it a mirror, son, because it *is* a flaming mirror!"'

'No flies on you, dear.'

'But he said an *upper-class* person would say "looking-glass".'

Mrs Groynes shrugged and gave an exaggerated sing-song, 'Ooh.'

'I know,' agreed Brunswick. 'Talk about pointless. But apparently everyone's buying this book and talking about it.'

Mrs Groynes sighed heavily as if to ask what the world was coming to, lit a full-strength Capstan from a lady-like pack of ten, took a thoughtful drag and then handed the sergeant the latest *Police Gazette*.

'Hot off the press, dear,' she said, expertly exhaling at the same time.

'Oh, good.' He loved perusing the *Police Gazette*, which was just as well because it was part of his job to read it every day. It was Mrs Groynes's usual practice to read and digest it first, of course. The information in it was invaluable if you were a vigilant master-criminal with a network of around two hundred villains. But today it had arrived later than usual and she hadn't had the chance.

'Here,' Brunswick said, 'imagine when a toff goes to buy the *Daily Mirror* and he can't say it! He keeps asking for the *Daily Looking-Glass*!'

Mrs Groynes laughed. 'They wouldn't know what he meant! Poor bleeder would be there all day!'

Back at the Maison du Wax, things were less harmonious. In fact, they were quite sticky. Constable Twitten was pointing at a full-length mirror propped against the wall in the measuring-room, to the confusion of his senior officer. And he was beginning to wish he had never started it.

'That mirror, you mean, Twitten?'

'Yes, sir. But please let's drop the subject, sir. I'm sorry. It's just a book. By Nancy Mitford. *Noblesse Oblige*, sir. It's been quite controversial. It's basically about the differences between what she calls "U" and "Non-U", and truly, sir, it's bally fascinating, and I'm sure the whole field of socio-linguistics has practical applications for police work, you see, but people keep getting annoyed when I talk about it, so I should probably bally well belt up about it, sir.'

'No, look, hang on. You started this, Twitten. You're asking me what I would call that mirror?'

'Well, yes.'

'I'd call it a mirror, Twitten. Good grief.'

'So, not a looking-glass, sir?'

Steine swallowed hard. 'I don't understand what you're getting at, Twitten.'

'There's no need to be irritated, sir.'

'But it *is* a mirror, Twitten. Of course I'm irritated.'

'Even if I tell you that "mirror" is a "Non-U" indicator, sir?'

'Especially if you tell me that.'

At that moment, luckily for Twitten, the great blind model-maker Pierre Tussard made his entrance, wearing a crimson velvet cap-and-robe ensemble and shuffling behind his daughter, his hand dramatically on her shoulder, his head strangely angled, his eyes closed. Despite the ridiculous picture they made, Twitten couldn't have been more pleased to see them. Would he be allowed to leave, now? To go outside in the sun and read the rest of his book?

The answer was yes and no. 'You make yourself scarce, Constable,' said Steine, still sounding agitated. 'But don't leave the building. We haven't finished discussing this mirror business.'

'Yes, sir. I mean, no, sir. I'll wait on the landing, sir.'

Meekly, Twitten donned his shiny white helmet and left the room.

Outside, at the top of the stairs, he stood for a while, just thinking. How defensive everyone got on this issue of U and Non-U words! It made no sense to him. Why weren't they fascinated by the revelation that upper-class people said 'preserve' instead of 'jam', or 'wireless' instead of 'radio', or 'mad' instead of 'mental'? Wasn't it worth knowing that an upper-class person would despise you for referring to your fish-knives or your cruet set, or (worst of all) your toilet? Snobbery was a living thing in modern British society! Surely it was important to know how it operated?

He was so deep in thought that at first he didn't notice the small crowd of visitors gathering on the staircase below him, looking up with interest. And then he realised what was happening, and froze. A policeman at the top of a flight of stairs in a wax museum! Did they think he was a model? Crikey. Thank goodness his tunic buttons and helmet were stylistically complementary.

The small crowd approached, to look more closely.

'That *is* bleeding lifelike,' said a young man with a Brylcreemed quiff and prematurely blackened teeth. ''Ere, what's the time, mate?'

Twitten stopped breathing. Understandably, he was tempted to reply 'Half-past nine, sir', but worried about the accident it might cause. What if alarmed holiday-makers stepped backwards into space and then tumbled in a heap down the stairs?

The teenaged girl on the Brylcreem-boy's arm laughed and gazed up. 'Shall I pinch him, Roy?' she said. 'Shall I knock his helmet off?'

'Go on, Em. I dare you,' said an older woman.

Twitten mentally braced himself, but luckily the girl decided she didn't have the nerve and the group passed on to the upper floor, giving him an opportunity to exhale. But at what point could he move? It was while he was pondering his predicament – and continuing to stand completely still with a fixed expression – that he happened to overhear a conversation between a pair of star-crossed young lovers that would – given what happened later – haunt him for the rest of his life.

———————

Back on the seafront, Brighton Belles Phyllis and Adelaide decided to stop at Luigi's for a refreshing glass of hot milk before continuing with their duties, and found themselves sitting beside a man in a felt hat with a heavy bag in front of him on the table.

'May I introduce myself to you lovely ladies?' he said. One of his eyes pointed in slightly the wrong direction, which was unsettling, but he had a beautiful voice.

'I'm the Fifth Marquess of Colchester,' he said, in a confiding tone. 'But you can call me Melamine.'

They smiled at him and shook his proffered hand. He registered the names on their little lapel badges. The brunette was Phyllis; the girl with the rich brown hair was Adelaide. As it happened, Adelaide's hair was technically chestnut, while her eyes were almond-shaped, and hazel-coloured. As her mother used to say (presumably as a compliment), Adelaide had been born with all the nuts.

'Now,' Melamine said, shifting the bag a little closer to them, 'I'm wondering if you've ever heard the story of the gold from the battleship *Potemkin*?'

The two women exchanged glances. They'd been warned about con men, but they'd somehow imagined that a con man would be a little bit harder to spot.

'I don't think so,' said Adelaide, amused. 'Have *you* heard of the gold from the battleship *Potemkin*, Phyllis?'

'Not me,' said Phyllis.

'Russian gold! Imperial gold!' enthused Melamine. 'It was thought to be lost during the uprising of 1905, sunk in the depths of the Black Sea. But in the 1920s it turned up in the possession of none other than Rudolph Valentino!'

The Belles raised their eyebrows at each other. This man was possibly the least convincing liar the world had ever seen. They now understood the comments they had overheard from a young couple they had bumped into outside Luigi's. 'He was hopeless, Alfie!' the woman had said, and the man had replied, 'Yes, but you can't fault him for trying! Rudolph Valentino!'

'Gosh,' said Phyllis, now, trying to keep a straight face. 'Rudolph Valentino. That's very romantic.'

'Yes, it *is* romantic,' said Melamine, clearly making a note of a useful word that had previously not occurred to him. His faraway look was weirdly enhanced by the fact that his eyes pointed in different directions.

'But the Nazis sadly got hold of it, and then – ' He leaned closer, surreptitiously pushing the bag towards them, and quickly opening it to reveal the presence inside of several large gold-coloured bricks ' – General Eisenhower liberated it from

Berlin. And he placed it in the safe-keeping of my father, the Fourth Marquess, not realising that the poor, sad man was seriously mental and would forget where he had left it.'

'What a truly incredible story,' said Adelaide, between lady-like sips of warm milk. She turned to her friend, eyes twinkling. 'That is literally incredible, isn't it, Phyllis?'

'It is, yes. Literally.'

Melamine seemed pleased. 'Thank you very much,' he said.

'May I ask why you're carrying it around, sir?' said Adelaide. 'The gold? It's rather careless of you. Someone might steal it.'

'But I have to get rid of it, that's the point! I don't usually go around talking about my family's Russian gold to total strangers in coffee bars. No, I'm in a fix, my dears, and I need help.'

'Here it comes,' murmured Adelaide.

'Ladies,' Melamine announced, solemnly. 'For complicated reasons too shaming to relate, I'm willing to sell this gold of mine to you for as little as twenty-five pounds a brick! What you see before you is a desperate, desperate aristocrat.'

A less convincing story would be hard to imagine, and the kind thing would have been to stand up, plead an appointment elsewhere and go. But Adelaide had indeed been born with all the nuts, and was enjoying herself.

'Oh, I'm so sorry to hear that,' she said, reaching over to pat his hand. 'But I don't understand completely. What sort of complicated reasons? And why are they shaming?'

'Can't you guess?' he said.

'Well, no.'

'Tax!' he said, with what sounded like genuine frustration. 'It's all about tax and those dreaded new-fangled death duties. "You've never had it so good," the man says on the radio, but not if you inherit a country house and estate in 1957!'

'I see.'

'You can't imagine how hard things are for the landed gentry. My father dealt with nothing, being too mental. He didn't declare this hidden Russian gold, which is worth – each brick! – just under five hundred pounds! The ancestral home is on the verge of collapse. All over the country, families like mine are selling their silver cruets and serviette rings! Yes, it's a topsy-turvy world we live in, ladies, but the long and short of it is this: if I'm still in possession of Father's confounded gold at the end of the month, I'll be ruined!'

———

So what was the momentous conversation Twitten overheard at the wax museum? It was only because he had spent five minutes standing immobile on the landing that he noticed something that would never otherwise have caught his eye: at the top of the stairs, in the wall that (he calculated) ought to comprise the back of the building, was the well-disguised outline of a jib door.

'A secret door?' he said aloud. He wondered what to do. Should he stop pretending to be a waxwork and investigate? There was someone approaching the stairs below – he could hear footsteps echoing through the entrance hall – so he would have to make up his mind quickly. But too late! A scratching sound came from behind the secret door, then it opened and a young woman stepped out nervously.

'Peter?' she whispered.

It took Twitten all his presence of mind not to look round to see who Peter was.

'I'm here,' said a voice, and a thin young man came running up the stairs and put his arms round her. 'Deirdre! You came! Does this mean … ?'

'Yes, Peter,' she said, quietly. 'It does. I want to go with you. I want to run away. But we have to be so careful!'

'Oh, my love!' he said.

Twitten was extremely uncomfortable about overhearing all this private lovey-dovey stuff, especially when it emanated from people who might be minors. But again, he was also aware that if he exhibited the slightest sign of life, he might scare them out of their wits.

'Peter, stop. Stop!' said young Deirdre. 'This is serious. You know what my brothers would do if they found out. Or Mum! She calls you Weedy Pete! Weedy Pete Dupont! And the boys join in and laugh. They're all beasts!'

Twitten was just making a mental note about the reprehensible solipsism of the young when the girl said something that truly surprised him.

'And don't forget what they did to Uncle Ken! The police only found one bit of him in that suitcase at the station. No one's ever found his head!'

Staying completely immobile while this conversation was playing out was possibly the hardest thing Twitten had ever done. The urge to take out a notebook and lick the tip of a pencil was overwhelming. *Uncle Ken's head?*

'We'll meet tonight at nine at the coach station in Pool Valley,' said the girl, who seemed to be in charge of arrangements.

Nine, repeated Twitten to himself, silently. *Pool Valley. Peter Dupont. Deirdre who? Secret door to … where?* And again, *Don't forget: Uncle Ken's HEAD??*

'Don't say anything at work,' she reminded her boyfriend. 'Especially to Mr Blackmore.'

'All right, I'm not stupid!' laughed the weedy boy.

Mr Blackmore, Mr Blackmore.

And then the boy took Deirdre's hand and held it tenderly. They both hung their heads. Twitten's eyes moistened. For the first time, he realised that this scene being played out in front of him was jolly lovely, in its way; it was a privilege to witness it. He was reminded of those short-lived hopeful bits in tough modern films like *On the Waterfront*, where wide-eyed young love expresses itself so sweetly and poignantly (usually with a light woodwind accompaniment), against a backdrop of inevitable violence and doom.

Peter squeezed Deirdre's hand. 'I know what to do, don't worry,' he assured her, quietly. 'It's a good plan and you're very brave. But if anything happens to me, remember you can trust Hoagland.'

Hoagland? Who's Hoagland? Oh, bally hell, this is getting harder.

'Don't talk like that, Peter! Nothing will happen to you, so long as we get away now. I'll get the money from the safe. Dickie said he'll help me.'

The boy reacted with alarm. 'You didn't tell Dickie?'

Dickie?

'I had to tell *someone*!'

Yes, but why Dickie?

It was at this point that they both happened to look round, and spotted Twitten for the first time.

'That's new,' said the girl, frowning. 'That policeman. It wasn't there yesterday.'

Twitten felt his new helmet slip slightly on his forehead.

'It looks a bit good for in here,' said the boy, suspiciously.

But just as Twitten's legs began to tremble, the door to the measuring-room burst open, signifying the end of Steine's sitting, and the boy and girl sprang apart and scarpered with all the energy of the young – the weedy Peter boy back down the stairs, the girl with the de-boncified male relative back through her secret door.

'Ah, there you are, Twitten,' said Steine, beaming. He turned and waved goodbye to Angélique.

'*À bientôt*, Inspector,' she called.

'Yes, sir,' said Twitten, almost crying with relief that he could move at last. 'Shall we go, sir?'

They started to walk down the stairs towards the sunshine outside.

'Well, I don't want to rub it in,' said Steine, 'but you won't believe what you missed by being out here.'

Two

Although Sergeant Brunswick and Inspector Steine had been working together for several years, they knew very little about each other's personal circumstances. All the inspector knew about Brunswick was that he lived with an aunt in a flat on the London Road (name of aunt forgotten); that his first name was something like Jim or possibly Algernon (immaterial); and that he was a perennial sad case where women were concerned.

This the inspector knew not because he was at all curious about such matters, but because he had been unlucky enough to observe Brunswick's love-life at first hand. Even the nineteen-year-old rabbit-toothed Maisie, who sold colourful buckets and spades from a little hatch near the bandstand, could wind the thirty-eight-year-old sergeant round her provocative little finger.

James Brunswick (the name was indeed Jim) was also a war hero, of course. Having joined the so-called 'Boys' Army' at the age of fourteen, he served as a paratrooper in the Italian campaigns; but if the inspector didn't know the specifics of his sergeant's wartime career, he wasn't alone in this; like many a decorated soldier, Brunswick was silent about his own particular role in the defeat of the Third Reich. In 1957, the war had been over for only a brief dozen years, but it was rare for people to hark back to it – the subject was officially closed. Many children of the 1950's grew up knowing nothing of their fathers' part in the conflict; and being too cocky and self-centred, they never got around to asking.

As far as Brunswick understood it, there were many good reasons not to talk about the war: for one thing, the real heroes were the dead ones; for another, young people loathed being reminded of what their elders had been through (and no man of thirty-eight wanted to be called 'Daddy-o' if he could prevent it); on top of which, very few people chose what they did in the war, in any case; and finally, war heroes were not exactly few and far between. So plentiful were they in Brighton alone that you couldn't toss a humbug without hitting a veteran of Monte Cassino. Every hotel commissionaire or doorman along the seafront sported either an unmissable limp or a jangling row of tarnished medals on his chest (usually both).

Brunswick would have been disappointed to learn that Inspector Steine thought his name was possibly Algernon. However, he would in turn have to admit that he knew little about Inspector Steine's life beyond the station, other than that he was about forty-five years old, lived in the Queens Park area of the town, had grown up in London, drove a very nice car, was childless and long-divorced, had served in the City of London police during the Blitz, and that his given names were 'Geoffrey' and 'St John' (the latter pronounced, for some unfathomable reason, 'Sin-jern'). There was a rumour that in the evenings the inspector was writing a memoir, but that he kept it securely locked away in his desk.

Of course, Inspector Steine famously wrote and delivered a broadcast every week on the Home Service (entitled 'Law and the Little Man'), which often utilised anecdotes from his life, and sometimes shed an oblique light on his childhood, but he was careful not to give too much away about his origins, partly because – in terms of class, at least – these origins were so unusual and difficult to categorise. His stern and judgmental mother Honoria, now living in Kenya (pronounced *Keen-ya*), was originally from a snobbish and very wealthy upper-class family in Dorset, while his father Wilfred had been a humble career policeman from West London, who was unfortunately struck and killed by an army transport lorry on Chiswick Bridge in 1922, when little Geoffrey was only ten.

It had been an unlikely alliance, this marriage between Honoria and 'The Bobby' (as the family back in Dorset always termed him, refusing to learn his name). The strains of it had helped turn his mother into the bitter, gin-sodden battle-axe she now was. But nowadays, whenever she looked back on that ill-advised marriage, she had to be honest: she could blame no one for her misfortune but herself.

And how short the distance, really; how short the years. Living with a mauve-and-golden view of the far-off Ngong Hills – the baobab trees alive with birds and monkeys, the equatorial sun scorching the tall grass, the sound of lion (*not* 'lions') roaring on the perimeter of the compound – Steine's mother could close her eyes and instantly revisit the dingy, noisy, choking London of her youth. Sipping her second pre-prandial Tom Collins, she could bring to mind the very aroma of sooty smog on that fateful day when she fell into the arms of her unexpected hero, Constable Wilfred Steine.

The story (as children Gillian and Geoffrey heard it so many times) was a pretty good one. In the spring of 1910, the eighteen-year-old Honoria Penrose was up in London for a society wedding, and had been carefully steering the unwieldy family car – a Clifton F model 1905 Motor Cradle – through a sedate Bloomsbury square. Visibility was poor; the Cradle was so difficult to manoeuvre that it had been christened by her father 'The Utter Bastard' (or 'UB' for short); Honoria was also a little bit lost, and her favourite hat had blown off on the Marylebone Road (to be snatched up instantly by gleeful street urchins). And then a bizarre thing happened. As she drove down the side of Gordon Square, a group of rowdy young bohemians dressed in exotic Eastern costumes emerged from one of the houses and, before she knew it, had placed themselves in front of the vehicle!

It was terrifying. In their colourful turbans and robes, they looked like wild things. She tooted her horn at them, but it didn't help. They surrounded the Motor Cradle and deliberately blocked her way, making guttural animal noises and exchanging the nonsensical phrase 'Bunga Bunga'. (Upperclass young people at this period often breached the peace in such comical ways, wrecking the interior of the Café Royal, and so on. This bohemian bunch – led by the irrepressible prankster Horace de Vere Cole – had conceived the idea of impersonating Abyssinian royalty in order to board a warship at Weymouth, in one of the unfunniest hoaxes ever recorded.)

Having lived quite a sheltered life in Swanage, poor Honoria had never been exposed to bohemians at all before, let alone ones tastelessly blacked-up like American minstrels. Feeling threatened, she begged them to leave her alone, but they refused. They were too excited about the effect they were having. Her panic made them surge and Bunga Bunga all the more.

It was at this point that the handsome Constable Wilfred, who had been proceeding in an easterly direction along

Torrington Place, heard the piercing female scream that was to change his life. Instantly, he diverted from his beat and raced towards the source of the rumpus, blowing his whistle and waving his truncheon.

The bohemians scattered like startled exotic birds, and disappeared through various well-appointed front doors, uttering expressions rather less exotic than 'Bunga Bunga', such as 'Botheration, Horace! It's a fucking constable!' and 'Where's the key, Adrian? Where's the bloody key?'

Wilfred did manage to land a truncheon blow on the slowest of the group, which was a source of pride ever after – although the pride was slightly diminished when the desperado in question was later identified as Virginia Stephen (later Woolf), the mentally frail lady novelist.

At first, Honoria wasn't quite sure what had happened – those ghastly people had come and gone so quickly! But then she saw Wilfred's dear honest face in a sepia halo of London air pollution, and her heart swelled within her. The breathless young Constable Steine had only to utter the fateful words, 'Are you all right, miss?' and that was it: the world tipped on its axis. She looked into the blue eyes of her brave rescuer and decided on the spot that she had never felt more all right in her life, and that she must marry this paragon as quickly as possible.

The marriage was a terrible failure, of course, especially when Honoria's family disinherited her and never spoke to her again – and also took back the car. Honoria soon found that she hated being a policeman's wife. But Wilfred was a decent man, and an intelligent one, and the marriage did produce two children in quick succession, a girl and then a boy, the latter of whom grew up to be Inspector Steine of the Brighton Constabulary.

Honoria begged her only son not to follow in Wilfred's footsteps by becoming a policeman; but if ever a man idolised his father, it was Geoffrey St John Steine. His ideal of the police officer was set forever by the kind of public servant his father had been: a man who would, regardless of his own safety, rescue a clueless posh woman from out-of-control modernists intent on a racist prank.

It is a shame that Sergeant Brunswick knew none of this, when the adult character of Inspector Steine was so clearly influenced by his background. So much was explained by his unique beginnings: his intense, abiding loyalty to the law and all its officers; his touchiness about class distinctions; his loathing of the term 'bobby'; his interest in vintage cars, especially the (very rare, now) Clifton F model 1905 Motor Cradle. Even his quickness to classify any mystery as 'unsolvable' could perhaps be traced to his feelings of impotent schoolboy anguish when his unhappy sister Gillian ran away from home at the age of sixteen and was never heard of again.

On a lighter note, the family background also explained why he loathed fancy dress. As for the Bloomsbury Group, Steine abominated them one and all, once describing them in a live radio talk – to the surprise of both his listeners and his producer (it wasn't in the script) – as 'degenerate human scum'.

———

Their mission at the Maison du Wax successfully accomplished, Steine and his constable returned to the station, Steine regaling Twitten along the way with the various compliments paid to him in private by Tussard *père* – for example, about the spacing of his eyes being precisely the same not only as Napoleon's but also Dr Crippen's and Lady Jane Grey's.

'Something jolly interesting happened outside too, sir,' Twitten said, but he never got the chance to elaborate, what with Steine's eyebrows having reminded the blind French model-maker of Benjamin Disraeli and his ears of Teddy Roosevelt (although possibly it was the other way round).

After greeting Sergeant Brunswick, who was still engrossed in his *Police Gazette*, Steine retired to his own office to tinker happily with this week's instalment of 'Law and the Little Man', which would interestingly skewer the popular fallacy that a wife is barred from testifying in the trial of her husband.

If there was one type of subject that he loved to tackle, it was the common misconception in regard to the legal system. Why did the general public insist on believing things about the law that weren't true? Why did they not check their facts? Were there no public libraries? In this wonderful new information age, with encyclopaedias and reference sections and index-card systems in special wooden cabinets situated in public buildings *in every town*, it was well established that checking any fact would rarely take the average person (with the help of a trained librarian) more than a few hours; two days at the very most.

Meanwhile Twitten – almost too excited to say hello after what he had overheard between the two star-crossed lovers at the wax museum – quickly borrowed the heavy office typewriter, transferring it to his desk with a grunt of effort. He needed to type up the notes in his head before he forgot them.

Naturally, Mrs Groynes noticed his fervid, single-minded paper-feeding, so immediately set about trying to derail his concentration. Twitten might have capitulated to the charwoman's terms: he and she might now operate according to a secret truce; superficially, all might seem cordial, but there was no love lost between the keen young constable and the ostensibly motherly charlady. Young Twitten regarded Mrs Groynes as his own personal enemy, whom he must avoid as much as possible and eventually vanquish. Less respectfully, Mrs Groynes regarded Twitten as an endearing source of harmless entertainment.

'Cup of tea, dear?' she called, as he adjusted the carriage of the machine and began to type.

Without looking up, he shook his head. 'No, thank you, Mrs G. I'm a bit busy, I'm afraid.'

'Oh, go on, dear, you must be proper parched. Stop that silly typing for a minute and have a nice chat, why don't you?'

There was no response except typing.

'Here, I've been meaning to talk to you for the longest while about this dismal epidemic of myxomatosis. Are we for it, dear? Or are we against it?'

But Twitten, pausing in his work, merely bit his lip and scanned what he had written so far.

```
Door leads where?
What building is behind the wax museum?
Deirdre who? Who mother? 'All beasts!'
Dickie – who he? She said she trusted
him but Weedy Pete not so sure.
```

'It's just that I'm taking a vote, dear,' continued Mrs Groynes. 'And the results so far have been a bit of a revelation.'

But Twitten (who was actually keenly interested in the topical issue of myxomatosis, as Mrs Groynes well knew) was not so easily put off. He needed to imagine himself back at the top of those stairs, listening to that conversation. What else had those young people said? What else?

'*I'll* have another cup, Mrs G,' Brunswick volunteered. 'That last one was lovely.'

'Good for you, dear. Keep your strength up. Here, fancy a nice fig roll, and all?'

Twitten closed his eyes, willing this witless chit-chat to stop. He mustn't forget Peter Dupont, Uncle Ken, the *head* ...

'I don't suppose you've got any Garibaldis?' said Brunswick. (He was joking. He loved Garibaldis, but Mrs Groynes disapproved of them so strongly that she had been known to dismiss them as 'little sods'.)

Mrs G laughed. 'Now you know how I feel about Garibaldis, Sergeant.'

And they chuckled together at this mysterious joke, while Twitten closed his eyes and took a deep breath.

```
Peter Dupont.
Who he? Where does he work? Is he weedy?
If so, why?
Uncle Ken's headless torso in suitcase!
```

This last he underlined emphatically (skilfully employing the shift key) and tapped the number six so hard – and so many times – that even Sergeant Brunswick took notice.

'Oh, come on, son,' he said. 'What's so important you can't stop for a cup of tea?'

Twitten took a deep breath. 'Just a second, sir!' he said. 'Please, sir!' His train of thought had almost vanished, but he rescued it.

```
Weedy Pete said Deirdre could trust
Hogeland/Hoagland? Who he?
Blacksmith? Blackgang? Blackmore!
```

Mrs Groynes plonked a cup of tea on his desk. 'I brought you one anyway, dear,' she said, peering over his shoulder. He took a deep breath. He had one last thing to set down:

```
DON'T FORGET: 9 o'clock at coach station
in Pool Valley.
```

And then he ripped the sheet from the typewriter and folded it before she could see too much of it.

He smiled up at her in a kind of triumph. 'Lovely day, Mrs G,' he said. 'Did you say something about a fig roll?'

Out on the seafront, the two Brighton Belles who had so easily resisted the sales pitch of Lord Melamine, 5th Marquess of Colchester, paraded past the entrance to the West Pier, then took the steps down to the beach.

Their daily briefing had instructed them today to encourage the public, in the gentlest possible fashion, to partake of fairground activities and other entertainments, because in fine conditions such as these, visitors tended to frolic in the sea, sunbathe on the shingly beach and build sandcastles (when the tide was sufficiently far out to uncover the necessary raw material) – all of which pastimes profited the grasping town of Brighton precisely nothing.

'Good morning!' Phyllis and Adelaide called from the steps, generally, to the holiday-makers below in their deck-chairs. 'Have you heard about the new roller-coaster on the Palace Pier?' The Belles had been trained to wave and smile in the style of the young monarch; the man from Brighton Council had looked very funny when he demonstrated it the first time, but it seemed to work. 'Hello! Good morning! Can we help you with anything?'

Reaching the level of the beach, they paused and absorbed the scene. Families had erected colourful stripy wind-breaks to nestle behind and eat their home-made shrimp-paste sandwiches and hard-boiled eggs, and drink their flasks of tea; a Punch & Judy man was setting up his booth, whacking wooden posts into the shingle with a large rock and muttering a number of unrepeatable swear-words to himself in a Greek accent; a limping man in a doorman's uniform, with a row of shiny medals on his chest, clutched a parcel and headed for the steps; donkeys with names like 'Flora' and 'Ermintrude' poker-worked on to their bridles stood patiently while frightened toddlers were placed on their backs (and sometimes smartly lifted off again); and under one of the arches, a buck-toothed teenaged girl in dazzling white ankle-socks arranged brightly coloured plastic windmills in a red metal pail.

The Belles looked so sophisticated, it was hard to believe they weren't much older than the buck-toothed girl. But they were scarcely out of their teens. When they talked amongst themselves, the subject was likely to be make-up, or boys, or the price of nylons, or their plans for dancing the night away with a friend of Daddy's who'd invited them to dinner at the tennis club.

Of the six girls, Adelaide was the one who seemed most worldly, and she was also the funny one: she was apt to reduce her regular partner Phyllis to unstoppable giggles. And in fact they were just laughing at something Adelaide had said (about the self-styled Marquess of Colchester taking his name from a famous pub) when a small sunburned boy in sky-blue knitted swimming trunks ran up to them and pulled at Adelaide's sleeve.

He seemed distressed, and it wasn't just from the way his damp woollen costume was bagging to his knobbly knees, or from the painful scorching of his bony shoulders.

'Miss!' he said. 'You've got to come, miss! There's a man!'

'What sort of man?' said Adelaide, with a ready-for-anything smile. She was always having to put up with little japes on the beach – daddies buried in sand; being offered seaweed sandwiches; small translucent crabs being dropped down her neck.

The boy pulled a face. 'Well, miss. He looks to me like a dead one.'

'What?' she blurted. She tried to recover, but failed. 'I mean, *what?*'

Adelaide and Phyllis looked around, and saw that – alarmingly – they were surrounded by a crowd of people in dark glasses and colourful straw sombreros, who had jumped up from their deck-chairs and were now grasping each other by the arm, or holding their hands to their faces in shock.

Back at the station, there was now a bit of an atmosphere between himself and Mrs Groynes, but Twitten refused to feel bad about it. Keeping police intelligence from this wicked woman was a highly reasonable precaution. He had no intention of ever again speaking in front of her about the details of a case. He had no intention, either, of letting her see anything. He put the folded piece of paper in his tunic pocket and pointedly buttoned it.

Part of Twitten's daily torment, however, was that he could not prevent other people from unwittingly sharing the most delicate information with this most brazen of criminals in their midst. Just last week Brunswick had come in and announced, delightedly, 'Guess what I heard, son! The Albion Bank in North Street is taking delivery of its new safe next Wednesday, but they've already removed the old one, so for the time being all the deposits will be kept in flaming sacks in the basement! And their back gate in the alley's a disgrace!'

Twitten had been fascinated by the way Mrs Groynes received this news. She seemed not to react at all. But then, having made everyone a quick cup of tea, she reached for her coat and headscarf.

'Just popping out, dears. We're in need of some Handy Andy.'

'Okey-dokey, Mrs Groynes,' said Brunswick, distractedly, still chuckling at the shocking security arrangements of a bank known to deal in unusually large sums on summer weekdays.

Pausing at the door, she said, 'Did you say the Albion Bank, dear?'

'Pardon?'

'Did you say the Albion Bank just now? The one in North Street?'

'That's right,' he laughed. 'But don't tell anyone!'

When she came back later, she seemed to have forgotten the Handy Andy, but brought festive coconut ice wrapped in greaseproof paper, to the joy of all. And that very night, the Albion Bank in North Street was cleared out by a professional gang, gaining entry by means of the disgraceful back gate in the alley.

But now Mrs Groynes was about to hear some news that, to Twitten's surprise, unsettled her so badly that he almost felt sorry for her.

Brunswick looked up from his *Police Gazette*. 'It says here,' he said, 'that Wall-Eye Joe is back to his tricks, and that they're expecting him to turn up on the South Coast.'

'What?' she said, sharply, almost dropping the tray she was holding. The return of Wall-Eye Joe to business (which meant nothing to Twitten) was evidently a massive headline so far as she was concerned.

'Who are you talking about, sir?' said Twitten.

'Proper name Joseph Marriott,' said Brunswick.

'But known to all as Wall-Eye,' chipped in Mrs Groynes – this humble, uneducated charwoman with her miraculously exhaustive knowledge of crime and criminals. 'He's a hardened con man, dear,' she said. 'One of the hardest. And bleeding notorious.'

There was an edge to her voice that Twitten recognised but at first couldn't place. When had he heard that flinty tone before? With a shudder, he remembered. He'd last heard it when they were alone together in London, when he had first denounced her as a villain, and she had threatened to kill him.

Turning to Brunswick, she said, as lightly as she could, 'But I thought Wall-Eye had gone away, dear. Last I heard he was doing a tray on the cave-grinder.'

Brunswick looked blank.

'She means three months' hard labour, sir,' Twitten explained.

'Oh.'

Twitten watched as a ghost of a question crossed Brunswick's mind, but (as usual) didn't settle.

'Well, that's right, Mrs G,' he said. 'But he's been out for a month or more.'

Twitten was still on the back foot, information-wise. 'What does he do, though, sir?' he asked. 'Don't con men just swindle people?'

'Well, you might say this one goes a little bit further than that,' said Mrs Groynes, furiously picking up a bit of knitting and sitting down with it. She gestured to Brunswick to tell the story, and then, before he could begin: 'This one's like Neville bleeding Heath crossed with George Joseph bleeding Smith!'

'Oh, steady on, Mrs G.' Brunswick turned to Twitten. 'As far as I know, the worst one was when he and a female confederate set up a phoney dating-agency business, and targeted women with a bit of money. Is that the case you're thinking of, Mrs G?'

'Yes, it bleeding is!' she said with passion. 'And they didn't just target them, they *murdered* them, Sergeant. They both should have swung. It was a travesty.'

'No bodies were ever found, Mrs G. So you can't even say it *was* murder.'

'Pah!' she said, angrily.

'They probably used acid,' explained Brunswick, grimly.

Although the name had meant nothing to him, Twitten remembered the story. There had been a lot of coverage in the papers. Luckily, friends of the various missing women had come forward with details of how the con was managed, and as a consequence this Joseph Marriott and the female partner had been arrested and charged.

And as Twitten recalled, the basic 'trick' had been quite clever. It involved an unfinished house in the country, near London. The phoney dating-agency partner – an attractive woman ostensibly working from a second-floor office in Regent Street – would interview well-to-do lonely women (known in the trade as 'marks') and fix them up with a widower – always the same widower, of course, with a distinctive squint, but a plausible manner.

'I miss my wife so badly,' he would tell each mark, pathetically. 'Perhaps I'm not ready. But you seem so lovely, my dear. I have but one request. Please don't mention my existence to anyone, I'm so shy!'

Having thus engaged the woman's interest (but luckily not succeeded in stopping her confiding in her closest friends), he would court her expensively, until her head was completely turned. Then he would make his move. He would allow her to glimpse a photograph of an unfinished house, and reluctantly, he would tell her about it.

'But that house is my problem, my dear, not yours!' he would say, explaining (but only reluctantly, when pressed) that he needed several thousand pounds to complete the building work. Within a couple of weeks, the mark would usually stump up the money, and then vanish from the face of the earth.

Friends might get a postcard from Aviemore, or Oban, but then the trail would go cold.

'How many women fell for it?' Twitten asked.

'They reckon at least half a dozen,' said Brunswick. 'It doesn't bear thinking about. Wall-Eye Joe and the skirt were tried for it at the Old Bailey, but there was no physical evidence of foul play, you see, only of obtaining money under false pretences. Without the bodies there wasn't enough to convict on the murder charge, so they got off scot-free. It wasn't the legal system's finest hour.'

'But didn't you just say that he was recently in prison, sir?'

Brunswick shrugged. 'That's right. But that was for something else. He doesn't always get away with it, but nothing will stop him trying again – new place, new MO, new mugs. He's a regular menace, that man.'

Mrs Groynes, still knitting, shook her head. 'The thing is, dear,' she said, bitterly, 'there are just so many gullible people in the world. To someone like Wall-Eye Joe, do you know what the world looks like? Full of mugs, dear. Full of bleeding stupid mugs.'

Brunswick pulled a face in regretful agreement, while Twitten looked at Mrs Groynes with a mixture of astonishment, curiosity, hatred, mortal fear and sincere admiration. What gall to be angry about a man seeing the world as full of mugs, when it was precisely how she saw the world herself. But why was she so worked up about this? Why was she so adamant that Wall-Eye Joe and his accomplice should have hanged for their crimes?

———

Mid-morning in Grenville Street, and lounge singer Dickie George was sitting at the piano of the Black Cat night club, idly picking out the tune to 'Melancholy Baby'.

Dickie was not a cheery soul at the best of times. Finding himself up and about at half-past ten in the morning made him no happier. His ulcer burned; his hips ached; his bottom set of teeth wouldn't quite settle on his gums. On top of which, he could hardly keep his eyes open. Last night the Black Cat had stayed open (illegally) until around three-thirty a.m., and he had crooned ballads until the bitter end – 'For All We Know', 'Someone to Watch Over Me', 'It Had to Be You' – until the last, hateful, inebriated couple stumbling round the dance-floor realised they were seeing double and finally admitted it was time to call it a night.

Dickie always had mixed feelings when the night was officially over and the cocky Frank Benson hopped on to the stage to announce to a virtually empty room, 'That's all, folks. Let's hear it for Dickie George and the Black Cat Quartet!'

True, it was a relief that it was over, but at the same time, it was a source of sadness that yet again the evening had passed without igniting in any way; yet again, he'd had only the merest glimpse of the teenaged girl who had captured his tired old heart. He and the band were expected to wait onstage, manfully stifling yawns, while those last dishevelled punters drunkenly searched for lost ear-rings and tried to cram high heels back on, before they handed over fistfuls of cash without counting it properly, and finally left the premises.

At that point, Ma Benson would usually appear from her office and turn on the house lights (the worst moment of all), saying in a bored voice, 'Good job, Dickie.' Then, while her large sons Frank and Bruce started stacking chairs on tables, she would accompany Dickie and the musicians to the side door, let them out into the dingy alley, and then lock and bolt the door again from the inside.

None of the guys ever wanted a nightcap, for reasons Dickie respected: like him, they'd been in the business too long to think of this lousy job as a lifestyle choice. Across the road, at his modest digs on the top floor, he would open the sash-window to the night air, take a few calming breaths and then quickly undress – shiny tail-coat, bow-tie, braces, shirt and corset – and furiously apply a novelty long-handled back-scratcher to his itching skin, groaning aloud as he did so. Such was his unlovely bedtime routine. After popping his dentures in a glass of water and gargling with TCP (to preserve the pipes), he would sink gratefully into his creaky single cot, with the idea of not rising again until at least two o'clock in the afternoon.

But last night had been different. When he got back to his room, he'd found a note pushed under the door. And as a result, here he was, virtually at the crack of dawn, after just five hours' uneven sleep. Young Deirdre Benson – a girl to whom a jaded, overweight band-singer such as himself could aspire to be only a friend and confidant – was excitedly asking for his help in a romantic matter, and had thoughtlessly named this ungodly hour for the meeting. But he could not deny her. He would do anything for Deirdre. She was the light in his darkness, and when he sang 'Embraceable You' each night with genuine tears of longing in his eyes, it was Deirdre he was thinking of.

It wasn't wise to meet like this inside the club – when Deirdre's thuggish older brothers might be awake and listening in the shadows; when her thuggish mother might appear at any moment with a blackjack. Ma Benson was a terrifying woman, all right: this was his third decade as a singer, and he'd never worked in a joint as tainted as this before, where there were whispers of uncle-murdering and dismemberment. But on the other hand, he was too tired to care; too out of love with life, especially now that young Deirdre seemed to be planning to run away.

Sitting at the piano, while the girl made him a wake-up cup of Camp Coffee (which would be disgusting), he picked out more notes to his favourite song from the musical *Pal Joey*. Could he write a book about Deirdre, if they asked him? He was just beginning to think that he could, actually, when he felt a crack on the back of his head, and everything went dark.

'Here, talking of mugs,' Mrs Groynes carried on, in a hushed voice, 'did you know the inspector fell for that spaghetti-crop hoax on that BBC *Panorama*?'

She was evidently hoping to turn the conversation away from Wall-Eye Joe, aware that she might have given too much away about her feelings. And like most of her ruses, it worked. Even Twitten was momentarily diverted from the scent. *Inspector Steine had fallen for the April Fool's*

Day spaghetti-crop hoax on Panorama? *What on earth could be more interesting than that?*

'What? No!' said a delighted Twitten, his voice lowered. 'But it was so obviously a joke, Mrs G!'

Mrs Groynes pulled a face and leaned forward. 'I only just found out the other day when I was sorting through his bits in that precious locked drawer of his, where he keeps his memoir and whatnot, and the letters to his horrible old mum that he isn't brave enough to send. Yes, he only went and got a personal ticking-off from the Director General of the BBC himself!'

Brunswick squirmed. 'If it was in a locked drawer, Mrs G … ?' he said, gently.

'Oh, pooh, dear,' Mrs Groynes rushed to reassure him. 'That drawer was wide open when I looked in it!' (Which was technically true, but only because she had opened it with the aid of specialist tools.)

They all looked at Inspector Steine's closed door, on the other side of which he was being very quiet. Matrimonial law as applied to criminal prosecution was predictably turning out to be a bit of an unwieldy subject: he might remain in there for hours.

'So picture the scene, dears,' Mrs Groynes continued, her voice still low. 'There it was, April the first. You'd think the date would be a bit of a clue, wouldn't you?'

Twitten laughed, despite himself.

'So the inspector's in his slippers with a cup of cocoa, and there's that nice Cliff Michelmore on the television reporting how the pasta crop was early this year on the Swiss–Italian border.'

'I saw it with my parents,' said Twitten. '"*The last two weeks of March are always an anxious time for the spaghetti farmer*"! It was priceless. But how could anyone believe it was real? They'd just draped strands of spaghetti over bushes. They said what a miracle of nature it was that all the strands were the same length!'

'Well, it turns out that the inspector got so worked up about the dangers of the so-called spaghetti weevil that he only went and wrote one of his talks on the subject.'

'No!' said Twitten, while Brunswick (no less shocked) merely put his head in his hands.

'Apparently he wrote this impassioned plea, see, saying that this weevil needed to be stamped out completely or the people of Italy might starve, and many respectable restaurants in Brighton be put out of business!'

'But someone stopped him? They must have stopped him?' said Twitten, worried.

'Oh, yes, dear. His producer at the BBC.'

'Thank goodness.'

'But it was touch and go, dear. He had to dash off a completely new script in about half an hour once they realised what he'd done. And then he got this shaming memo from the Director General – the one I found in his desk – saying it had better not happen again.'

Down on the seafront, Adelaide and Phyllis peered along the row of hastily vacated deck-chairs to where a dark lone figure remained, unmoving. The crowd of holiday-makers helpfully shuffled into position behind them, leaving their way clear to go and investigate.

'There, miss!' said the child, pointing. 'Where he's not moving.'

'Yes,' said Adelaide. 'Yes. Thank you. I can see.'

This was a far cry from popping people's postcards into a pillar-box, or reciting the timetable of Volk's Electric Railway. But she was wearing a uniform, and that seemed to put her in charge.

'Phyllis,' she said, firmly, 'you go and find a policeman.'

'My Bert's already gone to do that,' a woman volunteered. 'He went as soon as he saw the blood.'

'Ah,' said Phyllis, in a quivering voice. 'There's blood?'

'I should say so!' the woman scoffed.

'Oh, dear,' said Adelaide.

She and Phyllis took a few brave steps towards the figure, which appeared to be that of a man – a long, thin man slumped back in his deck-chair, dressed in the dark clothes and shiny laced shoes of an office worker, his hair uplifted by the wind, arms hanging lifeless at his sides. They both saw something liquid was dripping from the bottom of the chair and accumulating in a small, dark puddle underneath.

Adelaide, feeling it was now or never, took control. 'Look, he might still be alive, Phyllis,' she said, quietly. 'You wait here.' Then she turned to the little crowd and said, in a re-assuring tone, 'I'm sure the police will soon be here, so please don't be alarmed. But if you did want to find amusement else-where, may I recommend the Hall of Mirrors on the Palace Pier? Children get in for a penny!'

Then, with all the composure she could muster, she approached the body, while the crowd made a collective suck-ing-of-teeth noise.

And there, still bleeding from the deep knife-wound across his throat, sat the body of a somewhat weedy young man, his eyes open, his mouth forming a horrible 'O' and his life-blood accumulating – drip by drip – in a crimson puddle beneath his chair. Next to his right hand lay a knife.

'Is he dead, miss?' people called (from a safe distance).

'What did he die of?'

'Who is he?'

'Which pier has the Hall of Mirrors again?'

'What's his name?'

'How much is it for grown-ups?'

'What time do you get off work, miss?'

'Do you recognise him?'

'How many pebbles on this beach, do you think? More than a thousand?'

But for once, enquiring of a Brighton Belle was fruitless, as Adelaide stood frozen in front of the ghastly scene, fighting the urge to scream.

Three

It didn't take long for Inspector Steine to reach a considered view on the body in the deck-chair.

'Dead,' he called.

Brunswick and Twitten were holding back the crowd, but in truth there was little danger of anyone surging forward. Having already stood there for forty-five minutes, they were mostly quite bored – but, at the same time, refusing to disperse. Most of them didn't want to miss anything; others had paid good money for their deck-chairs, and were determined to reclaim them the moment the coast was clear.

The inspector's verdict of 'dead' was scant reward for their long forbearance. On hearing it, they let out a jeer of contempt.

Steine, unaware of the cynical mood of his audience, summoned Sergeant Brunswick to join him.

'Suicide, of course,' he confided, privately.

Together they looked at the body, with its open eyes, expression of horror and gaping scarlet throat.

Brunswick coughed politely. 'You think so, sir?'

'Oh, yes,' Steine said, in a tone of regret. 'You can see where he dropped the knife. Even more tragically, an unknown suicide. We may never know what drove this young man to commit such a horrid deed. We may never know even who he was. Look, Brunswick, can you and Twitten get those people to go away?'

'What if someone saw something, sir? Shouldn't we interview them?'

Muttering to himself something that sounded like 'Oh, give me strength', Steine turned and called out, 'My sergeant thinks some of you might have seen something, although I personally have my doubts. Is it possible that any of you can help?'

Most people shook their heads, but then Adelaide emerged from the throng, to a general gasp. She stepped forward, gripping the arm of the skinny, sunburned child in the knitted swimming trunks. (These had now thankfully dried out; their former droopiness had been a tad obscene.)

From the way he needed to be dragged towards Steine, the boy's presence was not entirely voluntary.

'Nigel, come *on!*' she urged him.

Adelaide was, by her own standards, horribly dishevelled: one long, beautiful strand of chestnut hair had escaped from her little hat and was dangling near a hazel eye that happened to be shaped like an almond. And on the hem of her perfectly pressed and laundered skirt, Brunswick noticed, there was a smear of blood.

'Tell the nice man what you saw, Nigel,' she said, gently. 'It might be important.'

The boy shook his head vigorously. He was desperate to get away. Everyone was looking at him. Everyone was looking in particular at the sky-blue trunks specially made for him in fancy cable stitch by his block-of-flats nanny in Bethnal Green. Years later, when he was grown up, he would successfully manage a sports equipment emporium in Romford, and would make it a firm policy never to stock knitted swimwear of any sort.

Inspector Steine wasn't going to wait for some street urchin to favour them with his testimony, and was about to tell

Adelaide just to go away when she announced, 'Nigel saw something, Inspector!'

She crouched down in front of the boy, so she could look him in the eye. 'Now, come on. You cared enough to come and fetch me. Tell the nice man.'

But the boy refused. 'Grass to a ruddy copper?' he said. And making an exceedingly rude hand-gesture at the inspector, he wriggled free from her grip and darted off towards the sea, with Sergeant Brunswick in limping, futile pursuit.

Steine rolled his eyes. 'All right. You tell me,' he said. 'What did the little lad see? But tell me first who you are and why you're dressed in that ridiculous uniform.'

'Well, sir,' she said, looking down at herself. She saw the blood on the hem of her skirt, and quailed. 'I'm just—'

She was reaching the limit of her courage. Steine's peremptory tone was the last thing she could cope with right now.

'My name is Adelaide Vine and – and I'm a Brighton Belle, and no one warned us that this sort of thing might happen.' Steine hardly noticed the catch in her voice. He was too busy puzzling over the name 'Brighton Belle'.

'A Brighton what?'

Looking round, he saw another young woman in identical uniform. This was Phyllis, sitting on a bench, sobbing. It seemed that Twitten (without authority) had brought this other Belle a mug of tea from one of the rougher places along the seafront where they barked; 'With or without?' when they took your order; and when you asked, confused, 'With or without *what?*' they said, 'Handles'.

Adelaide took a deep breath. 'What Nigel told me,' she said, 'was that he saw this young man arrive and sit down in that chair. He seemed edgy.'

'Well, he would. He was about to kill himself. You'd be edgy too.'

'He was holding a package, wrapped in brown paper.'

Steine waved an arm towards the body. 'So where's the package now?' he said.

It was at this point that Constable Twitten came forward. He had been looking at the corpse for the first time, and was excited.

'Sir,' he said. 'I believe I know who the dead man is, sir.'

'Oh, shut up, Twitten. Of course you don't. You've only been in Brighton three weeks.'

'But I do, sir. I even know quite a bit about him. His name is Peter Dupont; cruel people called him "Weedy Pete". His girlfriend Deirdre has access to the wax museum through a secret door and they were planning to run away together tonight. Look how weedy he is, if you don't believe me, sir.'

'This nonsense can wait, Constable. It's not every day we get a suicide in a public place.'

'But this can't be suicide, sir. He was planning to run away.'

'Look,' said Steine, firmly, 'when I said shut up, Twitten, perhaps I wasn't clear. I meant *shut up, Twitten*. Now, where was I?'

He turned back to Adelaide, who was unsure what to do. Should she go on?

'Oh, ignore the constable,' said Steine. 'He's always like this. You were telling us what else that loathsome little street child told you.'

'Well, he thought that the old ladies sitting either side of the young man were dozing.'

'Convenient,' muttered Steine.

'Meanwhile the young man appeared to be waiting for someone, and kept looking at his wristwatch. Obviously, this being low tide, Nigel had his sandcastles to think about; he was working with his dad on an ambitious scale model of Wormwood Scrubs – to show the rooftop route his dad's friend Chalky had used to escape – and they were busy with the watchtower.

'But he was aware of a sudden, violent movement – the young man's long leg kicked up very high, he said – and when he turned to look, there was a figure running off towards the bandstand, and the package had gone, and the young man wasn't moving, and a knife – a knife – ' She took a deep breath ' – fell to the ground.'

She staggered, and Twitten instinctively offered her his arm. 'Are you all right, miss?' he asked her, earnestly.

It was just then – as the constable offered this kindness to a beautiful young woman in distress – that something mysterious stirred deep in Inspector Steine, something like a memory.

Are you all right, miss? Why did this simple question move him so powerfully?

Brunswick came back, panting from his fruitless chase after the boy.

'He got away, sir,' he explained, unnecessarily.

But Steine said nothing. He had adopted his trademark thoughtful, faraway look, as if searching the universe for the meaning of life. Usually, this expression was actually quite vacuous – just a means of mental escape from an unpleasant situation. But this time it was genuine: *Think*, he urged himself. *Think, Inspector Geoffrey St John Steine of the Brighton Constabulary, twice winner of Policeman of the Year! Think! Think!*

'Excuse me, miss,' Twitten continued. 'But why don't you come and sit down with your friend? Then the sergeant and I could escort you home. You've had a bally enormous shock.

May I get you a cup of tea? I think I'll be able to obtain one with a handle this time. They took me by surprise before.'

'Tea?' she wailed. 'Oh, yes, please!'

And it was at this moment, to Inspector Steine's extreme surprise, that his heart went out to this young woman – this beautiful, helpless woman with all the nuts.

Deirdre Benson was confused when she came back into the sparsely lit bar of the Black Cat Club (bearing two cups of disgusting chicory coffee), and found that Dickie had dis-appeared. Hadn't she heard him picking out the notes to his songs at the piano only a few seconds before?

'Dickie?' she called, quietly. 'Are you there?'

She was a pale girl, and thin. You might say that their common weediness had been the thing that attracted her to young Peter. However, while the boy's etiolated look was genetic (he came from umpteen generations of unhealthy stock, some of his ancestors scarcely living long enough to reproduce), her own was more the effect of nurture: she'd been brought up virtually in the dark.

'I expect he had to pop out,' said her mother, from the gloom.

Deirdre swung round, peering into the shadows. She put a hand up to shield her eyes.

'Oh, Mum, you haven't? Not Dickie?'

Ma Benson laughed, and emerged into the light.

She was wearing an electric-blue nylon housecoat; her hair was in tight curlers; she was accompanied by a smell of setting lotion, fresh nail varnish, eau de cologne and (her favourite indulgence) sweet pipe tobacco. She was quite a sight, Ma

Benson: a broad-shouldered woman, she was six feet tall, with big legs and thick wrists, and to top it all she smoked (bizarre choice) a long churchwarden pipe. Her unusual stature and exotic smoking preference served her well in the very masculine world of night-club entrepreneurship. Most men, when dealing with her, were automatically thrown off kilter: when a woman can look down on your bald spot (and can also blow smoke in your eyes), you somehow don't know quite how to go about patronising her.

''Course not, Deedee,' she said, not entirely convincingly. 'Dickie's one of us!'

But when she approached her daughter, the girl backed away.

'Look, darling, I expect he had a bit of a headache, that's all. Or a change of heart. And who could blame him? I mean, you've hardly done that man a good turn, darling, involving him in your stupid schemes to run off with that kid from the council.'

Deirdre sat down at the piano, where the seat was (a bit gruesomely) still warm from Dickie's bottom. She sighed. It wasn't a sigh of thwarted grand passion; more of resignation. It had been a long shot with Weedy Pete. But in her defence, she never met *anyone*.

'I'll be sealing up that door to the wax place, by the way,' Ma Benson said. 'It's long-since served its purpose.'

Deirdre's chin quivered. When she had discovered the door behind a fake wall upstairs in an unvisited stockroom, she'd assumed it was her own little secret. But here was her mum talking about it having had a 'purpose'. What possible purpose could it ever have served? To save the tuppenny entry fee to the Maison du Wax?

'You promise you won't hurt Peter, Mum?'

'Me? Of course not. You just let him know you changed your mind, and we'll say no more about it. One of the boys can deliver the note.'

The girl, accepting defeat, placed her hands on the keys, and played the first few bars of 'Stardust'. She was a good pianist. Her musical uncle Kenneth had taught her the basics in the old days (before he was sawn into pieces).

She pictured Peter boarding the cream-and-green Southdown coach at nine p.m., and laying his raincoat along the back seat; begging the driver to wait another minute; checking his wristwatch; scanning the faces of the surging, anonymous seaside crowd. And then, when the coach driver insisted on setting off, he would meekly take his seat, and vanish from her life forever.

It made her want to sing Judy Garland's 'The Man That Got Away'. She started to pick out the notes to the opening line, but Ma Benson snapped, 'Don't do that, Deedee! You're always doing that!' and the girl obediently stopped.

Having a song for all occasions was young Deirdre's special curse. It's what happens when you grow up in a night club: the Great American Songbook gets into your blood. It drove the rest of the family mad, but she couldn't stop herself. Weedy Pete wouldn't have minded it. He loved the way she could sum up (with lyrics) the feeling that he was the one, 'night and day'; or that when he touched her fingertips, her heart was aglow.

———

Back at the police station, Mrs Groynes had bustled through her chores and then bolted down the back stairs. There were people she needed to talk to around the town. If Wall-Eye

Joe Marriott was already at large, and possibly heading for Brighton, she intended to be ready for him.

Normally, she would tolerate a certain amount of unauthorised villainy on her turf. The odd freelance con man getting himself arrested in the town was actually helpful to her: such small fry could be fed into the justice system to keep it happy, with no danger to herself or her many vassals and associates.

Just last month, for example, a teenage 'whiz gang' (pickpockets) working on the London platform at the railway station had been successfully brought to book by Sergeant Brunswick, with benefits to everyone. If truth be told, it was Mrs Groynes the charlady's innocent prattling on the subject that had set him on their trail in the first place, but he'd done a good job catching the kids in the act. He had felt very pleased with himself; the inspector had been pleased with him too. Meanwhile Mrs Groynes had been the most pleased of all, because while police attention had been focused on the petty pilfering of insignificant junior villains, her top team in the Kemp Town area had stripped all the lead off the roof of St Michael and All Angels.

But if Mrs Groynes was willing to tolerate such outsider activity, it was important that she always knew what was going on. Currently in Brighton, she was aware of several housebreakers operating around Fiveways; some minor rackets at the race course; money changing hands over a proposed ugly new convention centre in the grounds of the Brighton Pavilion; and of course the continuing reprehensible thuggishness of the Benson clan (mother and sons, not the girl) operating from the Black Cat night club at the seaward end of Grenville Street.

Actually, the Bensons had been suspiciously quiet recently – in fact, ever since the so-called 'trunk murder' of 1955.

Having a discreet and well-remunerated informant working for her at the club (he played percussion in the quartet and kept his nose clean), Mrs Groynes was well aware of whose torso had been found in that famous suitcase at the railway station. According to Tommy Drumsticks, Ma Benson's younger brother Kenneth had disappeared at precisely the time the body was deposited in Left Luggage. Drumsticks had admired Kenneth, who was a musical director on some of the big shows up in London. He had possessed sheet music signed 'With thanks' by the legendary Richard Rodgers! Kenneth had given Dickie and the band a few excellent tips on phrasing. But then, one day, he had disappeared – just after angry words had been exchanged between him and Ma Benson.

And although the press had had a field day with the trunk murder, and called for the police to make our left-luggage system safe from deposits of grisly human remains, no formal identification of Kenneth's torso had ever been made. Inspector Steine had personally lost interest in the case very quickly.

'Too little to go on until the head turns up,' he had decided, and Mrs Groynes had whole-heartedly supported this decision, because it would give her leverage with the Bensons in the future if she needed it.

'And look at it this way, dear,' she had said, while pouring the inspector a nice cup of tea. 'What's the rush? Without legs, he's not going anywhere.'

And so the torso's original owner went untraced. Poor Sergeant Brunswick couldn't help thinking that there had been a *few* useful clues, such as the fingerprints on the locks; the lingering smell of sweet pipe tobacco when you opened the case; the initials 'KB' in the leather; the small fragments of coloured glass found embedded in the skin of the shoulders (as from the footlights you might find in a night club). But unluckily, he was over-ruled.

So far as the Bensons were concerned, then, Mrs Groynes was biding her time, with an ace up her sleeve. So far as the boys at the race track were concerned, she could – up to a point – live and let live. But Wall-Eye Joe Marriott was another kettle of fish altogether. Twitten had been right to detect an unusual personal animus in her on this subject.

On her way to the seafront, Mrs Groynes approached a boy dressed like a shoe-polisher's lad, leaning against a wall, perusing a copy of the *Dandy*. As it happened, the lad lurked there every day, from nine to six, in precisely this spot, retained by Mrs Groynes. He looked up when she drew near.

'Morning, madam,' he said, smiling. 'What can I do you for?'

'Shorty,' she said, 'tell Vince to leave the Punch and Judy and meet me in Luigi's in fifteen minutes. Then get Diamond Tony from the Metropole.'

And even though she said no more than that, the boy frowned all the way as he raced off to deliver the messages. It wasn't every day that she required the special services of Diamond Tony.

'Something's up, Vince,' he reported to the Punch & Judy man, when he arrived. 'She looks proper cross,' he told the spiv having his nails clipped in his top-floor suite at the posh seafront hotel.

So what was it about Wall-Eye Joe's unfinished-house scam of 1949 that so agitated Mrs Groynes? Had she perhaps been a friend or relative of one of the female victims? Had the unfinished-house scam perhaps been her own idea, nicked from her by Wall-Eye? What reason had she to feel so aggrieved?

What no one knew about the unfinished-house scam was that it wasn't just women who fell for it. There were male victims too. Marriott's young woman accomplice (The Skirt, as Brunswick called her) had herself courted lonely, gullible, big-hearted male clients, and spun them the identical story about the house in the country. And one of those men had been very dear to Mrs Groynes. He had been the love of her life. She carried in her handbag his last letter to her. She had treasured it for years.

As she sat now in Luigi's, waiting for Vince, she felt a scream well within her when she thought of what must have happened to her darling man. During the war he'd been a captain in the bomb-disposal unit of the Royal Engineers; he had risked his life dozens of times for the sake of other people; he had lost members of his team; he had himself suffered both psychological trauma and bodily injury. To be murdered after all that … murdered and then dissolved in acid, perhaps! His name was Philip Hoagland, but at his invitation she had called him by his nickname 'Hoagy', the way his men had done.

Their time together was just after the war. They had met on VE Day, in fact, in the jubilant crowds of Trafalgar Square, when she accidentally elbowed him in the eye. He bought her a gin to show there were no hard feelings, and the attraction (which was powerful) grew from there. In the few short weeks they were together, she had been thrilled by Hoagy's attentions: she had never expected to consort with a man who was either so selfless or so posh. But their closeness also caused her anguish: she felt like a fraud. Surely she and Hoagy had nothing in common? Wasn't he just too good for her, in every way? Look at their contrasting histories: while Captain Philip Hoagland had been crawling in muddy East

End craters to disarm German explosives, she had been hijacking GPO vans on the Holloway Road, learning her trade from the young, up-and-coming London gang-boss Terence Chambers. Hoagy was also, socially speaking, from quite another world: a true toff. If ever there was a man who said 'looking-glass' instead of 'mirror', it was he.

But what tipped the balance was when Chambers started making unmistakable romantic advances towards her, and asking if she had a boyfriend already. She refused to expose her dear Hoagy to the danger of being Terence Chambers's rival: she simply had to forsake him. He had been hurt and confused. The scene in the bustling Lyons Corner House on the Strand, during which the stricken Hoagy openly wept huge manly tears on to his uneaten egg on toast, she would never forget. She kept telling herself, *I'm doing this for your sake, my darling; I'm doing this for you* – but it did not assuage the guilt. And later, when she learned that the unfinished-house scam had brutally torn the good and guileless Philip Hoagland from this world, she felt deeply (though irrationally) that she herself was to blame, for not protecting him.

She hadn't known till much later what his fate had been. After years of silence, she had assumed he'd forgotten her. But then in London a year ago, she had bumped into his best friend Hoppy coming out of a bistro in Dean Street (all Hoagy's army captain friends had nicknames like Aspers, or Hoppy, or Dicko).

'Not seen Hoagy for yonks,' said Hoppy, sadly. 'Last I heard he was in the pink, though, so don't you go worrying about him. Word is, he visited one of those agencies in Regent Street, and fell in love with the handsome woman who ran it!'

At the council offices in Marlborough House, Mr Blackmore was beginning to get annoyed. It was nearly eleven o'clock, and there was still no sign of his junior clerk.

He slid open the little wooden hatch beside his desk.

'Still not in?' he asked his secretary Lillian. 'Where *is* the boy?'

Lillian, who had been giving her full attention to the pleasurable smoking of a full-length Bristol Tipped, pulled a face and shrugged.

'Why are you asking me?' she said, stiffly, brushing ash off her desk and not looking at Mr Blackmore. 'I'm not his mum.'

A stranger to the office would have spotted at once that this particular department of Town Planning (Sewerage and Waterworks) was not, as they say, a nest of singing birds.

Blackmore sighed. Sometimes he felt very hard done by, having Lillian as his secretary. Mr Statham down the hall had the beauteous Nancy; Mr Phillips in the treasury had the virginal Iris—but Blackmore mustn't let himself think about Iris.

'Lillian, have you typed up the minutes of Friday's meeting?'

'Not yet, no. They only just came in.'

He knew this to be a lie, but let it pass.

'Well, we need to get them signed off by the Borough Engineer this afternoon, so please could you do it as soon as possible?'

'All right, all right,' she muttered. 'Keep your hair on.'

With the half-finished cigarette clamped between her lips, and eyes half-closed against the smoke, Lillian mutteringly fed new paper (two sheets, with carbon paper between) on to the heavy Remington carriage and then aggressively commenced the clattering high-decibel *bang-rattle-bang-rattle-rattle-bang-rattle-rattle-ping* that was the soundtrack

61

to busy office life everywhere in the world in the age of the manual typewriter.

Mr Blackmore slid his little hatch back again, muttering under his breath. He had no idea what Lillian's problem was, and he refused to enquire. In his defence, had he known that her main grievance concerned gender differentials in pay, he wouldn't have understood anyway.

But that was exactly what she was fed up about. Two weeks ago, an unfortunate mix-up with pay packets meant she had found out that junior clerk Peter Dupont (seventeen years old; first job) was paid twice as much as she was. Lillian was thirty-two years old, and could type seventy words per minute. She'd worked in local government for fifteen years and had a mother to support. Unsurprisingly, since her discovery, she'd been smoking considerably more at her desk, and speaking considerably less. She had also stopped wearing make-up and deodorant. As for clothes, she was opting increasingly for ugly skirts and shapeless cardigans.

It was odd that Dupont was so late, though. Pausing in her work, she looked over to his empty chair and orderly desk, and decided she had never liked him; and she hoped he got in serious trouble. What a pipsqueak! And so nakedly ambitious, too: always volunteering to run things along to the various planning departments down the corridor, and helping the women in Archives with their unwieldy Gestetner machine. He probably thought Lillian didn't know about those Archives visits, but several times recently he had come back to the office smelling to high heaven of the distinctive purple ink that was used in those machines.

Needing a fresh box of matches, she opened her desk drawer, and inside it found something peculiar. It was a Manilla envelope with 'Miss Ross' written on the front in

Dupont's handwriting. She looked at it in confusion, and was just about to get up and rap on Mr Blackmore's hatch when she heard the telephone ring on his desk and noticed that, in any case, the boy had written 'For Your Eyes Only' under her name.

'Blackmore speaking,' she heard her boss say (a bit muffled), next door. Using her favourite paper knife, she slit open the envelope and found inside a handwritten note.

Dear Miss Ross,

This is just to say goodbye, and also to say I was shocked to see how little you are paid. It is an outrage.

By the time you read this, you will know what I have done. Please do not think less of me. I know what I am doing. I could not just stand by and do nothing.

People will say I have abducted Deirdre, but I assure you she is coming of her own free will.

Keep cheerful and please remember me with affection,

Peter

The hatch slid open.

'Lillian, that was Mr Reinhardt upstairs,' said Blackmore. He looked pale and anxious. He was wondering whether the hatch was really the most fitting conduit for news of this magnitude, but it was too late now to change his mind.

'What's that you're holding?' he said.

'It's nothing.' Lillian slid the note into the pocket of her cardigan.

'Look, there's no easy way to say this. It seems that the entire contents of Mr Reinhardt's safe have been taken. And he thinks it was our young Mr Dupont who did it! He's going to call the police!'

Dickie had not had a change of heart, as Ma Benson had told her daughter; but he had certainly had a change of location. As he regained consciousness, all he knew was that he was on the floor – on a cold concrete floor, somewhere indoors, in the dark. His various aches and pains had not been improved by being dumped there. His head was sore; worst of all, his bottom set of dentures was not in his mouth. The only good news in all this was that he seemed to be alone.

Did he have matches in his pockets? With an effort, he sat up. If he had some light, he could find the door and perhaps get out.

'Yes!' he said, with relief. It was his habit to keep a Black Cat match-book in one of his trouser pockets, for lighting the cigarettes of attractive female customers between songs. This practice had done him no good for as long as he could remember, but it was certainly a godsend now.

'All right, where am I?' he said quietly to himself, striking the first match – which gloomily revealed a sort of store room, with shelves. Dark shadows danced on the walls. The shelves held rows of indistinct grey objects, each the size and shape (roughly) of a beachball. He narrowed his eyes and scrambled up to take a look – but as he reached his feet, the match went out.

Had he paused for thought before striking the second match, he might not have emitted the scream that echoed round the room. But what a fright, on first seeing the glassy eyes of Napoleon Bonaparte staring right back at you: a ghoulishly severed head, complete with imperial kiss curl, stacked on a shelf amid dozens of others, all wild-haired and florid. Next to Napoleon was (judging from the thickness of its hair and the dyspeptic expression) Ludwig van Beethoven. Next to Beethoven was (judging by the helpful yellowed label stuck to his cheek) Charlie Chaplin.

'Waxworks!' Dickie spluttered, in relief. 'Oh my God!'

And then, just as his second match blew out, he said, puzzled, 'Kenneth?'

Brunswick and Twitten, under instructions from Inspector Steine, were accompanying the stricken Brighton Belles back to their accommodation in the centre of town. It was honestly one of the best orders Brunswick had ever received: to escort beautiful women through the most populous streets of Brighton, to the envy of the entire male population. Twitten noticed that there was an unprecedented lightness to the sergeant's gait.

Twitten was less enamoured of their mission, however, having several pressing questions on his mind concerning the murder (not suicide) of Peter Dupont. Surely there wasn't a moment to lose, so why was he having to trail through the streets with a pair of stunningly pretty young women when he could be researching the inadequate investigation of Uncle Ken's murder in 1955, or finding out which building backed on to the Maison du Wax? To make this pointless peregrination even more annoying, the sergeant kept stopping, as if he were a tour guide, to regale the Belles with incidental facts about the town ('And there's the famous Maison du Wax, founded in 1924'), all of which information they already knew better than he did.

It was because the sergeant was so inclined to dawdle and stretch things out that from outside Luigi's ('This is Brighton's most famous ice-cream parlour'), he spotted Mrs Groynes on the other side of the glass having an intense tête-à-tête with the aggressive Punch & Judy man, Ventriloquist Vince, and another man, with a scar on his cheek, who was stirring sugar into his frothy coffee with what looked like a foot-long stiletto.

'Oh, look, there's Mrs Groynes, the station charlady,' said Brunswick. 'She's with some friends. Is that *tutti-frutti* they're having? I've got to say hello.'

The sergeant tapped on the window, making every customer look up in alarm at the sight of two policemen outside. A couple of Teddy Boys guiltily knocked over their milkshakes, while another athletically dived for cover behind the jukebox. But Mrs Groynes just waved back, cheerily, and with her mimed encouragement her two hard-looking companions waved half-cheerily too, indicating in dumb-show that the *tutti-frutti* was excellent. Twitten felt a twinge of weary sadness. Here was a villain having a blatant top-level meeting with two other villains, observed by two policemen on duty, and it was going to be the story of his life that he alone could see past their not-so-fascinating choice of ice-cream flavour.

'Sir,' Twitten said, when they were all walking along again, north this time, away from the sea, and Brunswick's travelogue commentary had temporarily run dry. 'Mrs Groynes was bally upset about that famous con man you saw mentioned in the *Police Gazette*, wasn't she?'

Brunswick, shocked that Twitten would raise such a subject when they were in the company of civilians, shot him a look as if to say 'not now', and pointedly changed the subject. 'We are entering the area known as *The Lanes*,' he said.

But Adelaide and Phyllis knew all there was to know about The Lanes, thank you very much; they could also tell you the quickest way to the station in most Indo-European languages;

they were far more interested by this tantalising mention of a con man. Also, given what they had just been through, they were desperate for something to take their minds properly off the subject of slaughtered youths and bloodstained deck-chairs on the seafront. They both brightened.

'A con man, did you say, Constable Twitten?' said Phyllis.

Twitten bit his lip. 'I did, yes. Sorry, miss, I probably shouldn't have.'

'But don't be sorry! It's just such a happy coincidence! Because we *met* a real-live con man today, didn't we, Addy?'

'You what?' said Brunswick.

'Oh, don't worry, we saw straight through him, so there was no harm done. It was in that very ice-cream place where we just saw your friend. He had a bag of *Russian gold*!'

At which Phyllis burst out laughing, and Adelaide joined in.

'He was hopeless!' she explained. 'He tried to sell us each a gold brick!'

'He did!' spluttered Phyllis.

It felt so good to laugh after what they'd seen on the seafront that both Belles were, for a while, unable to elaborate further, despite Brunswick demanding (unheard) to know why they hadn't reported this encounter directly to the police.

'He said he was a lord!' exclaimed Adelaide, literally hold-ing her sides. 'But, you see, virtually every word out of his mouth was *Non-U*! Do you know what I mean by that?'

'I do, yes,' said Twitten, triumphantly shooting a glance at Brunswick. 'I happen to know exactly what you mean by that.'

'You've read the book, Constable?'

'Yes, I've read the book.'

'He actually said the reason he had the gold was that his father was "mental"!'

'No!'

'He talked about cruet sets and serviette rings. He mentioned the "radio" as well. He was obviously a fraud.'

Twitten felt the urge to hug this young woman. How many times in the past few days had he insisted on the value of learning about U and Non-U? And how many times had he been dismissed with a flea in his ear, on the grounds that new-fangled socio-linguistics had no practical application in detective work?

'He actually said "mental" and "serviette"?' marvelled Twitten. 'Did he say "toilet" and "mirror" as well?'

'No, but I'm sure he would have. Such a posh voice, but the vocabulary – all wrong!'

Adelaide was breathing more calmly now, but still enjoying the story. 'But the whole thing was preposterous, not just the words he used. The story about how he got the gold, the reason for selling it, Rudolph Valentino's role in its history – just everything.'

Phyllis took some deep breaths. They were both growing calmer now. They were finally aware that their police escort, while interested, were still not finding their story remotely amusing. If there was one thing Brunswick was never light-hearted about, it was criminals.

'It was just hilarious,' said Phyllis, by way of summing up, 'but perhaps you needed to be there.'

'Well,' said Brunswick, sternly, 'perhaps when we get back to your accommodation and you've had a chance to collect yourselves, you can make a proper statement.'

'We would love to,' said Adelaide. She put a hand on his arm.

And then, despite herself, she burst out laughing again.

'You didn't mention the funny eyes, Phyl!' she cried. 'He had one eye pointing one way, and the other eye pointing somewhere else!'

Four

The so-called 'gold-brick scam' was pretty widely recognised in the world of crime detection at this time.

'Watch out for anyone offering gold bricks!' was a well-worn joke from one bobby handing over to another. Or, 'Don't buy any gold bricks that I wouldn't buy!'

The regular procedure was for a stranger to offer for sale gold bricks at a bargain price, using some far-fetched story about why he needed to get rid of them (he would sometimes affect an Australian or a South African accent). The brick he handed over for examination would indeed be twenty-four-carat (and he might even persuade people to take it away for tests), but the rest would be made of brass, with phials of mercury inside to bring the weight to the right level. One such brass-and-mercury brick was on permanent display in Scotland Yard's ghoulish Black Museum, alongside such other unsavoury items as the enormous, thick socks worn over his shoes by an infamously quiet cat-burglar known to the police as 'Flannelfoot'. Recently, the star exhibit was a floorboard with a human incisor tooth gruesomely embedded in it, from the scullery of the so-called 'Kennington Butcher'.

But even if the gold-brick scam hadn't been well known to the police, not many innocent civilians were likely to fall for it. Something had happened to the populace since the war: they had wised up. Perhaps they'd just been fleeced too many times by spivs. Perhaps they'd seen too many world-weary Hollywood movies. Either way, now that rationing was finally over, and they could walk away when a deal looked too good to be true, walking away (and laughing) was what they mainly chose to do.

A true con man such as the infamous Wall-Eye Joe, therefore, would not have bothered with this particular scam in Brighton in 1957. Which is why an important deduction can be made: that the man doffing his hat and calling himself 'Lord Melamine' was not a con man, as previously supposed. Despite his unfortunate optic misalignment, he was not Wall-Eye Joe. We simply have to accept that this man was exactly what his embossed card said he was: the newly encumbered 5th Marquess of Colchester, son of a mental father. And by extension this means that the gold in his bag was all real, and that he genuinely wanted total strangers to take it off his hands.

In the years to come, the instructive story of Lord Melamine would become common knowledge, but in 1957 it was not well known. He had spent most of his life up to this point in Herefordshire – it being the first rule with aristocratic families that if you're called the Marquess of Colchester, your ancestral seat is at least two hundred miles away, and reached diagonally. He had never before visited Brighton. The splendid Colchester House on the seafront was but one of five major establishments owned by the family, and the least regarded by the 4th Marquess (the current Marquess's late father, known and often mocked for his 'funny ideas'), who had refused to visit for many years, because Brighton tended to annoy him.

It is worth noting here that the many funny ideas of the 4th Marquess were so pronounced that they earned him the nickname 'Lord Loopy' in the Rothermere press. Among his particular hobby-horses were the rigidity of the class system and the nature-versus-nurture debate, which led him – in the spirit of experiment – to deny his only son the usual education of an aristocrat. Thus, instead of being sent away to prep school (to mix with his own kind), young Melamine had lodged from the age of six with a lowly family on the estate. Instead of following his father and uncles to Eton, he had attended a normal grammar. Lord Loopy had no qualms about using his son and heir as a sociological test case, especially after the convenient early death of his wife, who'd been a bit of a stickler for convention.

And it had worked! The current Lord Melamine – raised, as it were, by wolves – gave almost no thought to matters of rank. Where the difference between U and Non-U indicators was concerned, he was innocent as Sergeant Brunswick. In fact, it was remarked by several onlookers that when Lord Loopy lay on his death-bed, it was the wording of his son's pledge to dispose of all the worldly goods – 'every home, every fish-knife, every serviette!' – that had precipitated his final seizure. His heart had been simply unable to contain such joy. 'My son! My greatest achievement!' he had rejoiced. It was in particular his son's unaffected use of the word 'serviette' – *as if it were an acceptable word* – that had (all agreed) sent the 4th Marquess of Colchester out of this life a happy man.

And now the 5th Marquess was in Brighton, and becoming desperate. He confided in everyone who would listen, 'My father told me to get rid of it all. And not the easy way, giving it to charities: give it *directly to the people*. That was his message to me, from the cradle. You have to help.' At first, he had tried giving people the gold bricks as gifts; then he had hit on the idea (more face-saving for them, surely) of offering the gold for sale ludicrously cheaply. Nothing worked. One afternoon, running out of patience, he had tried simply leaving a gold brick in one of the shelters on the seafront, in the hope that an impoverished pensioner would totter along and find it. But he'd walked only thirty yards when just such an impoverished pensioner tapped him on the shoulder and handed it back to him. 'Nice try!' the old man panted, breathless from the effort of chasing him.

Luckily for him, the Brighton house was a beautiful one. Built in 1818 by one of the former marquesses, under the guidance of John Nash, it was a large, imposing Regency mansion on the seafront. So, why had Lord Loopy always eschewed it? Two reasons. First, he had discovered that, in the context of Brighton, he just wasn't halfway eccentric or free-thinking enough to make his presence felt (many self-styled non-conformists before and since have been similarly miffed). Second, he hated what had been allowed to happen to the back of his house.

No one knew how it had come about. But somehow, during the First World War, the valuable land immediately to the rear of Colchester House had been acquired by a rapacious builder in league with the local authority. What once had been a wide and stately walled orchard (with a famous aviary containing exotic birds, collected on foreign travels) was now the location of a pair of drab, flat-roofed commercial establishments: on one side (with its entrance in Russell Place), a squat, pathetic wax museum; on the other (entered from Grenville Street), a noisy neon-lit night club. The two buildings met back-to-back so that not an inch of space was wasted. No vestige of garden remained. The back of Colchester House was separated from the new buildings by a mere alleyway – an alley so narrow that the fire brigade was forever being summoned to release wedged-in couples stupid enough to attempt sexual congress in it.

The loss of the garden was a tragedy. The parakeets and cockatiels disappeared. Enquiries at the Zoological Society in Regent's Park confirmed that the birds had not been offered there: presumably, they'd been released into the air, only to be instantly pecked to death by gulls. Certainly, some very pretty feathers turned up in the hats of Brighton's domestic servants around this time. For Lord Loopy, the loss of the birds was a shock from which he never recovered. Whenever he spoke of a particularly long-lived parrot named Billy, a tear would form in his eye. Billy had been a much-loved bird, the pride of the collection, a brilliant mimic of street hawker calls such as 'Muffins, hot muffins!' It was said that Billy was old enough to have been present with the 2nd Marquess at the Siege of Sebastopol – but that, like many another brave war veteran, he could never be persuaded to talk about it.

With the garden and aviary long gone (and the natives of Brighton easily outstripping Lord Loopy in the eccentricity department), the 4th Marquess had therefore forsaken Colchester House, retaining a succession of live-in housekeepers to maintain it, and more or less forgetting it existed.

'Hoagy, it's hopeless!'

Such were the words heard every day by the trusty valet at Colchester House, upon opening the door to his master and revealing him silhouetted in a halo of sunlight on the top step. Today was no exception.

'Your lordship, I'm sorry. Allow me to take the bag.'

Captain Hoagland gently helped Lord Melamine off with his raincoat, and handed it to Mrs Rivers, the current housekeeper, who had lived comfortably alone in the house for the past ten years, and was still slightly reeling from the shock of having other people to attend to. Not that she minded the intrusion of Captain Hoagland: quite the contrary. A distinguished man of middle age, the valet was tall, handsome and well-made, but with an intriguing (and attractive) inward curl to the right side of his body, as if (possibly) he'd been injured by an explosion while heroically defusing bombs during the Second World War.

'No takers again today, my lord?' she asked, politely. Like Hoagland, Mrs Rivers knew all about Lord Melamine's doomed mission to distribute gold to the deserving poor.

Melamine threw up his hands. 'Not one!'

'I'm very sorry, your lordship,' said Hoagland.

'They assume I'm making it all up, Hoagy!'

'Oh, sir.'

'About the battleship, and Rudolph Valentino, even about Father being mental. Who would make up the story of a mental father? But I can see in their eyes that they think I'm lying!'

He looked as if he might burst into tears. Mrs Rivers turned to Hoagland – who had known Lord Melamine far longer than she – for guidance on the right words of comfort.

'Perhaps your offer just seems too good to be true, sir,' said the valet. 'There aren't many people genuinely giving away a fortune in this world. Allow me to put the bricks with the others in the safe downstairs, then I'll bring tea to the morning room. It will all seem better after a refreshing cup of Earl Grey, sir.'

Hoagland, carpet-bag in hand, took the stairs down to the kitchen, with Mrs Rivers watching after him.

'He's such a good man,' she said quietly to Lord Melamine. 'I don't think I've ever met anyone like him.'

'I couldn't agree more,' said his lordship, with a sigh. 'Now, what's been happening while I was out, Mrs Rivers?'

She smiled. She had potential good news for him.

'There's a letter on your desk from the council, sir.'

His lordship's eyes lit up. 'Do you think it's regarding the compulsory purchase of Colchester House?'

'I don't know, sir. But I do hope for your sake that they're going to knock this old place down to make way for a shiny new conference centre, or useful bus garage, or something.'

'Oh, so do I!'

As Hoagland reappeared, carrying a tray of preliminary tea-things, Mrs Rivers noticed he was wincing. Not for the first time, her heart went out to him.

'Not your shoulder playing you up again, Captain Hoagland?' she asked, gently.

'Well, a little, Mrs Rivers.'

'Let me take the tray, go on.'

'No, no. But damn those damn' Jerries, Mrs R, if you don't mind my saying so.'

He deposited the tray in the morning room and went back downstairs, with Mrs Rivers watching, unsure whether to follow. It had been such a whirlwind, having Lord Melamine and Captain Hoagland descend on the house like this, that she still didn't know how to fit in. But what an interesting pair these two were: Lord M with his unconventional upbringing, Hoagland with his war wounds. And how generous they were with their confidences. In cosy chats below stairs Hoagland had told her everything – even sharing with her his concerns about the human cost of the late Lord Loopy's sociological tamperings in regard to his son's education. 'He's a good, kind man, Mrs Rivers. He turned out very well. But he's also deeply lonely. Although how could he be otherwise, when he fits in nowhere?'

What Hoagland had also told her – and it was by far the most interesting story she had ever heard – was that he literally owed Lord Melamine his life. Wicked people had lured Captain Hoagland to an unfinished house in the country, and then tried to murder him! Lord Melamine had happened to be driving along a country lane and had found Captain Hoagland crawling along in the dark, terrified for his life.

'Oh, my goodness,' she gasped. 'You mean to say those fiends had wanted to kill you?'

'They had. And when I saw the headlights coming, I thought it was them! I thought, *This is it!*'

'No!'

'And then the car stopped and I heard his lordship say, "My dear fellow, what's happened to you? Let me help you! We need to get you to a doctor!"'

'Oh, my goodness gracious.'

'It was a miracle. Two minutes later, and those fiends (as you so rightly call them) would have caught up with me – the woman from the dating agency and her male accomplice who'd tried to strangle me in that cellar. Two minutes later, I would have been dead!'

Downstairs now, in the basement of Colchester House, Captain Hoagland opened the safe and stacked the five unclaimed gold bars alongside the one hundred and ninety-five others (it was a large safe) that had been sitting there since the Fall of Berlin. Then he went to make tea in the kitchen.

Upstairs in the morning room, the letter from the council was waiting for Lord Melamine. It contained more disappointment. He called Mrs Rivers in and told her the news. Evidently, the free offer of Colchester House had been considered by the Borough Engineer's office; there had been a vote last week and the offer had been rejected. The decision was final and not open to appeal. In no circumstances would the town accept the site for redevelopment.

'Oh, sir,' she said, sympathetically. Things did seem a bit topsy-turvy where Lord Melamine was concerned. He couldn't *give away* gold bars! Brighton Council, notorious from time immemorial for dodgy planning deals, *didn't want* a valuable prime site on the seafront at a knock-down rate?

Snatching up the telephone, Lord Melamine wasted no time however.

'This is Lord Melamine, put me through to the Borough Engineer,' he said.

But there was no answer from Reinhardt's extension, and when Melamine finally spoke to someone in the office of Sewerage and Waterworks, he was told by a rather hysterical secretary that the entire department was in such disarray this morning that she simply couldn't help with his enquiry.

'What has caused such disarray, Miss Ross?' he asked, politely. (He felt she wanted him to.)

So she told him. She couldn't help herself. There had been a mysterious theft by one of the junior employees!

'Oh, dear,' he said.

'And that's not the worst,' she said. 'He's not just done a robbery, taking everything from Mr Reinhardt's safe – ' her voice was shaky ' – he's only gone and killed himself as well.'

'No!'

'And he was only *seventeen*. And I wasn't very nice to him. It's awful.'

'Well, I'm so sorry to have phoned at such a distressing time,' he said. The idea of a seventeen-year-old boy killing himself was indeed almost too awful to contemplate. He tried to bring the conversation to a close, but it didn't work.

'In that case—' he began.

'And there's more!' said the excited secretary, who – now she had started – seemed to want to get it all off her chest.

'When the news came about young Mr Dupont being dead, and the stolen material from the safe all vanished, everyone just went nutty!'

'Nutty? Oh, dear.'

'Mr Blackmore fainted – dropped straight down as if someone had struck him. Someone's trying to revive him now, wafting him with his *Daily Sketch*. But Mr Reinhardt upstairs … you won't credit it!'

'Oh, yes? I mean, oh, no?'

'No! When he heard the news, he said, "Oh, shit, they killed him?" Pardon my French, but that's what he said! He said, "OH, SHIT, THEY KILLED HIM?" Then he runs down the stairs like the wind, streaks across the Town Hall car park, jumps in his car and drives off!'

———

Alone with Sergeant Brunswick at last, after dropping the Brighton Belles at their lodgings near the Clock Tower, Constable Twitten withdrew the typewritten sheet from his tunic pocket and unfolded it.

'Sir,' he said, 'I hope you don't mind, but I have some very urgent questions for you.' He scanned the page. 'Just to prepare you, they are mostly historical, criminological or topographical. But I think you will know the answers, so don't feel anxious – this isn't a test.'

Brunswick sighed. 'Well, so long as they're not about what I would call a flaming mirror, son, I expect I'll manage.'

Brunswick had hoped to talk about the relative charms of Adelaide and Phyllis. Personally, he had been attracted to them both, but he had acted with restraint and not asked either for a date – years of experience on the force having taught him the extraordinary, counter-intuitive fact that women are much less receptive to romantic advances when they've just been traumatised by (say) the sight of a dead body soaked in its own blood.

It had taken Brunswick quite a while to learn this lesson, by the way, but in the end he'd been obliged to accept the evidence of his own experience. Over the years, he had made many enthusiastic early moves on attractive women who had a) just lost all their possessions in a robbery, or b) just found their dead father electrocuted in the bath, or c) just been rescued from a house on fire. In each case, he had been soundly (though puzzlingly) rebuffed. What he had slowly come to accept was that, at times like these, women are grateful if you *don't* signal your keen sexual interest, but show selfless sympathy instead. Holding back might seem risky, but apparently it did make them think better of you as a person, and therefore increased your chances in the long run.

Thus, on the doorstep to the Brighton Belle lodgings, Brunswick had merely tipped his hat and said something about wishing it could have been under more pleasant circumstances – while Twitten tugged his sleeve, saying, 'Sir, sir. We did it, sir. We got them home. Now can I talk to you? Please, sir?'

It was just a couple of hours since Twitten had overheard the conversation between young Deirdre and her ill-fated boyfriend in the wax museum, but he felt he'd wasted precious time. As they walked downhill through the town towards the sea, it was a huge relief to be getting his investigation finally under way.

'The thing is, sir, the boy who died was planning to run away with a girl called Deirdre who came through a secret door in the wall from the building behind – which is what,

79

sir? What's the building adjoining the wax museum at the back?'

Brunswick stopped walking and screwed up his face, trying to picture the layout.

'Well, the wax museum is in Russell Place, so the next one along is Grenville Street. So that would probably be the Black Cat, son.'

'The Black Cat? What's that? A casino?'

'Night club. I know the singer there a little bit.' Something occurred to Brunswick. 'Here, that was a stroke of luck about Wall-Eye Joe trying to con the girls! I can't wait to see the look on Mrs Groynes's face!'

But Twitten wasn't interested in Wall-Eye Joe right now. He and the sergeant were on a wide street corner with no one to overhear them – not a bad place to stand and talk. The best thing was, there was no Mrs Groynes lurking behind, pretending to be absorbed in polishing a doorknob. He needed to press on.

'So who owns the Black Cat night club, sir?'

'Family called Benson.'

'Benson,' repeated Twitten. The name was new to him. 'So is there a Deirdre Benson?'

'Yes, I think there is. You think that was the girl you heard talking, then?'

'Yes, sir.'

'She's about sixteen years old, I think – and seems younger than that, apparently. She might be a bit daft. The singer talks about her sometimes; he's really soft on her. He's often in the Battle of Trafalgar at lunchtime, knocking back a few pints of Watney's before they call last orders.'

Twitten consulted his list. 'Is the singer's first name Dickie, by any chance, sir?'

Brunswick narrowed his eyes and huffed. Why did this always happen where Twitten was concerned? Just a few seconds ago, Brunswick had been the one airing his superior knowledge. In no time at all, Twitten had pulled that rug from under him.

Brunswick played for time. 'Pardon?' he said.

'Sorry, sir. I said, is this alcoholic singer of yours called Dickie, sir?'

'Yes, he is,' sighed Brunswick. 'Dickie George, well done.'

'Excellent,' said Twitten, making a note. 'Oh, don't look so glum, sir! Now we're getting somewhere.'

Brunswick put his hands in his pockets. He had started wondering how long the list was. He was also beginning to wish he'd had the nerve to ask Adelaide Vine for a date. Thinking about it, finding a stranger's dead body in a deck-chair was surely nothing like as upsetting as the electrocuted-parent-in-the-bath thing. It would be tragic to find out he'd misjudged the situation.

'Is there much more of this, Twitten? We ought to get back to the station.'

'Just a few more. Do the following names mean anything to you, sir: Hoagland, or Blackmore?'

'No.'

Twitten shook his head, disappointed.

'Last one now, sir.'

'Oh, good.'

'But it's quite a big one. Does Deirdre Benson have two big brothers and a scary mother, sir, who are basically thugs who literally get away with murder?'

Brunswick was outraged. '*What?*'

Twitten bit his lip. What had he said? Why was the sergeant so incensed?

'The Bensons *get away with murder*, did you say?'

'I did, yes. But – oh, I see.' Perhaps he should have employed a less offensive form of words. He hadn't meant to imply police incompetence, but evidently that was exactly what he'd done. 'I'm so sorry, sir. I didn't mean to suggest—'

'Look, we've never had anything on the Bensons, not all the time they've had that place. I personally have never even met them! What on earth makes you say they get away with murder?'

Twitten grimaced, and apologetically held up the list. Brunswick groaned. It was clear he was about to hear some big news.

'Oh, *what*?'

Twitten cleared his throat. 'What if I told you, sir, that the torso in the suitcase famously found at Brighton Railway Station was that of Deirdre's uncle Kenneth?'

'The torso in the suitcase? That was ages ago!' objected Brunswick – and then immediately regretted such a pathetic response. 'I mean to say, what do *you* know about that flaming torso in that flaming suitcase?'

'Well, more than everyone else, apparently, sir, since I know whose it was.'

This was the thing about Twitten, of course. However angry you were with him, he didn't back down. The strength of your annoyance was lost on him. You asked him, 'What do *you* know about this?' and instead of apologising, he answered the question.

'All right, *how* do you know that?'

'The girl told the boy this morning, sir. That's what caught my attention. She said Peter should be careful today because her family were capable of anything – she said, "*Don't forget what they did to Uncle Ken.*" Then she carried on, "*The police only found one bit of him in that suitcase at the station. No one's ever found his head."* So they *did* get away with murder at least once, sir. And now they might be doing it again.'

Twitten folded his list and put it back in his tunic pocket while Brunswick took some steadying breaths. Half of him wanted to demand to know why Twitten hadn't come out with this hugely important 'Uncle Ken' information earlier; half of him, however, was rapidly reviewing what they had known at the time about the torso and the suitcase, and praying that Clever Clogs Twitten would never hear about the initials 'KB' embossed in the leather. How had he not put two and two together at the time? Kenneth Benson had been quite a famous man in musical theatre, and there had been a national manhunt for him just around the time the suitcase had turned up. His disappearance had been on the front page of the *Police Gazette* every day for two weeks!

'Something wrong, sir?' asked Twitten.

Brunswick shook his head. He felt a bit sick.

'Look, Twitten,' he said, at last. 'That's good work.'

'Thank you, sir. So you think the body in the suitcase *was* this mysterious Uncle Ken?'

Brunswick made an effort to rise above his own feelings. 'As it happens, yes.'

Twitten beamed. He'd been expecting more of a battle to be believed.

'But listen,' said Brunswick, 'we can't just barge in and arrest them on the basis of something you overheard, son; we need evidence.'

'I know, sir. That's the law, sir. But it did occur to me just now, when you said you'd never met any of the Benson family: might that not be useful to us? Could this be the opportunity you've been waiting for to go undercover amongst villains in Brighton who don't know who you are?'

But before Brunswick could consider this presumptuous suggestion, they both noticed that on the corner of the next street, the light was flashing on top of the police box – a signal that (as Brunswick later reported) caused them both to proceed in a southerly direction.

'They've identified the boy as Peter Dupont, son,' said Brunswick, re-emerging from the box and locking the door. He looked excited.

'But I told the inspector that half an hour ago! I told you both!'

'All right, all right, clever clogs. He worked at the Town Hall, in the Borough Engineer's department. We have to get there at once. Apparently he committed a robbery, too!'

Back at the police station, Mrs Groynes was making a fresh pot of tea. Her meeting with Ventriloquist Vince and Diamond Tony had been most satisfactory. Given the efficiency of the bush telegraph operating within Brighton, within the hour a veritable army of villains would be on the lookout for an infamous con man of middle age with eyes that looked in different directions.

What was her plan? Well, it wasn't yet complete. But she owed it to her darling Hoagy to make this plan swingeing, permanent and sweetly perfect. This had been part of the reason for including Diamond Tony in the meeting at Luigi's: to impress on him that once she had located Wall-Eye Joe, she didn't just want him caught and killed in the usual way. Tony was a simple soul whose answer to everything (bless him) was a swift tug on a garrotte, a pair of concrete boots and a midnight splash off the end of the West Pier. As long as sea levels never drastically dropped (to reveal grisly stalagmites of Mrs Groynes's enemies in skeleton-and-concrete form sticking up from the waves), Diamond Tony was a neat and permanent solution to every problem. But this time, it was vital that he restrain himself.

'We're going to *con him*, Tony, do you see? If I get it right he won't suspect a bleeding thing. Only at the final moment when the scales fall from his eyes – when he realises how brilliantly he's been played – that's when you can step in and do him. This is revenge, not business. Don't you forget that for an instant.'

It was with such happy thoughts that she now innocently dusted the picture rail around the office, and whistled a tune from *Snow White*.

Back at the Black Cat, Deirdre was sitting at her dressing table, writing a letter to Peter. Her bedroom was a tiny, dark space in the back corner of the building. Despite facing south, her window got no sun: the entire view was of the back of Colchester House, just a few feet away. Interestingly, in the past few days the shutters there had been opened and for the first time she'd been able to see directly inside. Admittedly, all she could see was a fragment of staircase, but it was still like something from a fairy tale, after all these years.

Yesterday, she had actually seen a person going upstairs, and another person coming down. Such excitement: the outside world visible from her room! (The narrow alleyway that ran beneath her window didn't count: Deirdre had trained herself not to look down on it, for fear of seeing people tightly lodged there, engaged in unspeakable acts.)

Had everything gone to plan, of course, she would have been saying goodbye to this view forever tonight. At eight-forty-five, Dickie was to have opened the side door for her; fifteen minutes later she would have been holding hands with Peter on the bus, with her heart beating like wings in her chest. But now it was not to be.

Dear Peter,

Please forgive me for letting you down. I feel so bad. Mummy found out! She said they won't harm you, they will let you go away on the bus, but that I must stay here and not be silly, and she said that I hardly knew you anyway, which was true but I didn't like hearing her say it, and she doesn't know about the letters you wrote to me, which are so full of love, and I will treasure my whole life. I've still never played the record you made for me in the little booth on the Palace Pier that time, which was the happiest day of my life. I watched you through the glass walls while you were speaking, and I saw the look in your eyes, and I know it will make me cry and cry when I do get the chance to play it.

Under her bed, Deirdre had hidden a Lilley & Skinner shoebox with all her mementos of Peter inside. It included – along with the record – a paper bag with a couple of humbugs stuck to it, to commemorate their first sight of each other, just a month ago, outside a popular rock shop on the seafront, where twice a day a man in a white confectioner's coat demonstrated the strenuous processes of sweet manufacture to enraptured crowds. Deirdre had been out on an errand for her mother, and was expected home. Had she not stopped to watch Henry 'Humbugs' Hastings in the window of the shop, hard at his astonishing work twisting and rolling a striped bolster of warm molten sugar, she might not have found herself shoulder-to-shoulder with the boy from the Sewerage and Waterworks department who was there (apparently) to investigate a complaint about the drains.

What caught his attention was Deirdre's exceptional pallor. What caught hers was the same.

I love you, Peter. I know you think it's silly that I always have a song in my head, but if you want to think about me, or think about the happy couple we might have been, listen to 'It Had to Be You'. I keep thinking of the line, over and over – it does make me feel glad, even being sad, thinking of you.

I don't know how she found out. I'm sure Dickie wouldn't have said anything. He's always been my friend. The thing about Mummy is that people always want to be on her good side for obvious reasons, so it could have been anyone here tittle-tattling, one of the girls in the show perhaps, or someone behind the bar. Even the Humbug Man!

It was true that candidates for 'Deirdre Confidant' were few and far between at the Black Cat. The bar staff were lively people, but they reported directly to Frank and Bruce, which was as much as to say that they lived in fear; most of them Deirdre knew only by sight. The hat-check lady (Mimi) was a constant presence, but was not a friend. Obsessed with her own appearance, in particular her drawn-on eyebrows, she spent all her leisure moments checking their symmetry in a pocket mirror. The showgirls – a shifting population of bottle-blonde models and dancers, all much older than Deirdre, and inhabiting a different universe – concentrated entirely on keeping their hair in place, tweezing their moles in the communal dressing-room mirror and using their basilisk qualities onstage to bewitch/entrap any eligible male member of the audience.

This left only the band, who were (mostly) disgusting deadbeats with Brylcreemed hair and BO; she wouldn't have touched any of them with a barge pole. No wonder she'd chosen Dickie to help her. He was by far the most human person she knew, and she was aware he was a little bit in love with her. Tommy (the resident drummer) had been friendly to Deirdre a couple of times, but she found him creepy. Nothing about Tommy Drumsticks – as he insisted on being called – rang true, somehow. Even his gold tooth looked fake. He puzzled her. He asked odd questions about things that were none of his business. While everyone else seemed hardly to notice what was going on at the Black Cat, Tommy Drumsticks gave the impression of knowing much more than he ought to.

But I'm sorry if it's my fault and I hope you get away on the bus as planned, and live in Earl's Court and everything, and BLOW THE LID like you said you would, and I hope you will think kindly of me in later life and forgive me. You are a lovely person, Peter, with a good heart and a conscience. But I fear for you because of the weediness – you are not physically very strong. I wonder if your reporter friend tipped Mummy off? They are always working both sides, those people, like the police.

The reporter in question was young crime correspondent Ben Oliver, of the local *Argus*, who had made his name covering the shooting of critic A. S. Crystal at the Theatre Royal a month or so ago. Deirdre was wrong to point the finger at him. While seasoned crime reporters with famous bylines did indeed ingratiate themselves with criminals in order to get stories (which paradoxically enhanced their standing with their readers), Oliver was too young and honourable to have started compromising his integrity in this way.

Peter, I promised myself I wouldn't cry when I wrote this, but the thought of carrying on here without the hope of being with you – I'm not sure I can bear

But she didn't complete the sentence, because at this moment there was a knock at the door. Deirdre looked up, her eyes swimming with tears. She had never felt more wretched in her life.

'It's me, Deedee,' said Ma Benson, entering without waiting for an answer. 'Are you all right? What's that you're writing? Show me.'

Deirdre put the letter behind her back.

'It's just my letter to Peter. You said I could write one. You promised. And you said you wouldn't hurt him.'

Ma Benson frowned, puffed on her pipe and tried to remember. Had she really said that? It was sometimes difficult to keep track of all the lies she told.

'Of course, yes. Your letter to Peter. He's leaving without you, that's it. On the bus tonight. And we're not going to lay a finger on him. Have you finished?'

'Nearly.'

'Good. Bruce can deliver it to him at the bus station. Bring it down when you've finished. I'll be in the club. I'm auditioning for a new singer.'

Ma Benson was about to go when she noticed two things: the tears of misery rolling down her daughter's cheeks, and the fact that for the first time since the family had moved into the Black Cat, it was possible to see into the back of Colchester House. Which of these two things was decisive in her opting to stay a while and comfort her child is not for others to speculate.

'Deedee,' she said in a kindly tone, peering past her, and sitting on the edge of the bed. 'You do understand that we're only trying to protect you?'

89

'I suppose,' sniffed Deirdre.

'The thing is, Peter just wasn't the right one for you. You're too young for boyfriends.'

'I know.'

'And someone from Sewerage and Waterworks!'

Deirdre couldn't answer. She had been very impressed at Peter having such a responsible job.

'Look, why don't you tell me all about it?' Ma Benson patted the bed as an invitation for Deirdre to join her.

And then, when they were settled side by side, and Deirdre was weeping with her head resting on her mother's shoulder, she said, as gently as she could, 'So how long has the house next door been occupied, Deedee? And why didn't you think to bloody mention it?'

Five

The following morning, at ten o'clock, Inspector Steine boarded the train for London, Victoria, his radio talk safe in his briefcase. He had spent the previous afternoon polishing it in the usual manner, and was now very happy with the tone, which was, as always, authoritative and crystal clear but at the same time unintimidating, with occasional stabs at inoffensive sexist humour (because obviously the inferior legal status of wives to their husbands was universally amusing).

'Well done, Geoffrey,' he had said to himself after reading it aloud for the final time. He looked forward to saying on air the witty (but informative and cautionary) words, 'With all my worldly goods, *and all my criminal liability*, I thee endow.' Anyone listening to the talk would pick up no hint that in Brighton this week, the body of a seventeen-year-old boy had been found near the West Pier with its throat cut; nor that an obscure night-club singer had been reported missing by his landlady; nor that the Borough Engineer – a shady character with a giveaway Germanic name, as many people at the Town Hall were now pointing out to each other – had last been seen speedily boarding a cross-channel ferry at Newhaven, leaving no forwarding address.

Yes, no trace of these troubles could be found in Inspector Steine's 'Law and the Little Man' talk. It was as if the writer

– a high-ranking policeman – could somehow divorce himself from the realities of everyday criminal investigation to concentrate entirely on the subject at hand – namely, the fascinating anomalies in the law regarding married couples.

His morning had been so good that he briefly considered adding a few words to the manuscript he kept in his locked desk drawer (his memoir had reached 1922, the year of his father's death), but in the end his sense of duty prevailed. The Testing-of-Twitten took priority. Every day needed to begin with this ritual question-and-response, which (depressingly for Steine) had so far varied in its outcome very little.

'So, young Twitten,' he would say, ushering him into the room and closing the door. 'Sit down. Here we are, having a friendly private chat, just you and me, how very nice, don't be anxious.'

'Thank you, sir. Lovely morning, sir.'

'Precisely. Well, let's not beat about the bush, we both know why you're here.'

'Yes, sir. Thank you, sir.'

'So. How are we feeling about Mrs Groynes today?'

'I believe she is an evil criminal mastermind, sir.'

At this point, Steine would throw up his hands in annoyance.

'What, *still*?'

Sometimes this was the end of the conversation, and Twitten was dismissed with an irritated wave of the hand; on other occasions – which included this morning – Steine took a steadying breath and probed a little deeper.

'All right,' he said today, 'on a scale of one to ten, please tell me how convinced you are of this preposterous notion, bearing in mind that when you say "ten" it saddens and disappoints me and ruins my day unnecessarily?'

'Ten, sir.'

'Ugh.'

'I'm afraid there's just no bally doubt about it, sir. She was responsible for the raid on the Albion Bank in North Street last week, which netted her and her gang at least thirty thousand pounds. If you take no action she will continue to get away with it. I really appreciate this opportunity to reason with you, sir.'

'Reason with me?' Beads of sweat appeared on Steine's forehead. He rose slightly in his seat. Twitten, by contrast, was quite calm.

'Twitten, for the last time, I'm the one reasoning with you!'

'But, sir—'

'And you really should listen to yourself! You just talked about Mrs Groynes the charlady having a gang that does bank robberies!'

'Well, she could hardly pull a job like that on her own, sir. She'd need a driver, and a lookout man, and—'

'Stop it! Twitten, you have to stop this. You had a ridiculous idea planted in your head by a hypnotist, and I'm trying to help you to see it for what it is.'

After a pause to let the emotion subside, Twitten spoke, carefully, 'I understand that's what you thought you saw, sir.'

'A thousand people witnessed it!'

Twitten sensibly stopped arguing. He cleared his throat and stood to attention.

'I think I have it under control, sir. Please don't be concerned. I never mention it except at these helpful one-to-one meetings, sir. I try never to raise it with Mrs Groynes. And I am never – ever – alone with her.'

Steine shook his head wearily. 'And yet you won't say nine, will you? You won't just say *nine*?'

Twitten said nothing.

'Very well. We'll continue this tomorrow. Carry on.'

At which point, after Twitten had left the inspector's office, Steine said to himself, 'You did your best, Geoffrey.' And then he put the issue entirely out of his mind, and focused on how curious and interesting (and unfair) it was that while a man could go to prison for something his wife had done, the same rule ceased to apply when the case was the other way round!

Back at the railway station, the weather being warm again, the concourse was packed with day-tripping cockneys, all streaming excitedly towards Queens Road and the sea, and shedding litter like rose-petals as they went. Travel-sick children were being shepherded into the lavatories through the penny turnstiles; W. H. Smith was doing a brisk business in saucy postcards; young people laughed and screamed, and playfully shoved each other.

Few were travelling in the same direction at Steine – London-wards – but as he stepped up into a first-class compartment, he glanced back along the platform and spotted a young woman in a scarlet dress approaching; a young woman who looked familiar.

It was Adelaide Vine, the woman from the kerfuffle yesterday on the seafront; the one with (as her mother always said) the unusual concatenation of nut-like attributes.

He stepped back down on to the platform.

'Miss Vine?'

Adelaide looked up and frowned. She was evidently surprised to see the inspector, and not particularly pleased. He had been very abrupt with her at the crime scene yesterday. Obliged to acknowledge him, she performed a minimal nod of the head, but did not slow down; if anything, she quickened her pace. There were plenty more compartments up ahead.

The inspector thought quickly.

'Miss Vine?' he said again, and astonished himself by reaching out his arm as if to stop her.

It injured him to be cut by anyone at all – especially when the person was as attractive as Adelaide. But there was something more at work here. Last night, back at home, he had gone over the scene several times, of Twitten asking the agitated Brighton Belle, 'Are you all right, miss?' – just the way, fifty years ago, Steine's father had asked his mother. Those five simple words – those kind, respectful, quintessentially copper-ish words – seemed to churn inside him.

He decided to persevere.

'This is a happy coincidence!' he said. He clasped his hands together, in a show of supplication.

'I've, er, look … Miss Vine. I was thinking about what happened yesterday, and I've been wondering how I would get the chance to apologise. To apologise for my tone.'

'Your tone?'

With the train due to depart, the station guard had started coming up the platform, slamming the heavy doors shut, one by one. It wouldn't be long before he reached the first-class section. Meanwhile the train was getting up steam. Steine had to raise his voice.

'My tone, yes. I'm so sorry for it. And my words, of course. Both tone and words. In short, everything I said, and how I said it. Look, would you care to join me?'

He indicated the open door of the compartment. She pursed her lips and sighed.

'To allow you to apologise?' she said.

'Yes.'

She thought about it, and seemed to relent. 'Well, I do have a first-class ticket, as it happens,' she said, not quite smiling.

'Splendid.'

95

He held the door as she climbed up into the carriage, and then climbed up himself and closed the door just as the station guard waved his flag and blew his whistle for departure.

Twitten was growing a bit tired of the daily Mrs Groynes Litany: it reminded him too powerfully of his unique predicament, which was like something from ancient myth. He was the Cassandra of the Brighton Constabulary – all-knowing, all-seeing, and even able to predict bank robberies in North Street before they occurred, but fated always to be mocked, derided and generally disbelieved.

However, it's only fair to say that once his grilling was over each day, he gladly put it out of his mind, much as Inspector Steine did. After all, it was unlikely Mrs Groynes had anything to do with the murder of young Peter Dupont, or the consequent guilty dash for Dieppe of the seemingly respectable Borough Engineer – investigating which mysteries was the immediate job in hand.

It was the one positive aspect to knowing Mrs Groynes's secret: he could read her like a book. Thus he felt certain that the death of Weedy Pete was of no interest to Mrs G (she'd hardly reacted), whereas the news of Wall-Eye Joe certainly was (she had excitedly used the word 'bleeding' *five times*).

Sergeant Brunswick, by contrast, had noticed neither of these reactions, because he wasn't looking for them. How cleverly she had won his trust! This was the hardest part for Twitten to tolerate: having to stand by and watch his closest colleague being played (as they said in the gangster films) like a cheap pianola. Why didn't Sergeant Brunswick *ever* catch on? It wasn't as if Mrs Groynes was particularly subtle. Take that very discussion of Wall-Eye Joe, when Mrs G had lapsed, unguardedly, into specialist underworld slang.

'*Last I heard*,' she'd said, '*he was doing a tray on the cave-grinder.*'

'It means three months' hard labour, sir,' Twitten had translated at the time, but he'd watched Brunswick carefully. Would the sergeant start to put two and two together? Would he ask himself: *Is tray-on-the-cave-grinder normal charlady talk? Perhaps – perhaps—?*

But Mrs Groynes had likewise detected the first glimmerings of a dangerous train of thought, and diverted it neatly into a siding. It was her most accomplished regular manoeuvre. Recently, when the sergeant recovered a string of pearls from a sneak thief, he'd no sooner plonked them on his desk than Mrs G said, excitedly, 'Hang on, dear,' whipped out a high-magnification jeweller's loupe from her overalls pocket to examine the necklace, turned the pearls intently, and then pronounced, 'Nah, someone's took you for a steamer, dear.'

Twitten had watched, agog. *Now?* he had thought. And Brunswick had certainly looked a little puzzled, and had even started to say, 'Mrs G, why would you—?' But then Mrs Groynes said, brightly, 'How about a nice toasted teacake?' and in the sergeant's delighted surprise ('Ooh, lovely!'), the puzzled look vanished just as quickly as it had appeared.

On the morning of the inspector's trip to London, Twitten found himself alone in the office with Mrs Groynes for the first time in three weeks – the first time since she had explained to him, in fact, that he was utterly stymied so far as exposing-the-charlady was concerned, and should graciously accept his fate. The inspector had just left to catch his train; Brunswick was at the hospital to have his bullet-wound dressings changed. Twitten – who was anxious to get out and conduct interviews (there was a list of six people he was particularly anxious to talk to) – had been quickly typing up his notes concerning the evening of Peter Dupont's death.

At 8.45 p.m. I positioned myself at the Pool Valley coach terminus. I hoped to speak to Deirdre Benson, and question her about i) Peter Dupont's activities prior to his death vis-à-vis the theft from the Borough Engineer's office, and ii) her family's generally murderous proclivities. I realised I would have to break the news to her of Dupont's death. It seemed unlikely she would have heard of it any other way, especially if her family were responsible for cutting his throat in broad daylight as a means of warning him off.

Deirdre Benson did not come to Pool Valley.

At 8.50 p.m., however, a large man of intimidating appearance, with a cauliflower ear, arrived at the terminus and moved through the waiting crowds, asking for the London bus. He was carrying a letter. I approached him and said: 'I am a Brighton police officer, as you can tell from my uniform and distinctive white helmet. Please tell me your name.' He said he was Bruce Benson, out for an evening walk, and what would I like to do about it, Constable Pipsqueak? These were his precise words. I asked him about the letter. He said he was going

to post it, wasn't he, and how would I
like a bunch of fives? He was still looking round at the faces in the crowd as
if in expectation of seeing someone. I
pointed out that the letter did not have
a stamp on it. I then noticed it was
addressed to Peter Dupont.

I said, 'If you are looking for Peter
Dupont, I am sorry to inform you that he
is dead. We have reason to believe he
was murdered.' He said, 'Oh.' It seemed
to be news to him. I then said, 'I will
need to take that letter as evidence.'
He said, 'Really? I don't think so,
how will you make me?' I said, 'I am a
Brighton police officer.' He said, 'Yes,
but I am bigger than you.'

At this point the movement of the
excited crowd boarding the bus became
violent and the letter was knocked from
his hand and picked up by an unknown
person. I think I saw a child running
off towards East Street but I cannot be
certain as I was being elbowed roughly
in the face by people anxious to board
the bus. Mr Benson seemed to be as
confused as I was.

With the letter gone and the bus
departed, I said goodnight to Mr Benson.

Twitten looked up. He had heard a noise.

'Mrs Groynes!' he said, in shock. He had been so absorbed
in typing his report, he hadn't heard her come in and start
making tea. They were alone together! He stood up. 'Shall I
go?' he said.

She smiled at him. 'Why do you say that, dear? No, no, you sit down. Let the chair take the weight of that gigantic brain of yours.'

Looking him directly in the eye – and deliberately prolonging the smile well past the usual dropping-point – she held the large brown office teapot in both hands, and moved it slowly in a gentle circular motion so that the tea leaves inside steeped evenly in the hot water. He had seen her perform this ceremony many times before; it had never seemed so sinister.

'Just showing it the pictures on the wall, dear,' she explained, still smiling.

Twitten felt extremely uncomfortable. He was suppressing an actual whimper. What did Mrs Groynes want with him?

'The inspector's on his way to … on his way to London,' he said, faltering slightly. 'And the sergeant's at the h—' He found that he couldn't get the word out. He tried again. 'He's at the h—'

'That's all right, I know where he is,' Mrs G interrupted. 'Do take some deep breaths and calm down, dear. I'm not going to hurt you. Although I expect you think I'm mad at you for saying "ten" to the inspector every bleeding day – '

Twitten bit his lip quite hard, and Mrs Groynes laughed.

' – but I'm really not, dear! Oh, no.'

Turning away, she poured their tea, but carried on speaking. 'It's yourself you're hurting by sticking to your pathetic story, you see, dear, not me. One day you'll say to the inspector that you're a hundred per cent positive you've copped the right man, you see, and he'll say, "Yes, but you're also a hundred per cent positive that Mrs Groynes the charlady is an inveterate villainess!"'

She turned, a cup of tea in her hand. She handed it to him. 'See what I'm getting at, dear?'

'Yes, thank you,' he said, quietly. He was torn. On the one hand, it was worrying that she knew about the scale of one to ten, and even more worrying that she could so casually use the word 'inveterate' correctly in a sentence. But on the other, he had to admit that she did have fantastic instincts about when a nice cup of tea would hit the spot.

'I put three sugars in.'

'Super. Thank you.'

She sat down at the sergeant's desk, and opened a tin of biscuits. A tempting aroma of cocoa powder was instantly detectable in the air.

'I just thought we ought to have a little chat, dear. What with having the place to ourselves for once. We've got a lot of things to discuss. Bourbon cream?'

Twitten declined the biscuit (which was difficult), and sipped his tea. He was nervous. When someone with a history of killing people – and who has a pretty good reason to kill you, too – starts off by saying 'I'm not going to hurt you', it's never completely reassuring.

'I don't want to be rude, Mrs G, but I think the less I discuss things one-to-one with you, the better.'

'Really? You think that?'

'Of course.'

'Well, I see it differently, dear.' She stirred her own tea, and took a sip. 'This situation is as new for me as it is for you, dear; you must see that. I can feel your little forensic-observation eyes on me all the time, and I can't say I'm in love with it. But it does seem to me that having this special relationship, as it were, we could help each other.'

Twitten spluttered into his tea. 'Help each other? You want me to rob banks?'

'Rob banks?' she laughed. 'Of course not! What good would you be to me banged up for robbery? No, let's come at it another way: let's think first of how I can help you.'

Twitten took another sip of tea, playing for time. 'I don't think there are any ways you can help me, Mrs G, and I'd far rather you didn't. I suspect the quid pro quo would be bally unacceptable. And I'm sure Sergeant Brunswick will come back very soon, so I say, let's bring this awkward discussion to a close.'

'All right, dear. But you can't say I didn't offer.'

She sighed, replaced the lid on the biscuit tin and stood up. 'I'll just throw this away, then, shall I?' she said, taking from her overalls pocket a familiar-looking envelope.

Twitten froze. It looked like the letter from last night.

Producing a flick knife from her overalls (she kept so many interesting items in those pockets), she slit open the envelope, pulled out the contents and began to read aloud. '"*Dear Peter. Please forgive me for letting you down.*" Aww, how sweet. Young love, you see, it never gets old.'

She raised an eyebrow at Twitten and then, shrugging, replaced the letter in the envelope.

'How did you get that?' he said, quietly.

'Someone dropped it at the bus station, that's what I heard.'

It briefly flickered through Twitten's mind that for Mrs G to offer him this vital piece of evidence was quite similar to her offering Sergeant Brunswick a toasted teacake.

'And I don't like to boast, dear, but I can also show you the place downstairs where they put that suitcase they found the body in, dear. You'll have a bleeding field day with that. It's got more clues on it than a dog's got fleas.'

In that moment, Twitten wrestled with the complicated ethics of the situation – but mainly, he just held out his hand.

'May I see that letter, Mrs G?'

'Of course, dear. You can have it. With my compliments.'

Emerging from the hospital, with the wound to his thigh freshly dressed, Sergeant Brunswick crossed the street and made his (slightly hobbling) way downhill towards the centre of town. The doctors had said that he was healing nicely, but this wasn't news to him: he was a man who knew the score when it came to flesh wounds. While it was well known that Brunswick had been shot in the leg by the former Brighton gang boss Fat Victor (now in prison), in fact there had been three more occasions in his police career in Brighton when – close to significant arrests – something had gone wrong at the last minute, with the result of small-calibre firearms being drawn, and 'Bang! Take that, you lousy copper!' And it had been right in the leg, each time.

'It's like you're bleeding doomed, sergeant!' Mrs Groynes would often say, laughing, while lightly patting his latest bandaged area and handing him a plate of fig rolls.

On one occasion, it had actually been Mrs Groynes herself (bless her) who had been the innocent cause of his undoing!

Having skilfully infiltrated a gang of thieves in the Preston Park area, headed by the infamous Stanley-Knife Stanley, Brunswick had been poised to spring his trap. Going under the soubriquet Limpy Len, Brunswick was to be the driver of the getaway van. The job was fixed for midnight. The target was a furs warehouse on the London Road, full of high-ticket Russian sables. Last-minute instructions were taking place inside the van; meanwhile the warehouse was surrounded by well-briefed uniformed police awaiting an agreed signal. In short, all was going perfectly. And then, when Brunswick and the others emerged from the van, who should be strolling on the other side of the road but Mrs Groynes!

'Evening, Sergeant Brunswick,' she had called out. 'See you at the station in the morning?'

Well, what a calamity. Three months' work unravelled in a matter of a few seconds.

'It's a trap,' shouted one of Stanley's minions, drawing a weapon. 'He's a lousy copper!'

In the commotion, there was a lot of noise, but Brunswick thought he heard a woman shout, 'Stan! Remember! In the leg!' just before the bang that brought him down. But when he asked Mrs G afterwards at the station whether she'd heard this shouted instruction in a female voice, she said, mystified, no, dear; she definitely hadn't; he must have imagined it. And then she carried on bathing the wound, and explaining how – because of the kerfuffle bringing all the police raiding party running to Brunswick's aid – the desperado thieves had managed to get away with a van full of furs worth several thousand pounds.

Perhaps it was true, then: what Twitten had said to him. That his days of going undercover were over, for the simple reason that all the local villains now knew him by sight. But it had been a good run. As Limpy Len, he had got very close to arresting Stanley-Knife Stanley. As Eduardo the Italian ice-cream seller on the West Pier (for which disguise he had assumed an accent, worn nose-putty and messily dyed all the hair on his forearms), he had observed an operation to rob the amusement arcade, and had again arranged elaborate multiple arrests – but had once more, sadly, been shot in the leg just at the point of raising his whistle to his lips.

His last undercover job was the one he was (perversely) most proud of. Posing as a cellist (he had learned both the cello and the trumpet in his youth), he had infiltrated an amateur string quartet that he was sure was planning a bank job, on the grounds that their practice room was in a basement next door to a vault, with a large screen always suspiciously positioned against the party wall (presumably, to mask the large hole they were drilling in the evenings).

The inspector told Brunswick repeatedly that he was wasting his time, and that the plot of *The Ladykillers* was all well and good but should never be confused with real life.

'Some string quartets really are string quartets, Brunswick,' he had memorably said. 'Some people enjoy the music of Luigi Boccherini for its own sake.'

But Brunswick was on the right track, as it happened. His mistake this time was that he didn't have a proper plan, and that he was never taken into the confidence of the other three 'musicians', despite dropping broad hints about a criminal background, such as, 'You remind me of a bloke I met in Parkhurst,' and 'You seen that *Rififi* yet, mate? Talk about thought-provoking.'

One Friday evening he turned up for practice, having learned a serene passage of Schubert for the occasion, and when he opened the door, was knocked over backwards by the other three quartet members, racing out of the building holding large, bulging sacks.

Scrambling to his feet, he shouted, 'Halt! I am arresting you on suspicion of—' And then there had been the inevitable bang, and that was it, he was down on the ground again.

But what about the Black Cat? Who would know him there? Was the annoying Twitten right, that here was his opportunity to get to the bottom of the torso-in-the-suitcase at last? The press had been so damning of the Brighton Constabulary's failure to identify the body. But in general was it bad policy – even in the interests of justice – to infiltrate a set of criminals who murdered people in cold blood and afterwards cut them up and deposited bits of them in Left Luggage?

He was just thinking about this – leaning against a low wall and enjoying a cigarette – when he noticed through a café window a man gesticulating towards a woman and waving what looked like a gold brick. Brunswick dropped the cigarette, stubbed it out with his foot (the swivel of the injured leg making him squirm) and moved closer. The man appeared to have eyes that looked in different directions! Could this be Wall-Eye Joe?

Brunswick walked back up the road a little way and waited for five minutes. He saw the man exit the café and set off on foot towards the centre of town. Brunswick followed him, quite excited. The man, who seemed to be in no hurry, wended his way through the older parts of Brighton, stopping occasionally to study a shop window, and eventually knocked on the door of a white-stuccoed mansion facing the sea – a building that Brunswick recognised as Colchester House, which had notoriously lain empty for many years. A man opened the door, and Brunswick heard him say 'my lord' (but not as an exclamation). And then Wall-Eye Joe went inside.

Pondering what to do, Brunswick was still standing on the corner of Ship Street when a domestic servant – she looked like a housekeeper – exited the house by a side door. He stopped her, showed her his badge and asked her some questions – the answers to which were so thrilling that he returned directly to the police station and burst into the office just as Constable Twitten was taking Peter Dupont's letter from the hand of Mrs Groynes.

In surprise, they both turned to look at him somewhat guiltily: they'd been caught in the act of collusion! But true to form, he didn't clock a thing.

'Mrs G, you'll never guess,' he said, triumphantly. 'I think I've found Wall-Eye Joe.'

Mrs Groynes let out a sound very much like a 'YES!' and then coughed and said, in a more measured way, 'I mean, well done you, dear. Well done you. What's he up to this time?'

'You won't believe it. He's posing as a lord and living in Colchester House.'

'Golly,' said Twitten. 'So do you think he's the one who tried to sell gold bricks to those Brighton Belles?'

'Yes, I do. He had some in his bag. But I don't think flaming gold bricks are what this is about, son.'

Brunswick looked expectantly at Mrs G. But if he was hoping for a congratulatory cup of tea, he was disappointed.

'Colchester House?' she said, thoughtfully. 'Well, I never.'

Twitten was fascinated. It certainly was entertaining being privy to the reactions of a callous and calculating criminal gang boss operating unsuspected in a police station. Never had he seen deviant mental activity written so clearly on a person's face.

Brunswick, undeterred by the curious lack of reaction to his news, pressed on.

'Yes,' he said. 'He must have really pushed the boat out on this one. He's got someone posing as his manservant; household staff of five; everything. Whatever he's planning, it must be huge.'

On the London train, things had not warmed up much between Steine and Adelaide Vine. He was wondering if he'd done the right thing, asking her to join him. But it was too late now.

'May I ask what's taking you to London, Inspector?' she said, stiffly. 'Don't you have a murderer to catch?'

Steine's first opinion having been that Peter Dupont had killed himself in remorse for stealing – and then apparently losing – sensitive documents from the place of his employment, he refused to rise to the bait. He was still smarting from the verdict of the police pathologist, who had this morning firmly reported that it was indeed a murder ('There is no doubt *whatsoever*, Inspector').

'Well, needs must, I'm afraid. I'm going to Broadcasting House to deliver my weekly talk. It's a bagatelle of a thing, really – called "Law and the Little Man". You might have heard of it. Often reprinted in the *Listener*.'

'Of course!' she said. 'They announce, "*And now, 'Law and the Little Man' with Inspector Steine of the Brighton Constabulary.*" Yes, I've heard it several times.'

Steine gave a modest shrug, in expectation of the usual elaboration and praise – but he was disappointed. Adelaide seemed to have nothing to add, and when Steine looked up, she had turned her attention to the window. This was keenly hurtful to his pride. Unqualified congratulation was so far Inspector Steine's favourite form of discourse that (as we have observed) when there was no one else present to offer a 'Well done, Geoffrey', he simply supplied it himself.

'And what takes *you* to London, Miss Vine? Shouldn't you be parading the seafront, directing people to the nearest eel and pie establishment?' (*Touché*, he thought.)

'It's my day off, thank goodness. A legal matter, as it happens. I have to see my solicitor in Earl's Court. It's concerning a will.'

'I see.'

Steine sighed and joined Adelaide in looking out of the window. He was at a loss. He'd apologised to this woman: what more did she want? The train rattled through a cutting, with tall dark trees on either side of the track.

'Inspector?' she said, suddenly.

'Yes, Miss Vine.'

'Would you mind telling me a little about your lovely officers who were so kind to Phyllis and me yesterday. We both liked them enormously.'

'You want me to talk to you about *Brunswick and Twitten*?'

It was as if she knew precisely how to rub him up the wrong way.

'Yes, please,' she said. 'Sergeant Brunswick has such beautiful blue eyes, and I felt I could sense unhappiness in him. The young constable seemed very clever. I would love to know if my first impressions were correct.'

The train had got only as far as Wivelsfield. A long journey lay ahead, and sulking throughout the whole thing would be tiring. So, with obvious bad grace, Inspector Steine started to tell Adelaide about Brunswick, and Twitten, and even Mrs Groynes.

———

Meanwhile, in Brighton, the real Wall-Eye Joe – who of course hated the nickname and considered himself to be Joseph Marriott, Esquire – was hearing rumours in which his name was connected with a gold-brick scam. His feelings were mixed. Even criminals take pride in their reputation – in fact they are more touchy about the respect due from their peers than any other section of society: it's the main cause of them so often falling out with each other.

But on the other hand, Wall-Eye had bigger schemes to think about. The current scam – hatched up, as usual, with his evil paramour Vivienne (a.k.a. The Skirt) – would set them up for the rest of their lives, and while it had already been set in motion, it couldn't be rushed.

'Viv!' he called over to her now. 'Did you hear about me trying to sell gold bricks?'

'It's common knowledge, darling,' she drawled.

Vivienne carried on painting her nails. This hanging about was torture, but she had a lot of faith in the plan. It was far better than the unfinished-house scam, which had involved all the bother of dispatching and disposing of umpteen victims, and had netted the gang of five less than twenty grand between them.

This new scheme had everything: a massive payout at the end of it, and only one murder. True, the principal victim this time would be a police officer, which certainly upped the ante. But if all went to plan, it would look like a tragic accident, and they could (once again) walk away scot-free.

The inspector's train was finally crossing the outskirts of London, and he was relieved. Suburban sprawl had started to replace verdant countryside, and he would soon be safely ensconced in his airtight studio at the BBC. What a miserable journey this had been – answering Adelaide Vine's eager and impertinent questions about his adorable sergeant and dashing constable; or (to be accurate) consistently failing to answer her questions adequately, because he took so little interest in their lives.

For example, was Brunswick keen on cricket? According to Adelaide, he had an 'athletic build'!

Wasn't Constable Twitten's father the famous criminal psychologist J. R. R. Twitten? No idea, was Steine's somewhat sulky reply.

What made such sterling chaps as Brunswick and Twitten want to be policemen in the first place?

Steine did his best, but he realised that most of his answers sounded oddly peevish and disloyal. For example, he complained that Brunswick was forever getting shot in the leg, because of his insistence – against strong, sensible advice from his superior officer – on going undercover and mixing with the sort of people who carry guns.

'How heroic of him!' interjected Adelaide, who seemed on all occasions determined to miss the point.

Meanwhile Twitten was to all intents and purposes hopeless as a police officer, despite the immense capacity of his brain, because he'd allowed himself to be hypnotised onstage into believing the station charlady was a master criminal.

'But poor Constable Twitten. How terrible that must be!'

And to top it all, Steine persisted, both sergeant and constable had blatantly ignored him when he said the death of Peter Dupont was suicide, and started investigating it as a murder – although, to be fair, the pathologist this morning had confirmed they were right, so in this complaint he was on fairly shaky ground.

It was only as the train was on its final approach after Clapham Junction that Steine thought to ask where all this interest in policemen came from. Subsequently, he often wondered what would have happened if he had never asked the question, because the answer changed his life. He might have remembered Adelaide Vine afterwards as just an awkward conversation on a train.

'Oh, it's just that my grandfather was a London bobby,' said Adelaide, pulling a comical face. 'I know it seems unlikely.'

It was the first time she had seemed to warm to Steine. He felt the force of it. She was dazzling when she smiled.

'A London bobby? That's what I used to be.'

'Well, what a coincidence. But back to my grandfather. Mummy used to tell the story of how he had met Grandmother in the course of his duties. It was very romantic.'

'Really?'

Steine was so relieved that they'd finally settled on a happy topic, he failed to notice at first where this story was going.

Adelaide beamed. 'It was in 1910, in Bloomsbury. Shall I tell you about it?'

'Go ahead,' he said, settling back in his seat. There were only a few minutes left to go; he didn't mind listening. If the story reflected well on the police, he might be able to use it in one of his talks.

'Inspector Steine,' she said, 'did you ever hear of a silly prank involving members of the Bloomsbury Group called the Dreadnought Hoax?'

Steine gulped and leaned forward. 'The *what?*'

'No, not many people have, I think. But it seems that this group of bohemians, including Virginia Woolf, dressed up like Abyssinians and got themselves received on a warship in Weymouth Harbour. It was just a senseless prank, but they happened to spill out of their house in Gordon Square just as my rather highly strung grandmother was driving past, you see – and in their costumes and make-up, they made her scream.'

Steine had stopped breathing. 'Go on,' he said in a strangled tone.

'Well, Grandfather was on his beat nearby and heard the commotion, so came running to save her, not realising that the threat came not from a gang of street criminals but a bunch of effete intellectuals wearing fancy dress. I mean, they wouldn't have hurt anyone!'

Steine struggled to say something. He had a million questions, but at the same time he couldn't think of one. He was so busy trying to grasp the ramifications of Adelaide's words.

'So that's why I'm always curious about policemen, I suppose. It's in the blood. Mummy loved telling that story, but otherwise I don't know anything about the family. She actually ran away from home when she was quite young.'

'What happened to your grandfather? The bobby? Do you know?'

'Oh, he died a long time ago, when Mummy was little. Struck by an army lorry on a London bridge, she said.'

She looked up. The train, which had been gradually reducing speed, was now alongside the platform and travelling at a trotting pace.

'Well, that's it. Victoria!' she said, and started searching for her ticket. 'Inspector Steine, is there something wrong?'

'Miss Vine,' he said, solemnly. 'I need to ask you. Where did you grow up?'

'In Newmarket. Why?'

'Newmarket near Cambridge?'

'Is there another Newmarket? Inspector, why are you—?'

'Your mother was horsey, I expect?'

'Yes, through and through. That's why she chose Newmarket as the place to run away to.'

'Was her name Gillian?'

'Well, yes. But how—?'

'Did she ever mention having a brother?'

'I'm not sure.'

Steine swallowed, hard. He couldn't believe this was happening.

The train was slowing to a stop. People who had already opened their compartment doors and jumped out were streaming past the window.

She laughed. 'What on earth is the matter? Inspector Steine, we really do need to get off, and you're looking very peculiar.'

'You're my niece!' he gushed, reaching out to grasp her hand. 'I must inform Mother immediately! Adelaide Vine, you must be my long-lost niece!'

Six

Young Peter Dupont wasn't the first clerk in the office of Sewerage and Waterworks to hear complaints about the smell of the drains in the environs of Colchester House, but he was the first to put his jacket on, take a notebook, run a comb through his hair and set off to investigate it.

He nearly didn't, though. Lillian the secretary tried to warn him off.

'Mr Blackmore always says we've got better things to think about than drains, young Peter,' Lillian had said, rather primly, looking up from her trusty Remington. (This was three weeks ago, before she found out about the discrepancies in their salaries; when she was still disposed to like him.)

'Yes, but he's not in today, Miss Ross,' Dupont pointed out. 'He's taken his wife to a flower show.'

'I'm only saying.'

She started typing again, and then thought of something amusing to say. 'Don't fall down any manholes,' she laughed.

He laughed as well. 'Right-oh,' he said.

This was the standing joke amongst the staff of the Sewerage and Waterworks department – but only when Mr Blackmore was out of earshot. Mr Blackmore was forever lecturing the maintenance team on the dangers of manholes, perhaps because their existence was the only part of his job that he fully understood. His particular hobby horse was the way British black-and-white comedy films got easy laughs from showing people walking blithely down the street (lifting their bowler hats to say 'Good morning') and suddenly falling down them.

'Take the new Norman Wisdom film!' he would splutter to the burly workforce, who reluctantly congregated in the department once a week for a briefing (they had to take their boots off, and weren't allowed to sit down). 'Yes, all very hilarious, no doubt, but yet again I think you'll find that audiences are invited to laugh at the tragic circumstance of someone falling down a manhole. Let me remind you that most people who fall down manholes do not climb back out again, brushing dust off their shoulders. Most of them break their necks!'

Peter had no intention of falling down any manholes – and certainly none of prising open a cover in a spirit of curiosity, either. He was aware of the potential consequences. Were a pen-and-paper clerical worker such as himself even to touch a manhole cover, it would be reported immediately to the shop steward of the Waterworks Operatives Union, and the entire works department would be called out on strike. One of Peter's predecessors (now spoken of only in muted tones) had once unthinkingly popped his head inside one of the stripy tents set up by the works team on the coast road, and found a game of three-card stud in progress. For this prohibited infringement of incontrovertible industrial demarcations, he was forced to resign, and moreover, give up all hope of a career in local government, and now sold socks and ties in a department store in Worthing.

But Peter was not likely to make a similar mistake. He was the most intelligent and well-educated recruit they'd ever had in the department – a future star – and Mr Blackmore could not always disguise how intimidated he was by him.

'You've been doing the crossword in *The Times* again, I see, Dupont?' he would chuckle in a mildly disapproving way – as if to imply it was the sort of trivial pursuit that Peter would in time grow out of.

Had Peter's home circumstances been more favourable, university would have been the next step – but sadly, Peter was an orphan with no expectations (his naturalised French father had died in the war; his mother had followed five years ago; charitable grandparents abroad could afford no further education for him), so the workplace beckoned, and to his immense credit, he felt no self-pity. He took this particular job because he liked the idea of being able to say, later in life, that he'd worked his way up from the sewers. Also, his father's favourite novel had been *Les Misérables*. Being clever, Peter was sometimes invited to interesting meetings in other departments, too – such as the one that convened to discuss the advertising of the Brighton Belles. It had been Peter who'd pointed out to the grammatically stumped committee that, strictly speaking, the Belles could be enquired 'of', but not 'from'.

So when he set off on his mission to investigate complaints about the drains, there was nothing vague about it. He had a good idea where to start. Having checked on a street map to see where the reports were at their most frequent, he reckoned that the epicentre was just behind the popular rock shop on the seafront – the one with the twice-daily demonstrations in the window. You could smell this shop from several streets away – the peppermint, the sugar, the aniseed. As Peter noted in his little book, any whiff from the drains had to deal with stiff olfactory competition in this particular corner of the town.

As he entered the shop, he realised he was just in time for the morning show: Mr Henry (a.k.a. 'Humbug') Hastings was preparing a heavy loaf of stripy molten sugar and food colourings, kneading and bending it, and – with an effortful grunt – flipping it over. It was a job that clearly took brawn as well as a lot of practice. Hastings's thin shirt under his confectioner's apron could not disguise the massive bulge of his neck and shoulder muscles; his biceps were like beach-balls. Hastings had been a commando in the Special Boat Service during the war, and had afterwards maintained both his physique and his air of mental preparedness. Looking at him now, it was still quite easy to picture him in a black knitted hat, jumping out of a landing craft in Mediterranean moonlight with a pointy knife glinting between his teeth.

'Good morning,' Peter said.

Behind the counter were shelves packed with colourful boiled sweets and soft fudge – some of the sweets loose, in glass jars, to be sold in paper bags after weighing; some in little white boxes with garish postcards of Brighton pasted carelessly to the front. A whole wall was given over to lengths of candy-pink Brighton rock, along with novelty sugar items such as pink dummies (unnaturally large), and outsize sets of dentures. And then there were the humbugs: this shop was a veritable shrine to the humbug; they were available in every size – from the small ones you could pop in your mouth and suck, to the gargantuan ones that weighed half a pound, and needed to be held in two sticky hands and just licked (and inevitably dropped on the carpet to acquire a coating of pet hair, grit and old fluff).

Peter was impressed and revolted at the same time. He genu-inely liked the clever, honest way the issue of dental decay was addressed by those dummies and false teeth. 'Eat here and be thou toothless!' they seemed to declare. The sheer abundance on show, however, was a bit much for him. Growing up in wartime, food shortages had been too prominent a feature in his childhood and young life.

'Mr Hastings,' he said, politely. 'I'm sorry to interrupt you but I understand you've complained about the smell of the drains.'

The humbug man looked up quickly from his work and rolled his eyes. 'I've complained eight times in two years, sonny,' he said. 'That smell is putrid, ruddy putrid. But that council of yours is rotten to the core, mate. You're all the same; all ... ' And here he stopped for a moment and rubbed thumb and middle finger together, in the internationally recognised gesture for dosh, shekels, readies and general ill-gotten gain.

Peter had heard this unflattering description of council employees from more or less everyone since taking up his lowly post in the Borough Engineer's office. He was used to it. If you cared to believe the rumours, the council was corrupt in every one of its dealings, from the way it granted planning permission down to the way it purchased Harpic for the lavs. Outrage and accusation were commonplace. But in his innocence (bless him), Peter had always assumed that the highly unsexy Sewerage and Waterworks department would be exempt from such reflex slurs.

'Well, I certainly will be looking into it, Mr Hastings,' he said, at the door.

And the sweet-maker, speaking with more prescience than he knew, said, as a pleasant farewell, 'Then I don't suppose you'll be lasting very long.'

It was perhaps because he was goaded by these cynical words that Peter decided he would indeed dig a bit. As it happened, Mr Blackmore would be spending the next few days enjoying several more free leisure excursions with 'the lady-wife' (a luxury steamer trip to Beachy Head, departing from the landing stage of the Palace Pier; a jaunt by limousine to the West End to see the hit show *Grab Me A Gondola*, so the coast was clear. All Peter needed to do, to get started, was knock on a few doors in the vicinity of the sweet shop and then get down to the Archives department to check what had happened to Mr Humbug's previous complaints.

It was while Peter was outside the shop, with his back to the window, making notes, that he first looked into the face of Deirdre Benson, and his fate was sealed. He had never seen such a lovely girl. And what an expression! While the other people looking up at the demonstration showed curiosity, puzzlement and even hilarity, this girl was watching through the plate glass in a kind of rapture – like Jennifer Jones gazing at a vision of the Virgin Mary in *The Song of Bernadette*.

But then she caught his eye and frowned, and he didn't know why.

'Can I help you?' he said.

She reached out a hand to him. 'Come here, quickly,' she said. 'You're looking the wrong way!'

So he smiled and turned, and joined her at the glass. It was a sort of omen, he felt. 'You're looking the wrong way' was what his mother used to say to him when he was little; she used to warn him that looking the wrong way would be 'the story of his life'. Time after time, he missed seeing Messerschmitts flying overhead, or peacock butterflies dancing over long grass on a meadow, or Arthur Askey in a brown double-breasted suit emerging from a jeweller's shop in Hove. Once, when he was seven, he even missed seeing King George VI and Queen Elizabeth driving past at a walking speed, despite having stood in the rain at the roadside since the crack of dawn. Afterwards he had an impression of white-walled tyres and a little flag fluttering on the roof of a car, but that was all.

Now, outside the sweet shop, being finally orientated in the correct direction, Peter could appreciate why crowds were so frequently drawn here. Mr Hastings was a true artiste: his skilful three-dimensional manipulation of a malleable solid was almost hypnotic, like watching geometry in motion. It was also (speak it softly) slightly arousing – especially the rhythmical stretching process, in which the anatomically god-like humbug man grasped and twisted and pulled; then threw a loop over a stout hook, for stretching; then again grasped and twisted and pulled. The term *Übermensch* came unbidden, several times, to Peter's mind.

Deirdre was clearly captivated. 'I come here as often as I can,' she said to Peter, quietly. 'Sometimes he looks up and waves to me!'

'I expect he's soft on you.'

'On *me?*' she exclaimed. 'Of course he isn't!'

Peter wanted to say, 'Why not you?' – but it would have sounded like flirting, so he said nothing.

'It's usually about now,' she said. And on cue, the humbug man looked up from his sweaty work, spotted her at the window and raised his hand – but the look on his face, when he saw Peter alongside her, was mainly of annoyance.

'Oh, what a shame you saw that,' Deirdre said, as they walked away afterwards – when the thinner humbug mix had been chopped into regular pieces and set aside to cool, and the humbug man had slipped into a back room (presumably to lie down on a stone floor). 'He usually looks much more pleased to see me.'

Peter stopped walking and turned to her.

'What is it?' she said, tilting her head.

Blame the heady smell of the peppermint, perhaps; blame the sight of those astonishing Charles Atlas biceps triggering an animal instinct deep within; blame Friedrich Nietzsche. For whatever reason, Peter found himself saying, '*I*'d always be pleased to see you, Deirdre.' And just like that, he became her boyfriend.

Over the next couple of days, Peter set his investigation in motion. It didn't feel like detective work; just like doing his job properly. He interviewed all the neighbours, studied maps and plans of the pipes and sewers, familiarised himself with the archives – and gradually began to notice that key pieces of the story were unaccountably missing from the files.

Luckily he decided not to take Lillian into his confidence, as by now she had discovered the pay discrepancy, and would have reported him directly to Mr Blackmore (assuming she could locate him).

And while he was busy with all this sleuthing, he continued to meet Deirdre on the sly. More importantly, he also met her mother.

At first, he hadn't understood why Deirdre was keeping him a secret from her family. How could Mrs Benson be so 'strict' when she was the owner of a night club? Surely broad-mindedness went with the job? 'Just tell her,' he pleaded, repeatedly. He liked things to be above board. He certainly wished he had a mother he could tell about meeting Deirdre.

But then he called at the Black Cat on his official business, and immediately grasped the problem.

'Frank! Bruce!' Ma Benson, in a scarlet padded dressing gown, had shouted in a gravelly voice, on opening to the door to him. 'Here's some squit from the council knocking at an ungodly hour!'

Upon which two enormous young men – barefoot, in dark trousers and string vests, with tufts of dark underarm hair – joined their titanic mother and stood behind her, one of them with a soapy wet flannel in his hand. Peter found it was the un-wrung flannel he kept looking at; in particular, the cascade of sudsy drips, and the puddle they were making on the floor.

'I've come at a bad moment,' he said.

The Bensons did not respond to this politeness. Frank Benson – perhaps remembering what he'd been doing when he was called to the door – decided to carry on washing the back of his neck with the flannel, so that water ran down his forearm, and dripped from his elbow.

'As I said,' Peter continued, with a nervous cough, 'I wondered if you'd had any reason to complain about the drains? Our records seem to be incomplete.'

'Drains?' said Ma Benson, witheringly. She was at least six feet tall, this woman, and at least three feet wide. Turning to the boys, she heaved a vast sigh and said, 'Drains, Frank?'

'No, Mum.'

'Drains, Bruce?'

'No, Mum.'

And after the interview was over, and the door shut, Peter heard from outside the sound of Frank's voice: 'That's the little weed that's been sniffing round Deedee, Ma.'

After this encounter, Peter stopped saying 'Just tell her' and assumed a more serious attitude to the entire relationship, but it never occurred to him to end it. He liked Deirdre more and more: she was funny and nice and observant, and she needed rescuing. She hadn't read as many books as he had, it was true. When he mentioned *Les Misérables* to her, she thought he'd made up the title as a joke, and had duly laughed. But she knew literally hundreds of songs – and it seemed she had an impressive ability to suit a song to any occasion.

How did she do it? Peter could quote poetry himself, but only by rote. There was never an occasion when a passage from 'The Burial of Sir John Moore After Corunna' came to mind because it summed up what he was feeling. But with Deirdre it was different. She would hum a melody hardly knowing she was doing it, hardly knowing that the song in question expressed precisely what was in her heart.

'What's that?' he'd say.

'What's what, dear?'

'That tune.'

'Oh.' Then she'd hum it a bit more and think about it, and smile, and say, 'It's about how I'm bewitched, bothered and bewildered.' And then she would sing him an entire song.

Deirdre's voice was far more mature than everything else about her: it was both true and expressive. To have her singing to him like someone on a stage was pretty romantic for a boy who'd never had a girlfriend before. One day, at the end of the West Pier, she sang – perfectly – both verses of 'You're My Everything', and he thought his heart would burst.

While Peter was out and about in Brighton, he was naturally oblivious (as we all are) to the people he didn't know. If, for example, he one day asked a keen young police constable what the time was, or on another day bought a newspaper at the same time as the wall-eyed man living in

Colchester House, these people meant nothing to him, and the sad thing is, they never would. Older people quite often find themselves chatting to a new acquaintance and marvelling (after a bit of mental calculation), 'But hang on! Our younger selves must have *both* been staying at the Railway Arms in Stoke-on-Trent on Christmas Eve 1993!' It is oddly comforting to discover such coincidences. More and more, as we get older, we wish we could just travel back to re-inhabit our younger selves, and in a room full of people, *see who's there.*

But the fact is, although he died without meeting nearly all of them, Peter Dupont had brief contact with everyone in this story at some point or another during those last couple of weeks of his life. Sergeant Brunswick, for example, on his way to work one morning, saw him knock on the door of the Black Cat at nine in the morning, and remarked, 'Ooh, they won't appreciate that, sonny.'

Mrs Groynes, rushing back to the police station after a meeting with some of her Kemp Town boys, brushed past Peter outside Hannington's department store, dropping a string bag ostensibly full of oranges. When Peter stooped to help her, he realised that one of the things he had picked up was not an orange: it was a roll of banknotes. He handed it back to her with the merest quizzical look.

'Ooh, well done, love; I wondered where that was!' she bluffed, stuffing the loot in her pocket. 'Honest, I'd forget my own head if it wasn't tied on with ric-rac!'

Meanwhile, Constable Twitten did indeed provide Peter with the correct time one day – which was perhaps why he was all the more perplexed when, on the final morning of his life, he spotted the unusually lifelike wax model policeman at the top of the stairs at the wax museum.

The wax museum had become so much his regular haunt in the mornings (he usually had to wait for Deirdre to appear through her secret door) that he became almost invisible there. The friendly elderly lady who collected the tuppenny admissions just waved him through every day when she opened the shutters; the frilly Angélique would barely notice him as she bustled through the galleries, grumbling to herself and carrying an oil can. It was her daily job to climb into the window, duck down behind the Sleeping Beauty exhibit and oil the bellows mechanism that made its chest go creepily up and down.

'Why can't you do it for once?' Peter heard Angélique shouting at her father one day (with no trace of a French accent, incidentally).

They argued a great deal behind closed doors, it seemed.

'Why can't I do it? Because I'm supposed to be blind!' was the reply.

Once, after another such loud argument, Peter saw Angélique come out of her father's workroom in such a state of frustration that she marched straight into the Tudor Gallery and kicked Anne Boleyn in the stomach.

Who else had glancing contact with Peter Dupont in those weeks? Everyone, to a greater or lesser degree.

Dickie George came out of the Cricketers one lunchtime (shielding his eyes against the sunshine) and bumped into him. All Peter noticed was that he reeked of beer.

Inspector Steine was eating an ice cream in Luigi's – in a booth next to Ventriloquist Vince and a safe-blower called Birthmark Potter, as it happens – one day when Peter walked past the window. Steine, with an Ovaltine to hand, was engrossed in *The Riddle of the Sands*, which he had read before but happily couldn't remember in its entirety; Birthmark and

Vince were poring over the floor plans of the Post Office in Ship Street and discussing the pros and cons of entering through a dodgy roof-light. For no reason in particular, at the moment that Peter walked past, they all looked up.

Mr Reinhardt, the Borough Engineer, drove past him on his way to an expensive dinner.

Adelaide Vine and Phyllis were helpfully applying a sticking plaster to a child's knee – and giving directions to the First Aid caravan – just as Peter was arriving at the humbug shop one morning, so he said hello. And, in fact, he unknowingly passed Adelaide on other occasions, too – usually when she was out of uniform. Once, quite early in the morning, he saw her chatting to the old lady at the wax museum entrance – apparently coming out of the building, just as he was going in.

Meanwhile, Shorty (Mrs Groynes's reliable messenger boy whose chosen form of camouflage was the *Dandy*) tailed Peter around town for a day or two, just for a bit of practice.

Drumsticks Tommy from the Black Cat Quartet stood next to him in a urinal on the pier.

And Vivienne (a.k.a. The Skirt) got him to buy her a port and lemon in the lounge of the Windsor Hotel, while he was waiting to interview the manager about a backed-up sewer report from 1955. She didn't introduce herself, but she appeared to be a hotel resident, and he got the impression that she never paid for a drink if she could get someone else to do it.

Last but not least, there was Captain Hoagland, who had come down to Brighton a couple of weeks ahead of his master, to open the house. This encounter – unlike all the others – was not a glancing or unwitting one, and arguably had a deep effect on them both.

When Peter knocked on the door and enquired about the drains, Hoagland had been in residence just a day or two, and was simply glad to have some company other than Mrs Rogers. He invited the boy in, and they sat in the elevated morning room together, looking out at the sea and making small talk. Just as the housekeeper had done, Peter found the captain instantly fascinating; his posh and very British reticence was reminiscent of the quietly agonised teacher in Terence Rattigan's *The Browning Version*, the film of which Peter had seen twice with his mother in the year before she died.

But for all his inbred stiffness, Captain Hoagland was a fund of useful information. He knew a lot about the house and its environs, and explained to Peter about Lord Loopy and the great Regency garden that had been lost, with its aviary and famous parrot. He said it was a shame Lord Melamine hadn't arrived in Brighton yet; the new marquess had heard so much about the garden from his eccentric, obsessional father.

'A garden?' Peter marvelled. It was hard to believe that this area, crowded now with dismal buildings and tattered hoardings, could once have been attractively landscaped. Imagine if you could ever have looked out of a window in central Brighton and seen a living tree!

Hoagland suddenly remembered something and – standing up with an effort – reached with his left hand for a leather-bound book in one of the ornate walnut cases under the windows.

'There's an account in here,' he said, sitting back down and one-handedly riffling through it until he came to the correct page.

What he handed to Peter was an illustrated Brighton gazetteer from the 1840s, with a short description of the garden.

Peter read it with interest and then politely copied it into his notebook.

'I can see you're wondering about my arm, by the way,' said Hoagland. 'And my leg, probably, and my face.'

'No, of course not,' said Peter, blushing.

'Please don't be embarrassed. It was a long time ago now: just one of Jerry's unexploded bombs that went off at the wrong moment when we were defusing it. Three of my chaps copped it, so when you think about it, I got off lightly.'

'So you were in the Royal Engineers?'

'Yes. I'm proud to say I was.'

'But so was my father!'

'Really? That's wonderful. Did he … ? I mean, is he … ?'

Peter shook his head. 'He died in an explosion. I was eighteen months old.'

Hoagland sighed. 'So many did, I'm afraid,' he said. 'They told us when I joined the BD that the average life expectancy was twelve weeks.'

Dupont opened his wallet and proudly showed Hoagland a group photograph of four smiling men, their faces filthy from digging, standing next to a defused bomb.

'He's that one,' he said, pointing.

How did they get on to the subject of Deirdre Benson? Afterwards Hoagland could never remember, but he was glad that they had. From the back windows of Colchester House, he had already spotted her sitting at her sad little window; he had also been aware of the eye-watering stuff going on in the alley at all times of day. He thought it a splendid idea for the young, idealistic Peter to take her away from all this.

'Shall I tell you what I'm most afraid of, Captain Hoagland?' Peter said. 'It's not that something will happen to me because of Deirdre; it's that Deirdre will end it with me, to keep me safe from harm. She might dump me to protect me, do you see?'

And Hoagland shook his head and said, 'Well, I pray that doesn't happen to you, Peter. That exact thing happened to me once, and I can truly say that I never really got over it.'

Running away together wasn't the plan from the beginning. But they both knew this was no trifling summer romance. They could meet outside the sweet shop, where the crowd would shield them from view a little bit; they could be together in the early morning in the wax museum, because of the secret door. And on one glorious Saturday when Mrs Benson and both the boys travelled to London to meet with someone they always referred to just as 'Terence', Deirdre was able to spend most of the day with Peter – riding the roundabouts on the Palace Pier, and eating chips from newspaper.

It was on this special day that Deirdre first confessed to him that her family had killed and sawn up her uncle Kenneth. It seemed that in all the excitement of burgeoning young love, the perfect moment to mention this morsel of information had somehow failed to come up. But the way things were going, she felt that he had a right to know.

And then he was gripping on to the railings of the pier with his eyes closed, rocking back and forth, and she was wondering whether she'd done the right thing in telling him, after all.

'Does this change anything, Peter?' she asked, fearfully.

He swallowed a few times before answering. When he finally opened his eyes and spoke, he did it very quietly.

'Well, yes, I think it does, Deirdre,' he admitted. 'It does a little bit. Can you – can you – can you give me a while to let it sink in?'

'Did I do the right thing telling you?'

'Of course. I just … ' He trailed off. He felt sick.

'Really?'

'Yes, really. But I just have to … ' Faltering, he looked round for somewhere to think quietly for a moment and by bad luck spotted the old 'Voice-o-Graph' machine – the booth where for the cost of sixpence you could record your voice on to vinyl as a keepsake.

'Deirdre, would you like a record of my voice?' he said. And before she could answer, he was thankfully inside with the door shut, trying to suppress his feelings of terror and panic.

In some ways, luck was on his side when he stepped into the booth. For, despite his wide interest in comparative literature, he was unfamiliar with Graham Greene's *Brighton Rock*, so had no idea that this particular type of gift had been permanently tainted in terms of romantic gesture.

But in other ways, this was the very worst time to make a recording. He had never felt more scared in his life. He stared at the Bakelite speaking tube and quailed. What should he say? Deirdre was looking at him pleadingly through the glass; she obviously needed reassurance and comfort right now, but he was simply too traumatised to give it to her. *They sawed up Uncle Kenneth?* With his sixpence poised over the slot, Peter looked out at the general scene on the pier, and realised that standing a few feet behind Deirdre was a man in dark glasses who had surely been following them around all day. And now that he thought about it, behind the man in dark glasses there was a child who – well, was it possible that this urchin with the rolled-up comic in his hand had been following Peter around as well?

He made a last attempt to marshal his thoughts, took a deep breath and inserted the money. He told himself that all he needed to say was 'I love you, Deirdre'.

But there was too much vinyl to be filled. And after he had said, 'Deirdre, I love you', he rushed on, talking, spilling out feelings he scarcely knew he had – his fears that perhaps he was a bit young for all this grown-up stuff of criminal conspiracy at the council, and wishing he had gone to university after all, instead of dating the treasured daughter of a gigantic scary night-club owner who smelled like a tobacconist's and apparently thought nothing of murdering her own kith and kin.

Why was he blurting out this stuff? This must be what it's like in a confessional, he thought – as he found himself talking about what Mr Reinhardt might be up to, and how his landlady had received a brick through a window. On his way to work this morning, someone had deliberately driven a car up on to the payment and nearly knocked him over. This was stuff he'd been determined not to worry Deirdre with – yet now in his weakness he had recorded it! And the man in the dark glasses was pretending to take an interest in the helter-skelter, but was still watching Deirdre; and Peter, who had now completely lost control, started rambling about him as well.

By the time the little red light flashed in the booth to say he had just ten seconds left, Peter was more than grateful to stop. He was so ashamed of how badly he'd done this special thing; but in his defence, he had done it under extremely trying circumstances.

He came out of the booth with the disc in its paper sleeve, holding it tight.

'Is that for me, Peter?' Deirdre said, quietly. Her little chin wobbled. She was on the verge of tears. 'I shouldn't have told you, should I?'

'No, I'm glad you did,' he said.

'Really?'

'Yes, really.'

The man in the dark glasses had come closer, but was pretending to be part of the noisy crowd taking an interest in the coconut shy.

Peter pulled Deirdre towards him. It was the first time he had pressed his body against hers, and when he realised that her clothes reeked of the night club (tobacco, booze, sweat, perfume), it made his heart go out to her all the more. This girl ought to smell like a spring meadow.

'Deirdre,' he said, quietly. 'I've messed up the record, I'm sorry. But I'm afraid to throw it away where people might see me do it.'

She put her hand on his shoulder. 'I don't mind at all.'

'I suppose when it boils down to it, I'm quite scared, Deirdre.'

'Oh, Peter.'

She took the record from him, and slipped it into her handbag.

'We'll get away, Peter. We'll make a plan.'

———

And so to Peter's last couple of days. First he contacted Ben Oliver at the *Brighton Evening Argus*, and then he started to compile a dossier of material: his notebooks, containing records of his interviews; the various incomplete council records; some maps and historical material; and a fine print of a nineteenth-century watercolour supplied by Captain Hoagland. The missing parts of the puzzle (he calculated) would be found inside Reinhardt's safe. He also wrote to his auntie in Eastbourne, telling her about the joy of meeting a bomb-disposal officer who might have been known to his father.

On the morning of his death, after meeting Deirdre at the Maison du Wax to make final arrangements for their escape (unaware that a real policeman was overhearing every word), Peter clocked in at the office, took the clanking, self-operated lift to the third floor and waited in the corridor outside Mr Reinhardt's door for the sound of him unlocking his safe. Then he created a diversion.

'Mr Reinhardt, sir! Quick! Outside in the car park! Mr Blackmore has collapsed!'

'What?' said Reinhardt. '*What?* Cathy, come with me. This is serious. Blackmore owes me money.'

Once Reinhardt and his secretary had both left the room, Peter took the entire contents of the safe – including several uncashed cheques – and added them to his existing parcel. There wasn't time to sort through it all. He pushed through a heavy door marked 'No Entry' and took the tight, echoing back stairs, which on the ground floor (as he knew) opened on to a small locked yard surrounded by a high fence.

He was remarkably calm, but that was because he was prepared. He had everything worked out. With no one to see him (or, more importantly, to down tools on account of it), he opened a fairly large manhole cover and shifted it to one side. Holding the parcel carefully to his chest with one hand, he climbed down the iron ladder into a disused sewerage tunnel, at one end of which (just a hundred yards away) he knew he would re-emerge into daylight quite near the West Pier for his meeting with Ben Oliver.

'I'll be in a deck-chair,' he had told the reporter. 'I'll look out for you.'

Safely arrived at the seafront, he had paid his threepence, and taken his seat. And for a while, in the sun, he had closed his eyes and listened to the shingle dragged down by the waves, and the shouts of the children on the beach. He dared not think too much about the future, but yesterday Deirdre had sung to him, in her best jazz voice, that they had the world on a string. It was a memory to treasure – and he was treasuring it now.

But if looking the wrong way had been, as his mother used to say, 'the story of his life', it turned out to be the story of his death, as well.

'Hello, Peter Dupont,' said a voice from behind – and that was all he knew.

He opened his eyes and saw nothing but sky; he felt the sharp, cold metal against the skin on his neck, and then a great spasm of shock and pain that was over in seconds. As his body subsided, he felt the parcel torn from his arms.

The last, strange sensation that registered in his mind was, curiously, an overwhelming smell of peppermint.

Seven

The problem with informing two hundred criminal underlings that you are looking for a particular wall-eyed man in Brighton is that over the following week you will receive (taking into account a little slippage due to illness, laziness, stupidity and sudden death in suspicious circumstances) one hundred and ninety-two individual sightings, reported to you on one hundred and ninety-two different – and increasingly exasperating – occasions. At fault here was Mrs Groynes's rudimentary chain of command: people weren't authorised to tell others that the message had already got through. Thus, each and every minion who observed a suspicious wall-eyed man entering Colchester House on the seafront thought to himself, *That must be him! I need to tell the boss!* – and acted on that impulse immediately.

The first time the telephone rang at the station and the caller asked for Mrs Groynes, it was Sergeant Brunswick who answered. He was nonplussed.

'You'd like to speak to *who*?'

The person at the other end of the line sounded like one of the snotty herberts who hung around the railway station, nicking Granny Smiths from the fruit stall. From the band-music noise in the background, he appeared to be speaking today from the public call-box at the entrance to the West Pier.

'You want to speak to our *charlady*, sonny?' he said. 'On a private matter? On this telephone?'

'That's right, mister,' said the supremely confident child. 'And look sharp, won't ya? I ain't got much shrapnel.'

Sergeant Brunswick huffed.

'Listen, sonny. This number is for official police business. The reporting of crime and such like. The reporting of *incidents*. You're speaking to a police sergeant, not a secretary.'

'Yeah, but go on, mister,' urged the caller. 'Be a toff.'

And so Brunswick had summoned Mrs Groynes to the telephone, and she had shrugged her shoulders as if mystified, and then laid down her mop and taken off her heavy-duty rubber gloves.

Once on the telephone, she said, 'Now what's all this, calling me at work? Sauce, I call it.' And then, when the caller had introduced himself, she demanded in a businesslike manner, 'All right, Shorty. What's the lay?'

Twitten, pretending not to take an interest, listened intently to her slightly impatient 'Ah-ha' and 'Mm' responses. He noted that there was no inflection of surprise in her voice. Whatever this 'Shorty' person was telling her, she obviously knew it already.

'All right, ta-ta, good boy,' she said finally, and hung up.

She picked up her mop again and began bustling with it.

Brunswick and Twitten exchanged glances.

'Who was that, Mrs G?' asked Brunswick.

'J. Sainsbury,' she said, without a moment's hesitation. 'They got a new consignment of Vim. That was the manager.' She put her hands on her hips. 'Well, all this standing around jawing won't buy the baby a new bonnet, will it? How about a nice cup of tea?'

Five minutes later the telephone rang again, and this time Twitten hastened to answer it.

'Brighton CID, Inspector Steine's office, Constable Twitten speaking,' he said. 'May I ask the nature of your enquiry? Would you call it a crime or an incident?'

There was a hesitation at the other end. Then a lightly disguised, rough Greek-accented voice asked in strangled tones for Mrs Groynes. It was obviously Ventriloquist Vince.

'Are you calling from J. Sainsbury, by any chance?' Twitten enquired, in tones of concern. 'You see, sir, this line needs to be kept free as far as possible, and if you're calling about the important new shipment of Vim, I happen to know that Mrs Groynes has been told already.'

As he spoke, he watched Mrs Groynes's reaction. She showed no emotion other than polite bafflement. Vince, on the other hand, was definitely rattled.

'About what fucking shipment a fucking *what*?' he said.

'Vim. It's a kind of scouring powder.'

Twitten put down the receiver. 'He hung up,' he said, smiling.

At the first opportunity, Mrs Groynes put out the word through Shorty that she *knew already* about the so-called Lord Melamine, thank you all very much, but it proved impossible to stem the flow. For a whole week, everywhere she went, men with facial scars, tattooed knuckles, low hairlines and unorthodox hygiene sidled up to her and said out of the side of their mouths, 'I found him, boss.' Leaving home for work in the morning, she often found a cluster of shady characters loitering outside the front door of her house; in the end she started to climb out of a back window to avoid them.

'There's no reward, you know,' she said to them. 'Tell everyone, I never offered a reward and I *know already*.'

But back at the station, the telephone continued to ring all day for her, and she finally informed Sergeant

Brunswick that she feared she was the innocent victim of a hoax.

'If they ask for me again, just tell them to bugger off,' she said. And then she added, with a flash of the innate genius Twitten couldn't help admiring her for: 'And you'll never guess, dears. Even that so-called Vim delivery at J. Sainsbury turned out to be a wicked lie!'

It was partly because of the annoying phone calls that Mrs Groynes decided to help with the Dupont investigation. If Sergeant Brunswick were to work different hours – say, undercover at the Black Cat night club – he wouldn't be in the office when all these suspicious tip-offs came through. Tommy Drumsticks had already informed her of Dickie George's sudden disappearance, and of the recruitment of a new female singer whose musical arrangements suited a larger band. Three new musicians were required, and quickly. Pondering this, Mrs Groynes came up with a creative solution that was also (of course) entirely self-serving.

The next day Brunswick discovered an anonymous note on his desk, typed on the office typewriter, and smelling slightly of bleach. It informed him that the Black Cat required a trumpet player urgently, and that he should present himself for an audition at midday.

It was not what you'd call an impersonal note. It ended with the cautionary paragraph:

```
Try NOT to look like a POLICEMAN. Pay
attention in particular to HAIR and
SHOES. These are often a DEAD GIVEAWAY.
Be aware, the drummer is A FRIEND. And
BLEEDING GOOD LUCK, DEAR.
```

'Did you see who brought this, Mrs G?' Brunswick asked, having read it twice. But she said no, dear, she hadn't. It was on his desk when she arrived for work. Could have been anyone.

'And I didn't read it, neither,' she added, turning her back and bustling with a duster (she was the best in the business at seeming to bustle while at the same time doing nothing). 'What's it say, then, dear?'

'It's an anonymous tip-off that they need a trumpet player at the Black Cat.'

'Well, what are they telling *you* for? You play the bleeding cello.'

'*And* the trumpet, Mrs G.'

'No!' She turned to look at him. She seemed impressed. 'Blimey, you kept that dark.'

'I think I did talk to you about it once, Mrs G, when I kept going to see *Young Man with a Horn*.'

'Did you? Well, I never. I sometimes think I'd forget my own head, dear, if it wasn't stuck on with Araldite.'

He took a thoughtful sip of tea. Not many people knew this, but there was actually nothing he loved more than playing the trumpet. He had played it so much as a teenager that his auntie Violet had often joked (not entirely humorously) that he shouldn't be surprised to wake up one morning with a drawing pin stuck in his windpipe.

So this offer of his dream job combined with going undercover to spy on a heavy mob – this was nothing less than manna from heaven. However, a tiny note of caution faintly tinkling at the back of his mind did give him pause. Was this offer so perfect that he ought to question its provenance? Scatty old Mrs Groynes might have forgotten their relevant conversation, but *who else knew he played the trumpet?* For that matter, who else knew he longed to go undercover, or that the Black Cat was a location of interest in an ongoing inquiry? Such were the pertinent questions that floated just beyond the reach of his consciousness.

He held up the note and studied it through narrowed eyes (as if that would make any difference). It was a moment of truth: passion *v.* rationality; id *v.* superego; sensibility *v.* sense. Sergeant James Brunswick had pondered many such quandaries in his life, and the outcome was always the same.

'I'm doing it,' he said.

'Good for you, dear. Cup of tea?'

It was just too good an opportunity to miss. The stage at the Black Cat would be a perfect position from which to observe any nefarious goings-on. Up to now, his vague idea of working there undercover had involved lowly jobs such as washing up in the kitchens, or being a bouncer on the door. Now he would have the best view in the house.

'It's perfect,' he said. 'I'm off to buy a wig and some winkle-pickers.'

'Good idea, lovey. Look the part for once.'

'Tell Twitten about this development, would you?'

'I will,' she said. She resumed her bustling, and then broke off to say, 'Here, I just thought. You'd better not take that note with you, dear. Best leave it safe with me.'

'Blimey, you're right!' he chuckled, handing it over. Imagine if someone at the Black Cat saw it! Mrs Groynes might be just a harmless cockney charlady, but he had to admit that she was also very quick-thinking.

'Mrs G, I must say, sometimes you do seem—'

But he didn't get to say what Mrs Groynes sometimes seemed.

'Lovely iced bun before you go?' she interrupted.

And that was it. Within a couple of hours, Brunswick was posing as Kevin Mundy (a.k.a. 'Kevin on the Valves') in the Black Cat's newly expanded seven-piece band, complete with false quiff and sideburns, painfully pointy shoes, red bow-tie and shiny tuxedo jacket, belting out a jazzy solo verse of 'Melancholy Baby'. What a whirlwind. It was lucky that he was genuinely musical, and that his auntie had never followed through on that grisly drawing-pin threat, because although the anonymous note had used the word 'audition', it was actually a band rehearsal, and new singer Delores Dee had expected to get through at least a dozen standards along with four or five new songs, too.

There was just one awkward moment: when the double bass player (Bob) said in a spirit of welcome that he was sure he recognised Kevin from other jobs, possibly the Bora Bora Lounge in Portslade? Brunswick pretended to think about it, and agreed this was more than likely – while knowing full well that in fact they'd met when he arrested Bob three weeks ago in Church Street for drunkenly chucking a half-brick through an ironmonger's window.

As far as the music went, Brunswick acquitted himself, and loved every minute of it. But the main thing was, he was *in*! From his position on the slightly raised performance area, he would be able to watch all the club's arrivals and departures. Meanwhile, access to the back-stage dressing-room meant he had already formed an idea of the general layout of the building, and had spotted interesting unlit staircases going both up and down. The Bensons themselves he was yet to meet.

How much help he would receive from Tommy the drummer remained to be seen. Occasionally, in the sections of the orchestrations where Brunswick was not required to play – when he lightly held the trumpet on his knee, and tapped a winkle-pickered foot – he glanced across to Tommy and raised a quizzical eyebrow, but no acknowledgement came the other way, other than a flash from Tommy's gold tooth. Tommy, it seemed, was a bit of a pro.

So things looked very promising on the Brunswick Undercover front. When he left his auntie's flat at five that evening for his first night's performance with the band, he walked to the nearest phone box with a pocketful of pennies and called Twitten at the station.

'So what do you think happened to Dickie George, sir?' Twitten asked, eagerly. 'And have you seen Deirdre yet?'

Brunswick told him to calm down: he'd only been inside the place for a couple of hours so far.

'It was bally good luck about your getting the job, sir. I've been doing a little digging and everything seems to point to the Bensons. Scotland Yard have even confirmed a connection to the notorious Terence Chambers.'

'Really? What sort of connection?'

'Well, do you remember the big London Airport robbery, sir?'

'Of course. They couldn't pin it on Chambers, but they knew he was behind it. The problem was, none of the notes ever showed up.'

'They think the Bensons were involved. Specifically, Frank Benson, the older son, who used to be a boxer and is notoriously touchy and hot-headed. Apparently his mother keeps him in check; if she didn't, or so my contact informs me, Frank would be murdering people *all over the place*.'

Brunswick was impressed. 'Well done, Twitten.'

'Reading between the lines, sir, I suspect at root his problem is a bit Oedipal, so do tread carefully there.'

'A bit *what*?'

'Oedipal, sir. Being sexually attracted to the mother, and so on.'

'*What?*'

'But that's just my conjecture, sir, so feel free to ignore it. Bruce, on the other hand, has less violent tendencies, so perhaps you could befriend him. It's wonderful, sir. Just think! From this evening you will be operating incognito in the midst of extremely dangerous criminals, some of whom literally stop at nothing!'

Brunswick swallowed. Until the last couple of minutes he had felt quite bucked up. 'Well,' he said, trying not to sound as unnerved as he felt, 'that's a good job you've done there, son. You know what they say: forewarned is forearmed.'

'Thank you, sir.'

Twitten could have left it there, but he didn't. He wouldn't have been true to himself if he had.

'I suppose I ought to add, sir, that my contact at the Flying Squad also said he was shocked the Brighton police didn't connect the body in the suitcase with the disappearance of Kenneth Benson, sir – especially as he was last sighted boarding a Brighton train at Victoria.'

'Well, it's easy to say that now, but at the time—'

'And I'm afraid to say I have now examined the suitcase myself and it contains more clues to the victim's identity than—' Twitten stopped. He wanted the exact form of words, and after a pause for thought, it came to him. 'Than a dog's got fleas, sir.'

Brunswick huffed. He wasn't in the mood to hear any more. When the coin box beeped to tell him it needed more money, he was briefly tempted not to feed it, but in the end he inserted the pennies and pushed Button A. When the beeps cleared, Twitten started talking again immediately.

'Anyway, the point is, sir, the Bensons seem to have had more than one motive for killing poor Peter Dupont. I'm thinking that either they killed him because he was going to abduct Deirdre; or because he knew about Kenneth; or because of something to do with the council, because if you remember the Borough Engineer made the memorable remark "Oh, shit, they've killed him" before jumping into his car and heading directly for the ports. You're definitely in the right place to learn more. But I can't help wondering who wrote that incredibly helpful note to you, sir. Did you form any theory yourself?'

Brunswick shrugged. This was a slightly awkward question. 'Not really, son, no. I drew a blank, if I'm honest.'

'I'd look at it myself, but of course I can't.'

'Why not?'

'Well, I'm sorry to have to tell you this, sir, but I'm afraid the note has gone.'

'What do you mean, gone?'

'I did ask to see it, sir. But apparently – and to Mrs Groynes's credit she did say, 'You'll never believe it' before she supplied the astonishing details – there was a window open and a seagull hopped inside and took the note right off your desk, sir.'

'A seagull?'

'Yes, sir. Herring gull would be more precise, I imagine, but I wasn't there, so I can't be sure.'

Brunswick was stunned. 'A seagull?'

'I know, sir. Or herring gull. I'm tempted to say it's a blatant lie consistent with Mrs Groynes being a criminal mastermind operating complacently from inside the police station – '

'Oh, not that *again*, son! Not *now*!'

' – but I won't say that, of course, because it does no good and just makes everyone annoyed.'

'Listen, Twitten. You've got to get over this nonsense about the flaming charlady. It will ruin your career if you don't.'

'I know, sir. I do try.'

'But a seagull … ?'

'I know. Or herring gull. It really does *sound* like a lie, doesn't it, sir? Anyway, it means I didn't see the note and I'm sorry. But I don't think we should enquire too deeply anyway into how you got there. You're *in*, that's what matters, sir. You're *in*!'

———

Ordinarily, Inspector Steine would have had quite a lot to say about one of his officers going undercover, especially if the officer was Brunswick. But since his momentous encounter on the train with Adelaide Vine, he had paid almost no attention to what was going on in the station. He was utterly dejected.

Every day, he sat at his desk, staring blankly out of the window. He barely touched his little plates of assorted highland shortbread.

When Brunswick had popped in to announce that he was off to the Black Cat to play the trumpet and glean evidence against a patently dangerous heavy mob, Steine had merely advised, 'Well, try not to get shot again, will you?'

When Twitten asked him to sign a petty cash slip to cover an unspecified trip to London, he did not demand to know why.

And when his phone rang with news that another suspicious bag – with what appeared to be human blood seeping out of it – had been found at the Left Luggage office at the railway station, he merely sighed and sent Twitten to deal with it on his own.

Twitten was the main beneficiary of this change in the inspector's spirits, as it meant that the daily one-to-one interrogations took up much less of his time.

Knock, knock.

'Come in.'

'Good morning, sir.'

'Yes, yes. Blah di blah. Out with it, then.'

'Thank you, sir. The thing is, I still firmly believe—'

'Yes, yes. Out of ten?'

'Ten, sir.'

'All right, Twitten. You can go.'

And after that, the rest of the day was his own.

As for Steine, he just needed to think. He needed to go over the scene with Adelaide Vine again and again, trying to understand what had happened; recalling the dawning sense of joy and amazement when he realised this beautiful young woman was describing the meeting of his own parents in Gordon Square nearly fifty years ago. And then he would remember how that burgeoning joy was crushed when Adelaide, far from falling into his arms with a Shakespearean cry of 'Mine Uncle!', instead recoiled from him with a highly modern look of shock, horror and contempt.

The recollection made him physically shrivel at his desk.

'What a wicked thing to say!' she had gasped. And then she'd leaped from the train and walked briskly off, leaving Steine with his smile still frozen on his face.

Eventually, he confessed all to Mrs Groynes, which wasn't easy. But at least it stopped her enquiring all the time why he looked like a wet weekend in Weston-super-Mare.

She was surprisingly sympathetic and helpful.

'You see, dear,' she explained, 'from her point of view, you could be telling a great big porky pie. Pretending that this story of hers means anything to you.'

'But why would I do that?'

'I expect that's precisely what she's asking herself right now, dear. *Why would he lie? What's in it for him?*'

'And I knew that her mother's name was Gillian.'

'That's all to the good, then. Listen, I bet you hear from her when she's had time to calm down. Here, tell me who she is again, this Adelaide Whatever Her Name Is.'

'Adelaide Vine.'

'That's the one.'

For once, Mrs Groynes was not pretending to be vague about a detail. She genuinely had hardly registered the name of Adelaide Vine. In the past few days she had been preoccupied with other matters such as getting Sergeant Brunswick out of the way, plotting her revenge on Wall-Eye Joe and eluding her own well-meaning minions for their own safety (with the way things were going, she was afraid she might lose her patience and shoot one of them). This Adelaide Vine woman had not been on the radar.

'All I know is that she's a Brighton Belle,' said Steine, 'and that she's very nice-looking, and about twenty years old.'

'Blimey. A Brighton Belle, of all things.' She smiled. 'What will they think of next, eh?'

'Yes, apparently it was a bright idea of someone in local government. Of course, since meeting her I've seen the advertisements everywhere. They say, "Whatever you want to know, wherever you want to go, enquire of a Brighton Belle!" Apparently Miss Vine found out about it just as they were closing applications. She got in by the skin of her teeth.'

He let out a whimper of emotion. It was piteous. This Adelaide Vine woman had really got under his skin.

'Aw, what is it now, dear?'

'Nothing, nothing, it's silly. But I just keep thinking, what if she *hadn't* got that last-minute interview for the Brighton Belles?'

'How do you mean, dear?'

He sighed. 'I mean, I would never have known she existed. What if she hadn't been the person on the seafront who took control at the murder scene before we arrived? What if I hadn't bumped into her the next day at Brighton Station? What if I hadn't asked why she was interested in policemen?'

It was evidently a kind of pleasurable torture for him to think of all the ways he might not have met Adelaide Vine.

'You'd still be you, dear,' said Mrs Groynes, reassuringly.

'But I wouldn't know I had such a lovely and accomplished niece.'

Mrs Groynes nodded thoughtfully and patted his hand. Everything she had heard had sounded alarm bells.

'Do you know what, dear?' she said. 'I think she would have found you one way or another.'

'Really?'

'I reckon it was meant to be, dear! It was in the bleeding tea leaves! It was kismet! And I bet you anything you like she'll be in touch very soon to hear your side of the story.'

'Really?'

'I'd bet fifty pounds.'

He seemed relieved.

'Thank you, Mrs Groynes. You've been very helpful.'

'My pleasure. And tell you what, dear: why don't you go out for a nice little walk?'

'A walk? At ten o'clock in the morning?'

'To tell you the truth, dear, while I've been standing here I've been noticing quite a bit of nasty dust and dirt and cobwebs and whatnot adhering to your personal bits and bobs. If you could pop out for about an hour, dear – an hour should do it – I could get this place all shipshape and Bristol fashion for your return. What do you say?'

So Inspector Steine took himself off (slightly mystified) for a lovely walk on the seafront, and in his absence Mrs Groynes withdrew a set of skeleton keys from an inner pocket of her overalls, selected a small one, opened his desk drawer and carefully removed the first three chapters of Inspector Steine's memoir, without disturbing either the memo from the BBC's Director General in which he upbraided Inspector Steine for believing the spaghetti hoax on *Panorama*, or the recent letter from the Maison du Wax saying that his model would be ready in two weeks and that they planned a grand unveiling ceremony, which they sincerely hoped he would attend.

'Now,' she said to herself, 'what are you up to, Miss so-called Adelaide so-called Vine? What's he possibly got that you want? And who the bleeding hell *are* you, when you're at home?'

Ted Martin was the man in charge of the Left Luggage at Brighton Station. He had worked there for ten years or more, and only recently had started to wish he'd chosen a different profession.

In the old days, Ted had loved his job. For one thing, the Left Luggage office, with its heavy swing doors keeping out the cold and its ancient paraffin heater behind the counter emitting a steady (if always rather disappointing) warmth, was a fairly cosy place to work. For another, the tips weren't bad. And sometimes he could go home at six o'clock and regale his morose wife Iris with the daft things people had tried to leave with him that day (such as their overexcited toddlers fitted with reins), in the hope of cheering her up.

However, once the police started finding human body parts in the luggage, the shine went off the job somewhat. Sergeant Brunswick always regretted that he'd stupidly opened that suitcase in Old Ted's presence. An elderly man who remembered terrible things from the First World War, the sight of a newly dismembered corpse sent him over the edge, and afterwards he was out of action for several weeks.

It had taken a lot of pressure from friends and colleagues to make him resume his position; even having agreed, it took persuasion still to get him out of the house after breakfast.

'Try not to dwell on it,' his wife would say each morning, as she handed him his Cheddar cheese sandwich wrapped in greaseproof paper. 'It's not likely to happen again, dear, is it?'

So when he first noticed that a red stain had appeared overnight on the side of a canvas holdall, he hesitated about reporting it. For one thing, maybe the stain was only ink? (But it didn't look like ink.) For another, he had no recollection of the person who'd left it, so he could be no help to the police with any inquiries. (But this was really no excuse.) And for another, what if this time it was *the head*? (This was the obvious clincher.)

But how do you ignore such a bloodstain once you have noticed it? So in the end Ted made a decision, and called not only the police station but also Ben Oliver at the *Brighton Evening Argus* – because although Oliver was very young, he was gaining a good reputation as a crime reporter. Also, just after he was appointed to the job, Oliver had written a human-interest story about Ted's grisly torso experience, pointing out to the readers of the *Argus* that while we all enjoy reading about sensational stuff, we should never forget the real traumatic impact it can have on the normal, innocent people who work (say) in a Left Luggage office, and have to spend weeks in a rest home in Littlehampton to get over it. ('Being in Littlehampton was worse than being dead' was the quote that most Brightonian readers remembered from the piece, probably because it chimed so well with their own prejudices.)

Twitten was the first to arrive. He found Old Ted counting out the coppers he'd been given today – piling them into little towers on the counter. By the look of things, he'd got about two and sixpence. When he saw Twitten, he scooped the coins up and poured them back into his pocket.

'Good morning, Mr Martin, I'm Constable Twitten. I've come about the holdall; may I see it?'

Ted was surprised by Twitten's youth, but impressed by his politeness. He reached for the bag and set it gingerly on the counter.

Twitten immediately noted one key fact about the bag, which had not escaped Ted: that it was human-head-sized.

'So this is it.'

'Yes, sir.'

'Interesting size, Mr Martin.'

'Indeed, sir.'

Twitten felt his new helmet slip forward on his forehead, which (annoyingly) it always seemed to do when professional composure was required.

'Good. Excellent,' he said, affecting nonchalance. He picked the bag up by the handles and tested its weight. It was heavy. A human head would surely weigh about that much.

'Interesting weight.'

Then he spotted the stain on the canvas, and quickly put the bag down. He coughed.

'So you've made no attempt to identify the contents of this bag yourself, Mr Martin?'

'Me? No.' Mr Martin shuddered. 'Not on your ruddy life. Against the rules anyway, thank Christ.'

'Is it all right if we bolt those doors for a minute or two? We don't really want the public seeing this.'

'Good idea, son. I'll do it.'

But just as the old man in his shabby railway uniform reached the doors, Ben Oliver arrived. He was wearing a summer hat, and looked excited.

'Ted!'

'Mr Oliver.'

'Thanks so much for calling me. Oh, no, am I too late?' the reporter said.

And in a way, he was. Twitten, at the counter, had quickly opened the bag and was now staring down into it.

'What is it?' called Oliver. Then he said, 'Ted, you stay here. Don't move an inch.'

'No, it's all right,' said Twitten, with a look of relief. 'It's bally well all right. Come on.'

The others approached, but warily.

'No, really. There's nothing to be scared of, aside from the blood.' Twitten let out a slightly hysterical laugh. 'Come and look, Mr Oliver. It's a good thing you're here, actually. Because, look, it's addressed to you!'

By the time Inspector Steine had come back from his walk, it's true that no dust, dirt or cobwebs adhered to his personal bits and bobs – but only because there had been none adhering in the first place. Mrs Groynes was absent. His desk drawer, when he unlocked it, showed no sign of disturbance.

He needed to reply to the letter from the Maison du Wax, of course. But when he considered the idea of a grand unveiling ceremony, he had definite misgivings. He wanted just to feel simple pride: after all, not many people are chosen for the honour of being modelled in wax by someone with a French name easily confusable with 'Tussaud'. But there was fear of humiliation, too. As Twitten had heartlessly pointed out, a very high percentage of the models in the Maison du Wax were not only terrible, they were also weirdly grouped. By what rationale was Henry VIII placed with Kirk Douglas in shiny boxing shorts? Why was Marie Antoinette smirking over her fan at Tommy Trinder? Where would Inspector Steine turn up? Amidst Bill Haley's Comets? And what would the lovely Adelaide Vine think of *that*?

His phone rang. He answered it without enthusiasm. It was Twitten reporting that the bag at the Left Luggage office contained Peter Dupont's bloodied missing parcel of documents, addressed to Ben Oliver of the *Argus*. A preliminary rummage suggested that it contained 'bally dynamite, sir'.

'Dynamite?' repeated Steine in alarm. (He hadn't really been listening.)

'Not literally, sir,' laughed Twitten. The boy sounded faintly hysterical for some reason. Steine heard the constable turn to someone and whisper, 'He thought I meant real dynamite.'

'I heard that, Twitten.'

'Sorry, sir.'

'Who are you talking to?'

Twitten guessed (rightly) that he oughtn't to mention the presence of a reporter from the *Argus*, so avoided the question.

'Anyway, the main thing is, sir, it isn't a head!'

Steine shrugged. He had no idea why Twitten would say this.

'Well, good, good. Carry on.'

After hanging up the receiver, Steine folded his hands on the desk, swallowed and assumed his characteristic faraway expression, staring at a blank bit of wall. Aside from the occasional sigh, he was completely still. His brain emptied; his breathing slowed. This was what despair had always looked like in Geoffrey St John Steine. When he was a child, his father had once discovered him in just such a trance-like state, shaken him to his senses and exclaimed, 'Blimey, Geoff! You scared me!' And then, thoughtlessly betraying his origins, 'I thought you'd stuck your spoon in the wall!'

From there, things had escalated horribly. Sister Gillian had sneakily reported her father's cockney outburst to Mother (partly to ask what it meant), with the effect that Mother was angry with Father, and both of them were *very* angry with Gillian, and then – and there was no justice in this – all three ganged up together to be absolutely furious with young Geoffrey for unwittingly affecting death in the first place.

Dwelling on his childhood had become a habit over the past few days, for obvious reasons.

After fifteen minutes of staring poignantly into the middle distance, Steine realised that the telephone was ringing again, so he answered it.

'Inspector Steine?' said a female voice.

'Yes?'

He held his breath. Was it she?

'It's me,' she said. 'It's Adelaide Vine. I'm so sorry I ran away the other day. I was very confused. But I spoke to my solicitor that day in London, and he said you weren't lying to me. It seems you really might be my uncle.'

In the world of Mrs Groynes, there were usually few surprises, and even fewer mistakes. She thought ahead; she was well-informed; she was sceptical; and she was also preternaturally quick to grasp what was going on. So anyone hoping that she would carry on believing that Lord Melamine was Wall-Eye Joe and act accordingly *once she had actually met him* is in for a disappointment.

Prior to meeting him, of course, she had been planning a terrific sting operation, involving a *faux* diamond robbery that would first relieve him of everything he owned and then leave him dangling from a ceiling inside the Tower of London dressed as a Beefeater with a recently fired gun in his hand. A small gang had been put together to pull this wonderful con with her; a van had been stolen from Worthing and its number plates changed; facsimile floor plans of the Jewel House had been knocked up by Dave the Forger; a fake Koh-i-Noor had been fashioned (the idea being that the gang would leave this bit of 'jargoon' in the place of the real spark-ler). All that remained was for Mrs Groynes to make contact with 'the mark'.

But then she sat next to the poor man in a tea shop on the seafront, where he was ineptly trying to persuade a retired postman from Godalming to accept a gold bar in exchange for twenty-five pounds, and she quickly concluded that, whoever this so-called 'Lord Melamine' was, he was not the notorious and ruthless con man responsible for the deaths of multiple women at that horrific unfinished house in the country. This amateur magsman with the pot of China tea and the half-eaten custard tart evidently couldn't con his way out of a wet paper bag.

The sense of disappointment was immense, but she also felt an overwhelming sadness. It wasn't so much the wasted work and money (although replica Beefeater costumes don't come cheap). No, it was that over the past week she had felt Hoagy close to her again; planning revenge for his death had made her feel so much better about herself. And now, with the wall-eyed 'Lord Melamine' turning out to be just a hopeless beginner, unworthy of her attention, she felt the long-lost Hoagy slip away, back into the darkness.

But there was no sense dwelling on any of this now. Back in the tea shop, she wiped a tear from her eye and asked the skivvy for the bill. She had things to do. Without looking at Melamine, she put on her gloves and brushed marzipan crumbs from her skirt, and unclasped her handbag.

It was then that she realised Lord Melamine had been trying to catch her eye.

'Madam,' he said, smiling. 'I don't suppose I could interest you in a gold brick at a bargain price? Here's my card. I'm the Fifth Marquess of Colchester but you can call me Melamine. I'm very pleased to meet you. I was watching you in the mirror over there and I noticed you put your milk in before the tea. That's the way I like it too!'

Mrs Groynes, who had been on the verge of tears, was so amused she laughed aloud.

'Oh, you poor bleeder!' she said, patting his hand. 'Don't take this the wrong way, dear, but you are absolutely bleeding hopeless!'

'I don't understand. What did I say?'

And he looked so upset that – blame the Hoagy disappointment, blame the sugar rush from eating a marzipan fancy – she felt genuinely sorry for him. It just broke her heart that this man was so bad at his job, so bad at pretending to be posh; and as for choosing to flog gold bricks, that game was as old as the hills.

So she took off her gloves again, put her handbag on the floor and sighed. The least she could do was to offer him a few tips.

'Tell me again, dear. You saw me in the what?' she said. 'When I was pouring my tea.'

'Oh, I see. I saw you in the mirror.'

'And you're a lord, you say?'

'Again, I don't understand.'

'All right, we'll come at this another way.' She reached out a hand in a businesslike manner. 'Let me take a butcher's at one of those gold bricks of yours, then. Go on.'

Melamine, confused but not unhappy at this unexpected turn of events, obediently plonked a brick on the table. 'There's a very interesting history attached to this gold, actually. It has passed through the hands of some notable figures.'

'Yes, yes, I'll bet it has, dear. Now show me another one.'

He obeyed, shrugging, and produced another brick.

'It all started with the battleship *Potemkin*—'

'And a third, come on.'

'I don't understand,' he said, but he opened the bag for her to make her own selection. 'As you can see, they're all very much alike.'

'Oh, yes, I bet they are,' she muttered, helping herself.

But he had stopped paying attention to Mrs Groynes. A man in a hat had just entered the tea shop and was looking round. Mrs Groynes looked up briefly, but wasn't interested. She had examined all three bricks and was perplexed. They had turned out to differ significantly from her expectations. She tapped Melamine on the shoulder.

'This gold, dear,' she said. 'Where did you really get it?'

But he wasn't listening.

'Captain Hoagland! Over here!' he called.

Captain Hoagland?

'All of this gold is bleeding *real*, dear,' Mrs Groynes said.

'I know it is.' Melamine was evidently puzzled by the remark. 'Why wouldn't it be real? I described it as gold; I'm not a liar.'

Mrs Groynes, struggling to make sense of what she had heard, was still not fully aware of the man approaching their two tables. Had someone just said *Hoagland*? The name served only to make her impatient. What new imposture was this?

'Sir. Hello,' said a familiar voice.

She stopped breathing. Unable to look up, she concentrated instead on the gold brick she was unconsciously cradling in her arm like a kitten. None of this could be happening. Captain Hoagland? Emotion swelled within her. Her Hoagy had been callously murdered. He was *dead*.

But Melamine was still talking to this man, as if it were perfectly normal to meet him in a tea shop.

'I know it's your day off, Hoagy old chap, but perhaps you'd care to join us. Allow me to introduce you, although we've only just met. This is—'

He made a face at Mrs Groynes, hoping to prompt her to say her name, hoping to make her acknowledge the person standing in front of her. Finally, she did.

She looked up, and – well, let's face it, this is not a surprise but it's still lovely – it *was* the same Hoagy. An older, more careworn version of him, but still her noble, handsome man.

He beamed with pleasure to see her.

'Palmeira!' he said, smiling.

'Hoagy?' she croaked.

'What a truly agreeable surprise! But what's wrong, my dear? Why are you looking at me like that?'

'Because – oh, my good gawd!' There was an ominous catch in her voice. 'Oh! Oh!'

'Ah. Should I ask someone for a serviette?' said Melamine.

'Palmeira?' said Hoagland, gently.

'I thought you were dead, my love!'

And suddenly she was sobbing – sobbing in public, her hands to her face.

'Wah!' she cried, repeatedly. 'Oh! Oh! Oh! WAA–AA–AA–AAH! Hoagy, my Hoagy, WAAAAH!'

When she came to look back on the scene afterwards, Mrs Groynes was glad she had taken no backup with her, and that the shop was full of strangers. Her sobbing was lengthy, loud and uninhibited, and Melamine could only sit and watch as the gentlemanly Hoagland took the chair beside Mrs Groynes, offered her a hanky from his pocket and put his arm round her.

You would never have put these two people together, Melamine told Mrs Rogers afterwards; but here was the posh old soldier comforting this common (and somewhat offensive) little cockney woman, as if he really cared about what she was feeling.

'My dear Palmeira, I'm so sorry,' Hoagland was saying. 'I'm so sorry. I had no idea. I promise, I had no idea.'

Eight

Deirdre had gone missing. She had left no note. Ma Benson was so angry when she found Deirdre's bed hadn't been slept in that she kicked a hole in the wall.

'Frank! Bruce!' she shouted.

It had been a tense time for the Bensons. A week ago, the singer Dickie George had disappeared without trace; Deirdre's little boyfriend Peter Dupont had been murdered by a person or persons unknown; to cap it all, Terence Chambers had apparently sent a trumpet player called Kevin to breathe down their necks. It wasn't hard to identify Kevin as an imposter, first, because his shoes and hair were wrong, and second, because he clearly enjoyed making music much more than was remotely normal for a world-weary, cheesed-off professional.

But the most difficult thing had been protecting Deirdre from the knowledge of Dupont's death, after Bruce came back from the coach stop with the unexpected news.

'This meddling copper at Pool Valley said Weedy Pete was dead, Ma. Someone only went and cut his throat.'

'Good God,' she said, in genuine bafflement, puffing on her pipe. 'Who'd want to murder Weedy Pete?'

'I know, Ma. It don't make sense.'

The entire Benson clan (minus Deirdre) was nonplussed. For people who were usually in control of things, this state of nonplussedness was a novel experience, and they didn't like it.

'And then someone only nicked Deedee's letter, and all,' Bruce added.

'Who?' said Frank and Ma together.

'Search me,' said Bruce, unhelpfully.

At first, Ma Benson had been in favour of telling Deirdre what had happened, but the boys had dissuaded her. Bruce said that Deirdre was too delicate to cope with the shock. Not to mention, given her tiny circle of acquaintance, she might never find out – because who would tell her?

'But the main thing is, Ma, if we tell her he's dead, she's going to think we did it, ain't she?' said Frank. 'She'll never believe we didn't. Not after – you know, Kenneth.'

Ma Benson scowled. 'Ruddy Kenneth!' she said, bitterly.

'That stupid fucker,' agreed Frank. Normally his mother demanded an apology for this type of language, but this time she let it go. That Uncle Kenneth was indeed a stupid fucker was absolutely fair comment.

But that was a week ago, and now? Well, Deirdre had gone, and what turmoil! Where was she? How had she physically got out? And why? Had she perhaps found out about Peter Dupont's death after all, and left in despair? Or, *not* knowing about his death, had she run away to join him? And there was a further, much more worrying possibility: what if she had been kidnapped (possibly on behalf of Terence Chambers)?

The only thing they knew was that Deirdre had taken nothing with her. Not even her little Lilley & Skinner shoebox of childish treasures, which was still beneath her bed.

'We've got to think,' Ma Benson said. 'Bruce, go and ask at the wax museum if they've seen her. And make sure you speak to the woman in the stupid frock; she seems to be in charge. Don't use Deirdre's bloody trysting door: they might not know it's there. Frank, you go and talk to Hastings at the rock shop. Deirdre was always coming back with free humbugs. He must have been soft on her. And then one of you ask at the bus stop.'

'Are you gonna tell Terence?'

'No. Not yet. So make sure that trumpet bloke don't hear of it.'

'But maybe Terence could help, Ma.'

'No, Bruce. No heavy mob, do you hear me?' A chilling thought struck her. 'Has anyone checked downstairs? She couldn't have … ?'

Bruce nodded reassuringly. 'It's all fine, Ma. It's safe. No one goes in and out but Dave. Deirdre's never set foot down there.'

Frank put an arm round his mum. 'Deirdre might be weak and all that, Ma, but she's not stupid. She'll be safe, I bet you. And if anyone's harmed her, they'll bleeding well wish they'd never been born.'

For Twitten, it had been a trying week since Dupont was murdered. He had interviewed everyone present at the scene: he'd even been up to London's East End to coax a story out of the little boy Nigel, who had rewarded his journey by kicking him in the shins and running away; he had spoken to Dupont's council colleagues; he'd been shown the very manhole cover by which the murdered man had made his clever underground escape from the Marlborough House council offices (but had not been allowed to touch it). The only people so far to elude him were the two Brighton Belles,

Phyllis and Adelaide, who had both been allowed a week off work to recover. Whenever he called at their lodgings, they were out.

Although Deirdre ought to have been on his list of witnesses, he had held back from calling at the Black Cat to speak to her. This was a tad unprofessional of him, but he was torn: it was unlikely she could help him, and he was genuinely concerned about the unnecessary distress his questions might cause. And now that Brunswick was undercover, wasn't that enough? But both these reasons were masking the real one: he was just reacting to Deirdre's dreamy, faraway helplessness the way everyone else did, by feeling it was his job to protect her.

What an extraordinary effect this girl had. Everyone from the Bensons themselves, through Dickie George and all the boys in the band, through the Humbug Man, through Weedy Pete, through Constable Peregrine Twitten – somehow she put them all in touch with their inner Sir Galahad. Even as a baby, people had cooed into her pram, 'Hello, baby, come home with me, I'll look after you.' Captain Hoagland had spotted her just once from across the back alley at Colchester House (she was sitting like Rapunzel at her window), and he had instantly thought, *I ought to rescue that young lady.*

So to sum up, Twitten had done his best with the information available, but as he described it to himself, it was like trying to build a sandcastle with three parts water to one part sand. With the discovery of Peter Dupont's mysterious missing parcel at Brighton railway station's Left Luggage office, however, the sand-to-water ratio was suddenly drastically improved. Because what had looked at first glance like just the bloodstained stolen contents of a Borough Engineer's safe was in fact a bloodstained dossier intended for the press.

Which raised an important question in Twitten's mind.

'Tell me why this package is addressed to you, Mr Oliver. Did you know about it?'

Oliver bit his lip. 'I did, yes.'

'You did?'

Twitten was shocked.

'The thing is,' Oliver continued, 'I had an appointment to meet Dupont on the seafront that day.'

'Then why don't the police know this? Why didn't you come forward?'

Oliver shrugged and pulled a face.

'Well, to be fair,' he said, 'I did think about it. But look, Constable, Dupont meant nothing to me. He said he had a story, but he wouldn't tell me much on the telephone. He said he would bring the proof. And then he got murdered!'

'So?'

'Well, it suggests the story is quite big.'

'Which is all the more reason to come forward.'

Never having dealt with a reporter before, Twitten was at sea about Oliver's reasoning.

'Mr Oliver, can't you see this changes the official investigation completely? I could actually arrest you for choosing to keep this to yourself.'

Oliver put his hands up as if to apologise, and smiled for support at Old Ted – but Ted wasn't really listening. His main thought at this moment was that the doors to the Left Luggage office were still locked, and he could hear the telltale hubbub of disgruntled people gathering outside. So much for his tips. It was the universal law of the Left Luggage office: the longer the queue, the more meagre the haul.

Twitten was still far from satisfied with what Oliver had told him. He thought back to his training at Hendon, where he had repeatedly come top in tests for *never accepting the first explanation from a witness.* 'Look, Mr Oliver. The reason you didn't come forward … I know this might sound an ungenerous assessment of your character, so please forgive me if I'm wrong, but were you perhaps just scared that you'd be murdered too?'

'Of course I was scared I'd be murdered too!'

'Ha! I thought so!'

'They cut his throat, for heaven's sake.'

'Exactly. Ha!'

Twitten folded his arms and rocked back on his heels. He felt jolly pleased with himself. He had the package Dupont had been carrying; he now knew it to be a dossier, bound to contain important clues; he also knew why Dupont had been carrying it; he had remembered to put gloves on, so as not to leave his own fingerprints on the bag or its contents; and he had guessed correctly that even a crime reporter will risk breaking the law when apprehensive about being slit from ear to ear. All this represented a terrific breakthrough. If only Ted could remember the person who had left the bag.

'Will you try to remember, sir? And call me at the station if anything comes to you?'

Ted said he would apply himself, but couldn't promise anything.

'And may I use your telephone for a moment, sir?'

Ted sighed. Restive customers were actually knocking on the doors now, and the hubbub was growing louder. He could almost hear the snap and jingle of purses as the pennies and threepenny bits went back into them. But like a good citizen, he passed the instrument to Twitten.

This was the conversation with Inspector Steine, of course, in which an excited Twitten managed to alarm Steine by mentioning dynamite, but not to interest him in the Peter

Dupont case in any other way. And it would be fair to say that Steine's total lack of enthusiasm for uncovering the murderer of Peter Dupont not only annoyed and shocked Twitten, but caused him to make an uncharacteristic decision.

'Something wrong, Constable?' said Oliver, when they were outside on the busy concourse, and the hordes of frustrated customers had finally flooded into Ted's domain.

'I'm just thinking about what to do next.'

'Look. You know I *really* want to see what's in that dossier?'

Twitten's gloved hand gripped the handles of the holdall more tightly as he said, 'I'm sure you do.'

'Is there any way you could … ?'

'Of course not, Mr Oliver. It has to go directly to forensics.'

'Right.'

'They'll photograph everything, and dust for fingerprints, and test the blood against Dupont's. This material was taken by the murderer from the scene of the crime.'

'Of course. Of course. Forget I asked.'

But Twitten kept on thinking. He looked at the bag and he looked at Oliver, and then back at the bag, and then back at Oliver. This young reporter seemed to be the only person apart from himself actually interested in finding out what had happened to Dupont. He was also the sort of person who would understand that a reference to 'dynamite' could be metaphorical as well as literal.

So, as they were leaving the station, Twitten said, 'Look, Mr Oliver. Perhaps we *could* take a brief look at this dossier together at your office.'

Oliver, excited, said nothing. But he raised a questioning eyebrow.

'The way I see it,' Twitten carried on, 'much as I cannot condone your attitude to public duty, you are now an official witness in this inquiry, and this is a good opportunity to interview you accordingly. Moreover, I've only been working in Brighton for the past three weeks, and you live here and know lots of things I don't. Mr Oliver, would this perhaps be a good time to conduct the interview?'

And Ben Oliver said, 'Constable Twitten, I'm sure I can fit you in.'

———

Young Shorty was having a busy week. There had been very little slouching-against-walls time. He was seriously slipping behind with the adventures of Desperate Dan and Korky the Cat. Every day saw another message to be run around town. Today (the same day Mrs Groynes and Captain Hoagland were so dramatically reunited) the general alert was, 'The job's off. Everyone stand down. The mark is NOT Wall-Eye Joe, repeat *NOT Wall-Eye Joe.*'

As he dashed about, dodging between the shoppers and holiday-makers on the busy main streets, he sometimes felt like a character from one of his comics. The words '*DART!*' and '*ZOOM!*' ought to be visible in a little dark cloud trailing behind his heels.

'Hey, Shorty, got a minute?' he heard, as he was passing the rock shop on the corner of Grenville Street. He skidded to a halt. ('*SKID-D-D!*')

Looking round, he saw a familiar face. It was that bloke who played drums at the night club along here. He was standing in a patch of shadow, but his gold tooth glinted in the dark.

'Tommy?'

'Shorty, come here.'

'I'm on a job, Tom.'

'Look, it's important. It's worth a tanner. Tell the boss, there's things afoot at the Black Cat. That dodgy trumpeter Mrs G got me to vouch for – the Bensons tumbled to him right away, but they've got it in their heads he works for Chambers.'

'Oh, blimey.' (Shorty liked to pretend he understood what was going on.)

'And now the girl Deirdre has disappeared.'

Shorty closed his eyes and repeated the list: 'Dodgy trumpeter. Works for Chambers. Missing girl.'

'But the girl's the main thing, right? She needs protecting, and I can't protect her if I don't know where she is, can I? And *I don't know where she is!*'

'OK, OK. I'll tell the boss. But I gotta get on, Tommy.'

'All right. Good boy. Here.' Tommy pulled a bag of sweets out of his pocket. 'Humbug?'

'Oh, ta.'

Tommy helped the boy prise the sweet from the paper, then took one for himself.

'What about that tanner?' said Shorty.

Tommy dug a coin out of his pocket and handed it over.

'I can't get enough of these,' said Tommy, sucking the humbug wistfully. 'Just one of the many ways that me and Deirdre Benson are soulmates!'

―――――――

All this talk of Sergeant Brunswick being a spy for Terence Chambers, incidentally, needs to be set in context. If Brunswick justifiably assumed he was the only interloper in a band of professional musicians, he was wrong. Because Chambers did have a man inside the club's band already: he was the one who played the piano.

Of course, Chambers's pianist wasn't aware that the drummer worked for Mrs Groynes or that the trumpeter was an undercover policeman. Oh, no. But he had his suspicions about the guitarist, who in fact worked for MI5; meanwhile the guitarist had his suspicions about the alto sax, who (rather thrillingly) reported nightly to his superiors at Interpol.

Some of these men had joined the band at the same time as Brunswick. Others had been in situ for months. And it was all quite ironic. These men (mostly) all wanted the same thing: to find out how and why Kenneth Benson had been killed, and *what was going on in the basement area*. They all knew a little; none of them knew much. If only they had worked together! But instead, each of them believed he was the only cuckoo in the nest.

Incidentally, there was one person who knew for sure that Brunswick was a policeman. This was Bob on double bass, who (as previously mentioned) once threw a half-brick through a window and got himself arrested. The brick-throwing incident had been a calculated act on Bob's part, designed to throw any suspicion off him, because he was in fact a CID man reporting to Chief Inspector Jenkins at Scotland Yard. When he recognised 'Kevin' at the audition as his arresting officer, he loyally helped out a fellow undercover policeman by suggesting they had worked together in the invitingly named Bora Bora Lounge in Portslade.

So to sum up:

Terence Chambers was on piano
Scotland Yard was on double bass
Interpol was on alto sax
Brighton CID was on trumpet
Mrs Groynes was on drums
MI5 was on guitar

In short, only the trombonist was not living a double life. A life-long professional musician and a member of the union, he had no suspicions whatsoever that his fellow band members were not ordinary joes like himself. Occasionally, he would come across the guitarist emerging stealthily from Ma Benson's office (tucking a notebook into his back pocket), and he wouldn't give it a second thought. He once found Tommy Drumsticks having an emotional argument with Deirdre Benson on the back staircase – he thought nothing of that, either.

'It's really boring,' he would tell his wife in the mornings, when she asked what life was like at the club. 'It's the most boring job in the world. And the other guys: what a bunch of stiffs!'

———

On their way to the *Argus* office, Twitten nearly changed his mind about letting Oliver in on things. The newsman might be a useful ally when it came to solving the Dupont case, but he was also bally relentless when it came to asking awkward questions.

'There's something I've been meaning to ask you about, Constable Twitten,' said Oliver, casually, as they walked side by side downhill towards the newspaper offices.

'Oh, yes?'

'I've been wondering. What happened to that hilarious delusion of yours about that woman onstage with you at the Hippodrome – the one you were hypnotised into believing was a sort of female Professor Moriarty?'

Twitten stiffened. 'What about it?'

He felt sick. He'd forgotten Oliver had been present and seen the whole thing. He didn't know what to say.

'It occurred to me afterwards, you see,' said Oliver, 'that perhaps you were in on the act.'

'What?'

'But on the other hand, you were so convincing! Especially when you shouted out, *"But she IS a criminal mastermind, sir!"*'

'Ha ha ha,' chuckled Twitten, weakly. He looked round in an exaggerated manner. 'A lot of public houses in this part of the town, aren't there? I wonder what the historical reason is for that?'

They walked along in silence. But not for long.

'So *was* it all an act, then? What happened at the Hippodrome?'

'Could we change the subject, please, Mr Oliver?'

'It's a simple question. I just want to know, was it all an act?'

'Of course it was an act! In fact, "all an act" doesn't come close to describing how much of a bally act it was! Now, could we please—'

'No, sorry, perhaps I'm not being clear. What I want to know is, *were you in on it?*'

'I was not in on it, no.'

'I see.'

'I certainly wasn't.'

'All right.'

'The whole thing was horrible.'

'OK. But if that hypnotist—'

'Oh, *please!*'

'No, hang on. Listen. If that hypnotist *did* make you believe such a preposterous thing, what happened afterwards? Did the delusion just wear off, or did you have to get more hypnosis from someone else? Or perhaps – ' and at the thought of this Oliver started laughing ' – perhaps you still believe it!'

Twitten had had enough of this. Oliver was pushing him closer to telling a lie, and he refused to do it. So he took a gamble.

'Mr Oliver,' he said. 'The bally truth of the matter is that I do still believe the charlady Mrs Groynes is a clever criminal. I believed it before the stunt onstage at the Hippodrome, and I continued to believe it afterwards. And I'm promising you that one day *you and everyone else will believe it, too.*'

Oliver let out a low whistle. Then he looked at the policeman's earnest expression and started laughing. He held out his hand for Twitten to shake.

'Good for you, Constable; that was very funny.'

Twitten smiled, modestly.

'Sorry, Mr Oliver,' he said. 'But you did ask for it.'

Which made Oliver clap him on the back and laugh all the more.

And, thank goodness, they had at last reached Oliver's workplace, and the interrogation would cease.

At this time of day the *Brighton Evening Argus* building was a vision of industry. Vans were waiting outside with engines running, while men with barrows trundled weighty bales of newsprint and shouted instructions to the drivers. Presses were running ('First edition!' Oliver explained above the thundering din), and the whole scene was imbued with the incomparable smell of printers' ink. Oliver led Twitten upstairs to the newsroom, where hundreds of yards of telephone flex ran (bizarrely) in loops across the ceiling, and men (it was all men) hammered away on typewriters, or shouted into telephones, while other men in visors with pencils and sleeve-garters laboured over page proofs on outsized sheets of salmon-pink paper.

Oliver opened the door to a side office and ushered Twitten in, to a place of relative quiet, although the smell of ink came with them. Then he cleared a table and opened a desk drawer, from which he extracted a pair of leather gloves, pulling an expression that said 'Don't ask', before relenting.

'My predecessor left these,' he explained. 'He knew a lot of people who used them.'

'I see,' said Twitten. And then, as Oliver donned the gloves: 'So tell me about your dealings with Dupont.'

'There isn't much. Dupont contacted me the day before he died, saying he had a story for me involving the Borough Engineer's office. Now, I have to tell you, I didn't think it would be much of a story, if it was just about corruption at the council.'

'Why?'

'Because there'd be nothing new there, Constable! It's a story we could run every week!'

'I see,' said Twitten. He tried not to show how shocked he was. 'But you still think he was killed because he was the man who bally well knew too much?'

'Don't you?'

'Well, no. I mean, it sounds plausible now that you've said it. But I've been working on a completely different line of inquiry up to now.'

'Really?'

'Yes.'

'Why?'

'*Why?*' Twitten gave him a hard stare. 'Because you didn't come forward, Mr Oliver! You bally well didn't come forward!'

They worked quickly through the file, Oliver concentrating on the council proceedings – copies of minutes, and so on, some of them going back five years or more – while Twitten pored over Dupont's notebooks.

He was very impressed by the level of detail. If only this boy had opted for a career in the police, he'd have made a very good detective. Even when he was just idly waiting for Deirdre in the wax museum, Dupont would note down the hilarious behaviour of the preposterous 'Angélique', and the noisy arguments with her father about this and that. When Twitten read the line 'Because I'm supposed to be blind!', he actually burst out laughing.

'What do you know about Colchester House?' Oliver said, after a couple of minutes' purposeful page-turning.

'Recently reoccupied, so far as I know,' said Twitten. He didn't want to mention the station gossip about Wall-Eye Joe living there like a lord. 'It's been empty for years, though,' he continued. 'There are a few pages in this notebook, actually, about Dupont's meeting there with a Captain Hoagland, which was a name I'd been wondering how to spell, but a lot of it seems to be about whether this captain might have known Dupont's father from a bomb-disposal unit during the war, so it might not be relevant – "Tell Auntie Maud" underlined, and so on. Why did you mention the house?'

'Well, on the back of this picture it says, "Borrowed from Captain Hoagland at Colchester House – please return. Also read account in *Historic Brighton* by F. C. Grimshaw, 1937."'

'What does it show?'

Oliver pulled a face and held up the picture. 'A garden with an aviary. Some birds.'

'And what's this?' said Twitten, picking up a sheet with a list of dates on it.

'Ah, now this is something. These are the dates over the past four years when people reported the smell of drains. Attached are copies of the memos from Reinhardt to Blackmore, instructing him to ignore the complaints, saying they will be dealt with by a different department. And *here*—' Oliver picked up Mr Reinhardt's half-used bank book, and opened it at a random stub. 'Yes, you see? Here. A thousand pounds paid in. And here's another, and another.'

'A thousand pounds each time? That's a bally enormous amount.'

'I know. And see what he's written?'

'Yes. It says, "C House"!'

'And here are the minutes of a planning permission meeting just a couple of weeks ago.'

'Oh, yes.'

'It was a vote not to allow development on the site of Colchester House.'

'And that's a prime site, I suppose?'

'Exactly. To me, that's the most interesting detail of all. To vote *against* pulling down that house! In the context of what else has been going on in this town, that's extremely suspicious.'

'Mr Oliver, I'd like to thank you for helping with this.' Twitten sounded controlled but his heart was racing. Was he finally getting somewhere? Was he going to find out who had killed Peter Dupont, and why?

'Well, it's helping me, too,' said Oliver. 'Oh, and there's this other one.' He picked up another piece of paper. 'Dupont's put a star on it but it's not clear why. It seems to be about the formation of those Brighton Belles you see parading around.'

'That's odd,' said Twitten. 'What could the Brighton Belles have to do with any of this?'

'I don't know, Twitten. But Dupont put it in the package so he must have wanted me to see it.'

———

As it happened, Mrs Groynes was a guest at Colchester House at this very moment. After her sensational breakdown in the tea shop, Lord Melamine had insisted she come home with him to recover herself. And she had not declined. So overwhelmed was she by the coincidence of seeing her darling Hoagy again that she barely noticed (although she did notice) that Lord Melamine was toting a bag around containing three thousand pounds' worth of twenty-four-carat gold.

Melamine was clearly bemused by the whole thing. As he confided to Mrs Rogers in private later, Captain Hoagland's love life was his own affair, of course, but this impudent little woman hardly seemed the sort of person he would consort with. But Melamine gathered that they'd met after the war, and had enjoyed a romantic liaison. And that somehow she had known about poor Hoagland's experience at that ghastly unfinished house in the country – but not that he had survived.

'It was a friend of yours, Hoagy,' she explained now. 'What was his name … Hoppy Hopkins? He told me.'

'Old Hoppy? The Professor? That man defused more seven-teens than anyone else in the entire BD, you know. How is he, the old reprobate?'

'I couldn't tell you, dear. All I know is that I bumped into him around Soho one night and he told me you'd got yourself involved with a woman running a dating agency in 1949, and then were *never seen again*. So naturally I put two and two together.'

'I'm so sorry, Palmeira, that you were worried.'

'I wasn't worried, dear. I was in bleeding mourning!'

'Oh, Palmeira.'

'And not to put too fine a point on it, dear, I was planning to hunt down the devils who did it to you and have their guts for garters!'

'I'm so sorry. I had no idea. But as you see, I'm well.'

They were all three sitting together in the morning room, with the tall windows looking out to the seafront. Sun streamed in.

'Look, something's troubling me about all this, dear,' she said, softly.

'What? Tell me.'

'You survived an attempt to kill you, is that right? At that notorious ruddy unfinished house?'

'He tunnelled out,' said Melamine, proudly. 'You should have seen him.'

'So why didn't you come forward when Joe and The Skirt went to trial for all the other murders? I'm sorry to bring it up, dear. I'm sure it's a sore point. But they got off because of the lack of evidence, didn't they? But at your say-so I reckon they'd have hanged.'

Hoagland seemed dumbfounded. His face drained of colour.

'What have I said, dear?' she said. 'You look confused.'

'They went to trial? There were actual *murders*?'

'I can explain,' Melamine volunteered. 'Captain Hoagland, I—'

Hoagland held up a hand.

'Whom did they kill, Palmeira?'

'Probably about six women, dear.'

'No!'

'The bodies have never been found, that's the trouble. A big vat of acid was discovered at the house, though.'

Hoagland looked horrified.

'Oh my God. Oh my God.'

'You're saying you didn't know?'

'Of course I didn't know! All I knew was that it was night-time, and Vivienne suggested I take a look at this outbuilding, and then the door was shut and someone attacked me in the dark, and I fought back, and I must have knocked him out, and when I couldn't get out of the door, I scrambled out through some dirt. And the taste of the dirt in my mouth, and the fear, and the dark – I could smell the bloody bombs, Palmeira! It all came back: the dirt and the smell, and the blasted fear—'

'Oh, I'm so sorry.'

Mrs Groynes felt helpless. She wished she could comfort him.

'But still,' she persisted, gently. 'The case against Marriott was on the wireless and in all the papers. It was front-page news for weeks.'

Hoagland turned to Lord Melamine. 'Sir?'

'Look,' said Melamine. 'I'm sorry, Hoagland. I'm afraid it's all my fault.' He composed himself. 'Mrs Groynes, as you've probably guessed, after my part in Captain Hoagland's escape, I asked him if he would take a job as my valet. And then, about six months later, I heard a bulletin on the radio about the so-called murder house, and I realised it must be the place he'd escaped from. And I made a decision. I knew Hoagland was such a decent chap he would come forward if he knew about the case, and rightly or wrongly, I decided that the stress of having to relive his experience at the hands of those people would be too much for him. So I took us both off to Tristan da Cunha.'

Hoagland reacted to this news with something like a howl.

'So that was all for my sake, my lord?'

'Yes.'

'We took that whole trip to keep me from knowing about this blasted trial? So everything you said about wanting to emigrate eventually and farm ostriches … ?'

'All a ploy, I'm afraid.'

'I bonded with those ostriches, sir!'

'I know, and it did you no harm at all, Hoagland. The thing is, Mrs Groynes, I honestly had no idea the case would fail. I thought Captain Hoagland's absence would make no difference to the outcome. When we returned and I discovered that the hell-hounds had *walked free*, I could hardly believe it. I felt terribly, terribly guilty.'

'As you bleeding should, dear!' said Mrs Groynes, hotly.

'All I could do was keep the knowledge of that trial from Captain Hoagland for as long as possible. And I wish for obvious reasons I had managed it longer.'

With so much new information flying out, even Mrs Groynes couldn't quite keep up with this. Part of her was still wondering how you bond with an ostrich. What obvious reasons was his lordship referring to?

Hoagland was confused, too. 'What do you mean, sir?' he said, frowning.

'I'm sorry, Hoagland, but it's the main reason I have kept us on the move so much. Joe Marriott and The Skirt (as your friend here calls her) are probably still looking for you, aren't they? And if they ever find you, it stands to reason they will kill you.'

After dropping off the holdall at the forensics laboratory, Twitten called the personnel department at the council to get the name and address of Dupont's next-of-kin: a Miss Stanford in Eastbourne (his 'Aunt Maud'). She had already been informed of his death, of course, but Twitten wrote to her, to ask if he could visit. He also telephoned his own mother and had a consoling half-hour conversation with her, simply because it was jolly nice to hear her voice, and there was no one in the office to overhear for once (Mrs Groynes seemed not to have been in all day), so he could tell her that although the present case was shaping up well, in his darkest moments he did wonder whether being a policeman had been the best career choice, and whether it was too late to switch to studying kinship systems in the Fens.

Feeling bucked up by her encouragement ('I'm sure you're doing a super job, Peregrine darling'), he pulled himself together and said, aloud, 'To Colchester House, then.' And five minutes later, he was standing on the opposite side of the road, taking it all in. From the front façade, it looked well maintained and very handsome. From the side, however (from both sides, in fact), it was less impressive, with that narrow alleyway immediately to the rear of the house, and then the night club reached via Grenville Street and the wax museum in Russell Place.

He remembered the picture of the garden in Dupont's dossier. A Regency house as grand as this would have had such a garden, surely?

Which was why, ten minutes later, he was at the public library, looking at a copy of *Historic Brighton* by F. C. Grimshaw (1937). Colchester House was allotted two whole pages – the role of Nash; the Colchester lineage; a visit from the Regent in 1822, when the guests drank 'bumpers' of champagne. But the passage that caught Twitten's eye related to an account, written in 1835, of the garden:

*A very curious place ... full of little hills and mounds, covered
with trees, shrubs and flowers, all set a dozen feet or more
below the level of the street beyond the wall. Here and there
are arbours shaded by ivy and clematis; in some places are little
hollows surrounded by artificial rocks; in others are subterranean paths, besides railing, hedges, ponds, white tents and a
magnificent enclosure for birds. Over the whole are scattered
white statues and painted lamps, some on stands, others hanging from lofty arches which join the mounts. What I liked best
was the 'subterrane'. We entered a subterraneous passage, at
the end of which is a little polygonal chamber, curtained all
round with red and white, and carpeted with yellow-coloured
sheepskin.*

Twitten copied the entry word-for-word into his notebook. It
made him rather wistful. This area was now occupied by a club
run by gangsters who sawed up their relations and a tawdry
museum run by charlatans, one of whom was pretending to
be blind, and both of whom were pretending to be French.
Whereas it used to be an elegant place of statues and birds
and painted lamps, not to mention an underground polygonal chamber lined with a golden fleece!

With all these dramatic developments to think about – the
Bensons frantic to find Deirdre; Mrs Groynes coping with
the shock of Captain Hoagland's miraculous return from the
dead; Brunswick unwittingly working alongside representa-
tives of internationally renowned law-enforcement agencies;
Inspector Steine steadily bonding with his long-lost niece;
and Constable Twitten finally getting his teeth into the
Dupont case – it might seem strange to focus our attentions

on the rock shop on the corner of Grenville Street. After all, it was the same scene every morning and afternoon: the little crowd standing outside the window, making admiring 'Cor!' and 'Blimey!' noises as they watched while one enormous formless humbug was expertly stretched and twisted by Henry Hastings to make hundreds of small, stripy (and completely uniform) suckable humbugs in that somehow mind-confounding three-dimensional geometric form: the regular tetrahedron.

But today there was one small difference to the demonstration. Because about halfway through it, Hastings happened to look up from his muscular labours and see the surprising expressions on the faces looking back at him. It was bizarre. Instead of smiling like idiots, as they usually did, they all had their mouths open, and looked variously bewildered, appalled and horrified.

He didn't know what to make of it. The procedure was precisely the same as usual. Had he forgotten to put clothes on? A quick glance down confirmed that he had not. Had someone written a rude word on his window?

But when he looked again at his audience, there was no mistake about it. They appeared to be witnessing a highly disturbing sight. One woman actually screamed. And now that he thought about it, he could smell those drains again. The drain smell was in the very room!

Was there someone behind him? He suddenly felt sure that there was, not least because the people outside were pointing past him, over his left shoulder. Showing no alarm (but quickly calculating his next move), he squinted into the plate-glass window and saw in the reflection a pale figure to his left, not moving, but with one hand outstretched, as if possibly holding a weapon.

A feeble croak reached his ears. Afterwards he thought about it often. Had the ghastly figure tried to say 'Help me'?

But he would never be able to answer that question, because all of Hastings's commando training came back to him in this time of imagined threat. In a single move, he spun on the spot, grabbed a half-pound humbug from a shelf and used it to strike the side of the head of the ghastly, spectral and deeply smelly figure that had appeared behind him. To screams from the people outside, the man fell straight to the ground, dead.

It was Dickie George. The poor man had survived a week in the sewers only to be killed by a humbug. As the papers were to report over the coming months, this was the first case of manslaughter-by-humbug ever to be recorded anywhere in the world.

Nine

Sergeant Brunswick was beginning to realise that perhaps, before launching into an undercover career as a night-club trumpeter, he should have thought things through a little more carefully. Playing in the band every night was all very well (and his impressive solo breaks drew gratifying applause), but he was all too aware that the rest of the guys were watching his every movement; also that he had stupidly failed to establish a system for communicating safely with the station. Meanwhile it was clear that the Bensons suspected him, because Frank Benson – in between escorting portly male customers and their bejewelled wives to tables nearest to the stage – was always leaning across from the dance floor to pat him on the sleeve of his tuxedo and say, meaningfully, 'Settling in all right, *Kevin?*' or 'Look, *Kevin*, just tell him it'll never happen again, would you?' or (somehow most unsettling of all), 'Kevin! *Nice shoes.*'

The worst aspect of any undercover job, however, was simply the identity crisis that invariably came with it. Why did he not anticipate this? Why did he never remember that infiltrating criminal gangs threw up in him not just the obvious problems of loneliness and fear, but existential questions about who he really was?

'I am playing a part,' he would repeat to himself. 'I am *not* Kevin the trumpet player. I was a paratrooper in the war. I have advanced police driving skills, a desk waiting for me at the police station with a week's worth of *Police Gazette*s piling up on it, and I have been wounded several times in the line of duty. I am *not* Kevin the trumpet player.'

But still, shutting his eyes onstage some nights, lost in the glorious dance music, seeing all the little lamps on the tables and the flash of diamonds on the necks of the women – and trying not to obsess about the alluring curves of Delores Dee's satin-clad posterior – he could believe for a moment that he *was* a professional trumpet player for whom it was utterly normal to work until the small hours of the morning for a few bob a week, and to share tawdry digs in Grenville Street with a laconic pianist who affected a pork pie hat and kept a sharpened machete under his bed. Brunswick's other world – his auntie's bright little flat; Mrs Groynes bringing him a nice hot cup of tea and asking him supportively for the latest news from the big bad world beyond the police station – was swiftly slipping away from him, seeming every day more fanciful and unreal.

Still, there were a few things he kept a grip on. For a start, he took note of Frank Benson's mystifying message: 'Just tell him it will never happen again.' Tell who? About what? Was this something to do with killing Kenneth? Had the Bensons been told *not* to kill him by someone? Could Clever Clogs Twitten shed any light on this? But on the three occasions when he'd made a dash to the public call-box opposite the rock shop and dialled the number for the police station, there had been no answer from Twitten or Steine, or even Mrs G; the phone just rang and rang, unanswered, as if the whole place were deserted.

At least his shared room was the first-floor front, so he could pull up a chair to the bay window and observe the interesting foot traffic in the neighbourhood of the Black Cat. At least he could do some surveillance. Luckily the piano player used the room solely for sleeping, and made himself scarce in the afternoons. It meant that, for a short while each day, Kevin-on-the-valves could experience the thankful return of his full and proper Sergeant Brunswick-ness, because when he stared out of that window, and observed all the Hogarthian shenanigans in the busy, noisy street below, it reminded him that he not only knew all about Brighton, but in particular he knew all about Brighton's unattractive lowlife, in particular its exotically named (but lesser) villains.

This had always been Brunswick's fatal flaw: priding himself on his extensive knowledge of the small fry, of the blokes who chucked bricks through windows, or were caught red-handed jemmying a skylight, or lived off the earnings of tarts. For him, Brighton was packed with wide boys called Guido the Fish, Ronnie the Nerk, Dave the Forger – most of whom he had nicked in person on numerous occasions. He saw these people everywhere; they blinded him to the bigger picture. Because when a member of the true Brighton criminal aristocracy walked past the window in Grenville Street – such as the cold-blooded assassin-for-hire Diamond Tony, cleaning his nails with a long, pointy blade – Brunswick recognised him merely as a flashily dressed man often to be observed drinking whisky macs in the residents' bar at the Metropole.

Sometimes, sitting at the window was torture, his natural urge to nick wrongdoers being too great. After just a couple of afternoons in position, for example, he became aware of a pair of pickpockets working the street below – and he watched them with increasing frustration. But then something strange happened, as he continued to observe the operation: he began to feel a degree of awe as well. Their

MO was so simple: Irene from the Pretty Puss Club bumped into clueless holiday-makers, lifted their wallets and slipped them to Jimmy the Gimp, who (with impressive timing) was always at that precise moment sauntering past the other way. And that was all there was to it. On one afternoon, they did six wallets in an hour. It got so that Brunswick could spot the instant when each lift started. Irene would quicken her pace to draw alongside the mark, and Jimmy (leaning always against the same convenient sea-green lamp-post) would fold his newspaper and start his walk. 'Now,' Brunswick would whisper, and feel a strange mixture of triumph and despair when the job was executed flawlessly yet again. Just once their trick nearly failed, when Jimmy slightly fumbled the hand-over, and as the wallet slipped from his fingers, Brunswick embarrassed himself by jumping up and shouting (unheard), 'Watch out!'

On one afternoon, he took a look at the pianist's machete. But it was so terrifyingly sharp and heavy that he quickly put it back. He felt uncomfortable searching through his room-mate's stuff. Gerry was his name, apparently. Or 'Gerry on the ivories!' as Delores introduced him each night. Brunswick was glad Gerry-on-the-ivories chose to go out all day, but he did wish he'd be more forthcoming – about music, if nothing else. Searching through Gerry-on-the-ivories's chest of drawers, Brunswick found sheet music for *The King and I* that was not only stamped 'Theatre Royal Drury Lane' but was signed by Richard Rodgers 'With thanks'. It was very exciting. Thanks for what? Had Gerry-on-the-ivories played in the orchestra of the show? Brunswick longed to know. *The King and I* was one of his favourite scores and he had seen the film three times.

Sometimes he had the window open, sometimes not. But one day when the window was up, he saw a remarkable thing:

an off-guard Mrs Groynes. This was on the same day she met Lord Melamine in the tea shop, and was taken to recuperate in Colchester House. She was walking up the street from the seafront end, nicely dressed in a neat little suit and a pretty silk headscarf, arm in arm with a tall gent who stooped a little, and had a limp. It was the hardest thing for Brunswick not to shout, 'Hello, Mrs G! Up here!'

What stopped him was that the couple paused, right across the road from his window. And then the unknown man put his hand in his raincoat pocket and withdrew a paper bag of sweets, and when he offered it to her, she looked up into his face, shook her head and said something (Brunswick strained to hear the words) about how there were special moments in life that required more than a bleeding humbug. At which they both laughed.

And then – oh, flaming heck – the man bent down and slowly kissed her.

Brunswick watched, amazed. He thought Mrs Groynes would kick him and run off yelling for the police. But instead she positively melted in his arms!

───────

'Mrs Groynes?' said Twitten.

'Yes, dear?'

Mrs Groynes was just hanging her coat up. It was the morning after Sergeant Brunswick had seen her locked in the arms of Captain Hoagland, and she was surprised to find anyone already in the office at half-past seven in the morning. Normally she had at least half an hour by herself to fire up the water boiler, rub a duster over the doorknobs, have a quick cigarette and (most importantly) unlock her loot cupboard and stash anything incriminating from jobs the night before.

'Blimey,' she said. 'You been here all night? You look like something the cat spewed up.'

From the look of things, Twitten had indeed been in the office all night. He was sitting at his desk, with a dossier open beside him, the typewriter in front and papers all over the floor. There was ink on his face. He was bug-eyed. Three of his tunic buttons were undone. It was unsettling to see him like this. He looked positively off his rocker.

'Look, Mrs G, I know I said I didn't want any help from you *ever*,' he said, with a slightly hysterical edge to his voice. Was he shaking? 'And when I said that I *bally well meant it.*'

'I'm sure you did, dear. And there's no need to raise your voice to me, is there? I'm just here.'

'But … But I need to ask you something. Just one thing.'

'All right. Fire away.'

'I ought to warn you, I'm a bit tired.'

'I can see that.'

'I'm not myself. I think I'm experiencing the reality of the expression *at one's wits' end*. In fact, the phrase keeps going round and round in my head, and it's jolly unpleasant when you can't do anything to stop it. *At one's wits' end; at one's wits' end; at one's wits' end.*'

'I get the picture, dear. Poor you. Or poor *one*, if you prefer.'

'Thank you.'

He took a deep breath. 'So my question is: when I briefly left the station to get a breath of air early this morning and take a look at Colchester House for the umpteenth time, did I happen to see you emerging from the front door at around half-past six?'

Mrs Groynes smiled and blushed slightly. 'I don't know, dear. Did you?'

'Yes, I did!' he wailed. In his inexplicable anguish, he roughly undid two more buttons on his tunic. 'Oh, Mrs G!'

'Oh, my gawd, what's wrong, dear? Who's upset you? What do you want me to do about it?' She seemed genuinely concerned.

Twitten's face all but dissolved in misery. He had evidently been closer to his wits' end than either of them realised (despite the clues).

'Look. This isn't easy for me to say, Mrs G,' he snivelled, 'but I saw you coming out of Colchester House this morning, and it was just the final straw for me; it was the bally *final straw!*'

'Why, dear? I don't understand.'

'Because I had *no idea why you were there!*'

Mrs Groynes pulled up a chair beside his desk and put her arms round him. He did not pull away.

'There, there,' she said.

'I've only just found out that Colchester House is significant in my inquiries, and you're already bally living there!'

'Oh, you poor thing,' she said. 'Give old Mrs Groynes a hug, then. Come on. This is the problem with your being so bleeding clever, dear; I've warned you, and I've warned you.'

'But I need to know things like that!' he cried. 'If I don't even know your connection to Colchester House, how am I ever going to solve this bally case? Is it Wall-Eye Joe that's living there?'

She smiled. 'No, dear. It isn't.'

'*What?*'

'It's the real Lord Melamine. I thought it *was* Wall-Eye, I grant you, but I was wrong. Even the fake gold he's been trying to flog is the real bleeding McCoy.'

'There are so many things going on, Mrs G! I think it might be literally impossible to sort them all out!'

'That's silly talk, dear. I won't hear of it.'

'No, but really, Mrs G, what if I'm not clever enough? You see, we've got not just a council conspiracy and an absconded Borough Engineer and a dead council clerk – which is one thing; but then there's a historic sawn-up West End musical director – which is connected, I'm sure, but *I don't know how.* And now this Dickie George person who went missing from the Black Cat has come up through the floor of the rock shop and been killed with a bally humbug, which I'm sure is tragic for him but even worse for me because now he can't tell me what he knew!'

'He was killed how, dear?' laughed Mrs Groynes.

'It's not funny! None of this is funny, Mrs G!'

'No, of course not.' Mrs Groynes pulled a serious face, but she had rarely been more entertained. Twitten had been right. This was a demonstration of what someone at their wits' end looked like. It was pitiful, but at the same time absolutely hilarious.

'Mr Hastings at the sweet shop killed him with a big humbug and then immediately fled the scene of the crime, and I don't blame him, but who's going to look for him? Me? On top of *all this?*'

'Calm down, dear.'

'And meanwhile the inspector is completely uninterested in everything except for this bally woman Adelaide who might not be his niece, because she *might not*! And Sergeant Brunswick has just disappeared into the Black Cat, just *disappeared.* Does he not understand what going undercover means? It doesn't mean *becoming a professional trumpet player.* And we've recovered this vital dossier, but it's got so much in it I hardly know where to start. And then, on top of all that, to find that my arch enemy – my flipping *nemesis*, if you'll pardon my language – is now popping in and out of Colchester House as if she bally owns the place! Well, it makes me so cross!'

She patted his arm.

'You're all worked up, dear,' she said, kindly.

'I know! That's what I'm saying!'

Mrs Groynes got up and locked the door. Then she dropped the key into the pocket of her overall and came back to sit beside him. For a fleeting moment, Twitten thought she was going to calm him down for good by pulling out a gun and killing him. Unsurprisingly, the idea had quite a sobering effect.

'Now look,' she said. 'I'm very sorry to see you like this. Have you got a hanky, dear?'

'No.' His voice was suddenly very small.

She opened her handbag and handed him a freshly ironed man's handkerchief, monogrammed with 'PH'.

'I'll explain later,' she said. 'Go on, have a good blow.'

He applied himself to the hanky, and then steadied his breathing. He was not unaware of the position he was in: showing his weakest side to his Great Enemy was so foolish, and yet it had seemed the natural thing to do. Where else but to Mrs G could he turn?

'You're being very kind, Mrs G,' he said.

'Well, dear, to be honest I feel some of this might be my fault.'

'Really?'

'Do you remember I was quite annoyed when you refused my offer of help – do you recall that, dear? The other day, when I offered a very generous mutually advantageous arrangement between us, but you got all hoity-toity about the bleeding quid pro quo?'

'I do remember, yes.'

'Because you see, dear, I *can* help you. And it seems to me that I ought to help you. Because I know things you don't know. For example, dear, Deirdre Benson has gone missing.'

'Oh, no.'

'And at the Black Cat, they spotted the sergeant straight away as an imposter, because between you and me he just won't get the shoes right *ever*. But the good news is that they think he's working for Terence Chambers, so they'll probably leave him alone. Ooh, and you'll like this. They're saying his trumpet solos are out of this world; they're calling him the Harry James of the South Coast.'

Twitten managed to smile. He felt better for getting this stuff off his chest.

'The trouble is, I can't let you help me, Mrs Groynes,' he said. 'I just can't.' But he said it weakly, like a child protesting that it won't go to sleep, just before it nods off.

'Look, dear,' she said. 'Let's have a nice cup of tea, and then I'll help you sort the wood from the trees a bit, what do you say? I bet you've got everything you need right here – everything you need to work this out. Whoever did this horrible thing to that nice boy, we'll get him, you mark my words.'

'And will you tell me why you were in Colchester House with Lord Melamine, Mrs G?'

'If it means you'll pull yourself together, yes, I will. And if you're a very good boy, I'll also tell you what I've found out about Miss so-called Adelaide so-called Vine.'

That Inspector Steine had no doubts whatever concerning Adelaide Vine should not be surprising. He was a man with an almost superhuman capacity for accepting things at face value. He had been utterly taken in by the *Panorama* hoax about the bumper spaghetti harvest on the Swiss–Italian border; he had been taken in by the transparently fraudulent *ooh-la-la* nonsense at the Maison du Wax. He had also, let's not forget, been taken in by Mrs Groynes the harmless cockney charlady for many years, even when (on occasion) he stumbled across her piling unexplained bags of bullion into a taxi at the back entrance of the police station.

But, in his defence, he had pretty good reasons to believe in Adelaide's legitimacy. As far as he was concerned, no one but a member of the family could possibly know the story of his parents' momentous meeting all those years ago in Gordon Square. As he had said to Mrs Groynes, Adelaide had even known the make of the car! Moreover, she had been extremely stand-offish with him to start with, and had actually run away from him at Victoria Station when he dared to suggest that the story meant as much to him as it did to her. But most of all, why would anyone go to such lengths to defraud him? What on earth would they have to gain?

Meeting her had been very disturbing: no wonder he had been preoccupied ever since. When he had written those chapters about his childhood for his memoir, he had hoped to dispose of many painful memories – but with the advent of Adelaide, they'd been horribly raked up again. That awful trip to Swanage when Grandfather Penrose had met them on the drive with a shotgun, refusing to let them in. That children's Christmas party at Hammersmith Police Station that Mother had angrily dragged them away from because they were enjoying the company of 'common' children. The time Gillian announced firmly she would be walking backwards from now on, and kept it up for a week or more – just because the sole of her little shoe was flapping, and she wanted to keep it a secret from Mother (who, once she found out, would take it out on Father).

It was interesting that Gillian had told her daughter none of these other stories – after all, she was a year or two his senior, and more likely to remember. But as Adelaide explained to him, in that sweet, soft voice of hers: 'If these things were painful for you, Uncle Geoffrey, they were painful for Mummy, too. That's why she ran away from home. The only part of her family history she wanted to pass on to me was that happy day when out-of-control Bloomsbury-ites terrorised her mother and brought her parents together.'

On the morning of Twitten's breakdown at the police station, Steine told Adelaide some news. He said he had written to his mother in Kenya.

They were breakfasting in Luigi's, and from the way she clunked her coffee cup in her saucer, he could tell she wasn't pleased. Those almond-shaped eyes of hers (coloured hazel) flashed with annoyance.

'Oh, I do wish you hadn't done that, Uncle Geoffrey,' she said, in a reasonable tone.

'Yes, well. I know you didn't want me to, but it's done now.'

'I did ask you to wait for a bit, until – well, until after the ceremony at the wax museum. It's only next week. I'm sure that hearing you've been modelled in wax would have made her so proud.'

'How little you know of her, my dear,' Steine said, shaking his head. 'But on the other hand, surely she has a right to know she has such a beautiful and charming granddaughter?'

Adelaide patted her swept-up chestnut hair, as if to acknowledge the compliment. 'Oh, Uncle Geoffrey.'

She finished her coffee. She needed to go; Phyllis, who had been away for a few days, would be waiting on the corner.

'Well, off to the fray, I suppose. By the way, my solicitor in London needs to talk to you about that will of Mummy's. It's a bore, but he says now you've turned up it's possible you'll be getting everything instead of me, so I might have to stay a humble Brighton Belle forever!'

'What? But that's terrible, Adelaide. I would never allow that.'

'He thinks there's a way round it, if you're agreeable. Actually, now I think of it, he said he could meet you today – this morning, even – as he happens to be in Brighton.'

'Of course. I can see him whenever you like.'

'Good. I'll telephone his office now and find out where he is.' She smiled. 'I've always wondered, Uncle Geoffrey. Do letters take long to reach a place like Kenya?'

'About a week, I think.'

'And the same for a reply to come back?'

'I suppose so, yes.'

Adelaide buttoned up her jacket and prepared to leave.

'Have you been to Kenya yourself?'

'Yes, once. A few years ago. But I'd rather not talk about it.'

'Why? What happened?'

'Well, if you must know, there was an accident.'

He squirmed.

'Look, I accidentally shot dead the man my mother was in love with. But in my defence, he was lurking in some undergrowth wearing an old animal hide at the time – playing at Tarzan, apparently – it was entirely his own silly fault.'

With difficulty, Adelaide kept a straight face, but anyone better than Inspector Steine at reading expressions would have noticed the way her lips twitched and her eyes danced as she struggled to remain solemn.

'What a terrible story,' she squeaked, turning a laugh into a little cough.

'Mother was inconsolable, of course. She's never forgiven me. But then, when I think back, I don't think she's ever forgiven anyone for anything. Not even Virginia Woolf.' He thought about what he had said. 'Actually, I'm not sure I forgive Virginia Woolf completely either.'

Twitten was feeling better. He had not only drunk a restorative cup of tea, but also washed his face and done up his buttons. Ethically, he was very uncomfortable about accepting help from a villainess who could lock a door and pocket the key in such a sinister manner (and who, in his experience, had no qualms about murder). But pragmatism enters all our lives at some point or other, and today it was entering his.

'Now, that's better, dear,' she said, when he returned from the lavatory. 'You look much more like your usual annoying clever-clogs self.'

'Thank you very much for saying so, Mrs G.'

'So, I've been thinking about the killing of this Dupont,' she said. 'And I think your main mistake, dear, is that you've allowed *motive* to be your main concern at the expense of *method*. In short, you've neglected to think about the manner in which this particular murder was done, dear.'

'You mean, the actual throat-slitting?'

'Precisely. Throat-slitting in broad daylight, with potentially hundreds of witnesses. I mean, let's look at that list of suspects of yours.'

Twitten handed her a sheet of paper headed 'Suspects'. It said, at the top, THE BENSONS, and then underneath, in smaller letters: Frank Benson, Bruce Benson, Ma Benson. It was a very short list.

'Just all the Bensons, then,' she said.

'They've got so many reasons, Mrs G. One: Peter Dupont knew about Kenneth. Two: he was taking Deirdre away. And three: he knew about them bribing the council.'

'But you see this is what I'm talking about, dear. They might have had *reasons*, but be sensible: people like the bleeding Bensons don't go about slitting people's gizzards in public in broad daylight.'

'Don't they?'

'Of course not. They lure you up an alley at midnight and pump you full of lead. I mean, maybe occasionally they'd opt for hit-and-run, but – ' here Mrs Groynes, with head on one side, considered the running-over method ' – well, you see, speaking as a professional, running people over is messy, dear, because the daft sods often sprint off when they spot you coming; and even when you hit them bang, straight on, it's not a hundred per cent if you don't get the speed right. No, midnight up an alley, that's the best. Then shooting if you don't care who hears; stabbing or garrotting if you do. Do you see? No, I think you've got to cross off the Bensons, dear. Trust me, it wasn't them.'

Twitten reluctantly took the sheet from her. It was hard to let go of an idea he'd treasured since Day One.

'Tear it up, dear. Go on.'

Sulkily, he obeyed, and put the pieces in the metal waste-bin.

'You'll be telling me next that they didn't kill Uncle Kenneth,' he muttered, petulantly.

'Good point, dear. Nor did they.'

'Oh, come on, Mrs Groynes, you can't say they didn't kill Kenneth. I heard Deirdre tell Peter that they did! I heard it with my own ears!'

'Well, this is only a theory. But I reckon I know who was really behind that.'

'Who?'

'Terence Chambers.'

'Chambers?'

'Yes, dear. Legendary criminal and my own erstwhile – how can I put this? – *inamorato*.'

Twitten frowned. 'Why would Terence Chambers kill Deirdre's Uncle Kenneth?'

'As a warning, dear! To keep the Bensons in line. Blimey, Terry's done that sort of thing a dozen times. He'll have sent them the head, you see, as a nice little present. And then he's left the torso in the suitcase at the station covered in clues, so the whole world knows he's got the Bensons in his pocket.'

'So you think Deirdre perhaps saw the head and got the wrong end of the stick?'

Mrs Groynes nodded firmly. 'Absolutely, dear. Well done.'

This was all fascinating to Twitten. Much as he liked to work things out for himself, he was also fully prepared to rethink a case entirely if presented with new information. In fact, he enjoyed it. He just would have preferred it if the new information didn't keep coming from Mrs Palmeira 'Nemesis' Groynes.

'What's Terence Chambers's interest in the Bensons, then? Why does he want them in his pocket?'

'Well, wouldn't I like to know! I've had a man inside that club from the very start, hoping to find out.' She lowered her voice. 'There's a cellar by all accounts, dear, but so far *no one knows what goes on in it.*'

At the mention of a cellar, Twitten brightened. Peter Dupont's dossier had pointed him towards the underground polygonal room that was formerly in the grounds of Colchester House. Was it still there? Was it perhaps the cause of the drain smell? Was it to protect the unknown contents of this secret subterranean room that key people at the council were bribed in such an extravagant fashion never to investigate the drains or allow the development of Colchester House? Good heavens. This felt like a significant breakthrough.

'I can hear the cogs whirring,' said Mrs Groynes, kindly.

'Sorry, Mrs G. But this is bally exciting.'

'Well, I'm pleased to hear it.'

'Thank you.' He remembered his manners. 'This is very good of you, Mrs G.'

'Oh, you just needed a fresh eye on it, that's all. But back to the murder of Peter Dupont. There's something else telling you that the murderer didn't give a hoot about his investigation of the council stuff: after doing the deed, he put the dossier in that old holdall and left it at the railway station, full of incriminating evidence, instead of destroying it, do you see?'

'Oh, yes.'

'So I reckon you can narrow it right down, dear. By the method, this is either someone with military training, or a very, very hardened criminal. As for motive, my money's on it being personal. It was brutal and it was bleeding reckless. So I reckon it was someone who was in love with Deirdre himself and couldn't bear to see her go off with a boy – especially a weedy one. Who else was soft on her, do you know? Anyone a bit muscly?'

Twitten's eyes widened. The words 'soft on her' rang a definite bell. It was a phrase Peter had used a few times in his notebooks in relation to other men who knew Deirdre. He thought back to what he'd read.

'Well, Dickie George the singer. Dupont said he was *very* soft on her.'

'No. He was just *very soft*, poor bloke. I bet he wouldn't know one end of a shiv from another.'

'Then if memory serves there was someone called "Drumsticks Tommy".'

She laughed. 'No. Drumsticks wouldn't do it. He wouldn't dare.'

Twitten searched his memory. 'I'm sure there were more,' he said. 'I'll look again. But the thing about Deirdre, Mrs G, is that she seems to make everyone want to protect her, so although I like your theory, it doesn't narrow it down very much.'

Mrs Groynes had a little think, and then smiled. 'Well, how about this, then? If you can't work it out that way, how about a stratagem? You take that holdall back to the Left Luggage office.'

'Why?'

'Listen and I'll tell you. You take it back to Left Luggage and you get your pet *Argus* bloke to write a story saying that the mighty brains at Brighton Constabulary *blah blah* are searching high and low for the package of papers stolen from Peter Dupont *blah blah* – because they have reason to believe that the identity of Peter Dupont's murderer is indicated in those papers. You could even offer a reward. Then you stake out the Left Luggage office and wait to see who panics and collects it, dear!'

'That's jolly devious, Mrs G.'

'I know. I can't help it.'

'It pains me to say this, but you're a bally genius.'

'Oh, go on. But I bet it works, dear. Whoever collects that holdall, that's your man.'

Back at Colchester House, at eight o'clock, Captain Hoagland opened the wardrobe in his attic bedroom and found that the clothes he'd been wearing the previous day had already been hung up neatly on his behalf by a feminine hand. The discovery made him dizzy.

Sitting down on the bed, he considered the implications. It was of course a positive thing: on the basis of one night together, Palmeira was displaying considerate – even wifely – virtues. Perhaps this was her way of telling him that – this time – she wouldn't let him get away.

But the idea of her seeing inside his wardrobe seriously troubled him.

'Mrs Rogers?' he said. The housekeeper had appeared suddenly at his bedroom door, somewhat breathless, having run up four flights of stairs.

'His lordship needs you in the morning room,' she panted. 'He seems upset!'

'At once,' he said, but as he closed the wardrobe door on his suits and old uniforms, he still looked thoughtful.

'Look at this, Hoagy,' Melamine said, holding out a sheet of paper as his two trusty staff members approached. 'You can stay, Mrs Rogers,' he added, seeing her hesitate at the threshold. 'We have no secrets from you.'

'Thank you, sir,' she said, pulling a face. She was trying (in vain) to assume an expression slightly less of open-mouthed excitement, more of worried concern. Things had certainly looked up for Mrs Rogers since the arrival of Lord

Melamine. Life had never before been packed with so much incident.

'What is it, sir?' said Hoagland.

'Take a look.'

Hoagland took the paper and read it.

'Oh, no. I'm sorry, sir.'

'Yes, it's extortion.'

'Oh, *no!*' moaned Mrs Rogers in sympathy. Then, confused, 'Is that like blackmail?'

'It's just what I was fearful of,' Melamine went on. 'Someone threatening to tell that murderous pair where you are. Damn!'

Mrs Rogers's heart went out to both of them. But what could she do?

'Can you start packing things up, please, Mrs Rogers?' said Melamine. 'And, Hoagy, how soon can you have the car ready?'

'You're leaving?' said Mrs Rogers, with emotion.

'No choice, I'm afraid.'

'But I'll miss you!'

'I'm sorry.'

'I've been here on my own all these years! I thought you might stay – at least until the house was pulled down! That's why I hoped they'd agree to it.'

'I know. I'm sorry. But I can't think of anything else we can do, not now. Captain Hoagland, can *you* think of anything?'

'Do think, Captain Hoagland,' urged Mrs Rogers.

'Well,' said Hoagland, thoughtfully. 'I suppose I could telephone Palmeira. I know it sounds ridiculous, but in a situation like this she might know exactly what to do.'

Steine's meeting with Adelaide's solicitor turned out to be very brisk and straightforward. After a telephone call to arrange things, they met at the Windsor Hotel in Russell Place, just a few doors away from the Maison du Wax. The solicitor said he'd met another client there the night before and was glad to see Steine at such short notice as he was planning to catch the Victoria train in half an hour, so he hoped Miss Vine had explained everything thoroughly already.

'This will only take a few moments, actually,' the man said. He had a bright and businesslike manner. 'Now, did you remember to bring a copy of your will as I asked you?'

Steine handed it over for inspection.

'And you don't mind my keeping this for a few days?'

Steine frowned. 'Oh. Is that necessary?'

The solicitor shrugged. 'Not at all, Inspector, if you'd rather not. But I assumed you were here because you wanted to help Miss Vine, and not cause further delay. If I can press on straight away, and avoid chancery – well, you know how preferable that would be!'

He laughed, as if Steine would know precisely what he was talking about. Steine, mystified, laughed too.

'Then of course you must take it,' he said. 'But look after it. That's the only copy.'

The solicitor placed Steine's will in a briefcase. Then he consulted the clock on the wall. He was evidently worried about that train. He stood up. Steine politely stood up too.

'Is that it? Didn't you want me to sign something?'

'Of course, I nearly forgot.'

The solicitor withdrew a couple of legal-looking documents from his bag.

'I must say, Inspector, this must all be a lovely surprise for you. Miss Vine is such a charming girl. To tell you the truth, I'm quite smitten.'

He riffled through the documents to find the relevant pages.

'So if you would just sign *here* and *here*, I'll witness your signature and take my leave.'

Steine obeyed. He was very conscious of the time.

'I hope you've got your ticket already?' he said, as the solicitor quickly scrawled his name.

'Thank you, I have.'

The man took a quick look at the signatures and bundled the documents back into his briefcase, then offered his hand for shaking. And before Steine could utter the word goodbye, he had grabbed his hat and raincoat and bolted for the door.

Twitten sat in Ben Oliver's office at the *Argus*, waiting for news. He was very agitated. Just a couple of hours ago, he had been seriously wondering whether Dupont's murderer would get away with it (not to mention bawling like a baby on Mrs Groynes's shoulder). But now things were moving quickly. If the *Argus* editor agreed to it, this afternoon's paper would 'splash' the story of the missing dossier. By the time the Left Luggage office closed tonight, the culprit might be known.

Other stuff was speeding up too. It had been a packed morning – and it was still not eleven o'clock!

First: there had been a telephone call from Angélique at the Maison du Wax saying that Inspector Steine's wax model was unexpectedly ready ahead of schedule and was such an *absolument* triumph that they would like to invite the inspector for a private viewing this very afternoon. (Twitten considered explaining that '*absolument*' was an adverb, but decided against it.)

Then: Dupont's aunt in Eastbourne had replied to Twitten's letter, claiming to have information possibly relevant to the case. (Twitten resolved to make a visit to her as soon as possible, once the stake-out operation was over.)

Then: just as Mrs Groynes was about to explain her intimate connection to Colchester House, she'd been interrupted by a distressing phone call from someone she addressed as 'Hoagy' – presumably Captain Hoagland, the valet who had been so helpful to Dupont. Was he the 'PH' of the handkerchief?

'I can't lose you again, Hoagy,' she had said, rather melodramatically. 'I'll help you, whatever it takes.' (Twitten felt he was missing a big personal story here, but what with other matters pressing, it would have to wait.)

And on top of all this: Phyllis had asked for Twitten to call on her at the Belles' digs, because she'd remembered something about the day of the murder. (Twitten wondered why she couldn't bally well tell him on the telephone, but was too polite to say so. He had no idea that Phyllis had found him very attractive, and wanted an excuse to see him in person again.)

All of these urgent matters Twitten had left behind to race to the *Argus* office before half-past ten with the phoney news-story idea.

'We can do it!'

Ben Oliver flung open the door. He was very excited, too. 'The editor's main objection was that Inspector Steine ought to be the person sanctioning this, so I said if it went well, you'd be happy to give Inspector Steine the entire credit. You don't mind, do you? If we keep your name out of it?'

'Not at all. I think that's bally clever. It might even save me my job.'

'Good. So, if all goes to plan, and nothing bigger comes up, the story of the missing dossier will be the splash in the three o'clock edition. We'll have our best long-lens snapper positioned in the news-stand opposite the Left Luggage office from the minute the paper hits the streets, to take the incriminating picture when Mr X comes out with that bag.'

'Right.'

'Old Ted reckons he can manage not to give the game away.'

'Good.'

'You might have to wait out of sight, so Mr X doesn't spot the uniform.'

'Right.'

'Or indeed that very noticeable helmet.'

'Of course, yes.'

'And I'll pretend to be buying fruit. I'll get a good view from there.'

'Excellent.'

'Might you need a few other policemen to help with the actual arrest?'

'Well, I don't think I can ask for any without authorisation so we might have to manage between us. After all, I've got handcuffs, and a whistle … ' He trailed off.

Oliver seemed puzzled by Twitten's flat tones. 'Aren't you excited, Constable Twitten?'

'Well, I am, yes. Gosh, yes.' He grimaced. 'But, you see, Mr Oliver, there are any number of ways in which this could spell the end of my police career, and I'm only twenty-two. So I can't quite give way to outright excitement right now.'

'Oh, nonsense. They'll promote you after this.'

'On top of which, there's something else.'

'What?'

'You might not understand.'

'Try me.'

'It's this ruse. All this clever *flushing out*. It feels a bit like cheating.'

'Cheating? When it will mean flushing out a brutal murderer?'

'Yes. I know it's silly, but it feels underhanded to me. I'd so much rather have worked out in the proper way who the murderer bally well was, and then gone and arrested him!'

Ten

After two weeks of continuous sunshine, a promising day had turned misty. In a hundred boarding houses, landladies at breakfast-time had served salty fried bacon to hungry guests and cheerfully delivered the news that a cool sea fret was descending over the town; it was predicted to linger all day.

'I'd take a warm cardigan with me, if I were you,' the landladies had advised, briskly. 'And a mac.'

By nine o'clock, the view from every chilly window was the same: a blank of white, with the odd blob of washed-out colour. In most places, you could barely see to the other side of the road.

'Can we perhaps stay indoors this morning, Mrs Holdsworth?' a brave paying guest might have ventured to ask, shivering in anticipation of the cheerless day ahead. 'We could read our paperbacks quietly in our room.'

'You can come back at half-past four, Mr Chappell, same as always,' was the accommodating reply. 'Personally, I always go to the pictures when I want to keep warm.'

Mrs Groynes might never have heard of the pathetic fallacy, but she certainly recognised the way the weather had altered in the course of a few hours in direct accordance with her mood. At six-thirty this morning, she had left Colchester House with her heart fluttering in her chest and with other less mentionable parts of her body positively a-buzz with joy. At that time, the early sun had glistened on the flat, green-ish water of the sea, and the light breeze whipping inland seemed to whisper 'Yes!' and 'Isn't it good to be alive?' (And also, 'Palmeira Groynes, can you believe what just happened?') At the station, she had all but solved the Dupont murder case for young Clever Clogs Twitten, she'd been in such a generous and up-beat mood.

But now, as she made her way back to see Captain Hoagland, the sunshine was blotted out. He was in danger! What if she were losing him again? Could she bear it? The day was no longer saying 'Yes!': it was saying 'Are you kidding?' and 'What were you thinking?' and 'Well, that didn't last long, did it?' Some unknown person had written to Lord Melamine, threatening that Hoagy's whereabouts would be communicated to Joseph Marriott *within the day*.

'You came, Mrs Groynes,' said Lord Melamine, as he opened the door to her. 'I must apologise. We are in uproar, I'm afraid.'

Behind him in the hall was evidence of packing. Maids were scurrying about, under the sober direction of Mrs Rogers, who appeared to have been crying.

'Where's Hoagy?' said Mrs Groynes. 'Is he all right?'

'He's gone to fetch the car.'

'I can't believe this is happening. It's so bleeding sudden.'

'I agree.'

She felt sorry for Lord Melamine. He looked quite bewildered.

'Where will you go?' she said.

He pulled a face. He had no plan.

'Not Tristan da Cunha again, I hope?' she said, trying to lighten the mood. 'It would hardly be fair to those ostriches.'

Lord Melamine smiled bravely. 'No, not Tristan again. But I hear that Tierra del Fuego is extremely pleasant at this time of year!'

He showed her into the morning room, to wait for Captain Hoagland. On Melamine's desk was the letter. She wasted no time snatching it up. It became quickly apparent that Hoagland had not shared with her its entire contents. It was in fact an offer *not* to inform Joseph Marriott of Hoagland's whereabouts, in exchange for a payment of thirty thousand pounds in untraceable notes, to be left in a designated spot at a designated time.

When she saw the amount, she gasped. But then perhaps the sender knew that Hoagland was the treasured employee of a generous marquess with umpteen ancestral homes and a very large stash of gold bars.

'You shouldn't have seen that, Palmeira. Give it to me.'

It was Hoagy. He looked ashen. 'Please,' he said. 'Give it to me and I'll destroy it.'

'No.'

'Give it to me.'

'Look, Hoagy. I can't lose you again.'

'Well, you can't really come where I'm going, I'm afraid.'

It was an uncharacteristically blunt thing to say, which made her all the more worried for him as he threw himself into a chair beside the window. The view behind him – usually of blue sky and twinkling sea (not to mention the hustle and bustle of hard-working pimps and pickpockets) – was today nothing but white. Mrs Groynes sat down, too. She was so anxious about Hoagland's dismal state of mind that she struggled to breathe. What had he meant by *you can't really come where I'm going*?

'Look, Palmeira. I can see you're upset, but I have no words of comfort. I've been thinking about this confounded situation, and I've made up my mind. His lordship doesn't know it yet, but I have decided not to run away. Not again.'

'What do you mean? You've got to save yourself.'

'No. His lordship's too good a man to abandon me, so I can't tell him— ah. Oh, *blast*.'

Lord Melamine, they both suddenly realised, was standing in the doorway.

'Tell me what, Hoagy?'

'I'm so sorry, sir. I've packed up everything for you, and there's a van coming soon to take most of the things to Albemarle Street. The gold and so on. But as for me—'

'Does the vehicle have a reinforced floor, dear?' interjected Mrs Groynes. She couldn't help herself. She had visions of all the gold falling through and getting left in a heap on the north-bound carriageway of the London Road.

'It does, thank you, Palmeira,' Hoagland replied, with a pained expression.

'Sorry, Hoagy. You were saying something important to his lordship.'

'Yes,' he sighed. 'Yes, I was. The thing is, sir, I'm afraid you'll think me very ungrateful after all these years together, and I can't thank you enough for your kindness, but I just can't run away any more.'

'Of course you can,' insisted Lord M. He sounded stricken. 'You *have* to do this, Hoagy.'

'No. No, I really don't.' He shook his head. 'It's hard for either of you, I think, to understand quite how little I care for this life, sir. I know we're not supposed to dwell on that blasted war – '

'Oh, Hoagy,' breathed Mrs Groynes.

' – it's considered bad form, and I agree with that. We should put it behind us. But for some of us, there's just no choice. When you've diced with death day after day; when you feel you've all but died a thousand times already; when you've seen people – friends – sordidly blown to pieces … '

Mrs Groynes's eyes filled with tears. He reached over to pat her hand.

'I am so pleased that we found each other again, at least, Palmeira.'

She bit her lip. 'I love you, Hoagy. I always did.'

Hoagland sighed and looked away, shaking his head. Much as she willed him to do it, he couldn't bring himself to say that he loved her too. She knew why. It was because she had hurt him too badly in that Lyons Corner House of yore, over that damned congealing fried-egg-on-toast.

'I think we could have been happy once,' was as far as he would go. 'But I'm tired of it all, you see. I wish I'd never crawled out of that blasted unfinished house. I wish I'd never survived Borough High Street!'

'You often mention Borough High Street,' said Mrs Rogers, gently (she'd been listening quietly from the doorway). 'What happened there?'

Captain Hoagland's face contorted at the memory. Lord Melamine answered for him. 'It was a bomb in January 1941, Mrs Rogers. A bomb with – what was it – two fuses, Hoagy?'

Captain Hoagland sighed. 'Yes, sir. A seventeen *and* a fifty. Three men were killed as the device was raised by rope and pulley.'

'You hadn't defused it first, then?' said Mrs Rogers, puzzled.

Hoagland hung his head.

'As I understand it, this one wasn't ticking, Mrs Rogers,' said Lord M. 'And it had been in the ground for five days, which they believed at that time made it safe. But afterwards they said moving the bomb must have restarted the clock. Is that right, Hoagy?'

'Yes, sir. The men were raising it. All I knew was a blinding flash, and then I was thrown twenty feet against a wall. I was in hospital – in God knows how many hospitals – for a long while afterwards. I had a long time to think about what had happened.'

'It wasn't your fault,' whispered Mrs Groynes.

'But it was, my dear. There is simply no escape from that. It really was my fault. And if the time has come for me to pay for it, then *let it come*. That's what I say. *Let it come.*'

A knock at the front door made them all jump. Hoagland stood.

'That will be the van, sir. I'll tell them to come to the side entrance.'

Lord Melamine, Mrs Rogers and Mrs Groynes all exchanged looks. Their expressions were as blank and forlorn as the day outside. Hoagland, by contrast, seemed glad to have said his piece.

But he evidently hadn't changed his mind about facing Marriott. As he was leaving the room, he bent close to Lord Melamine and whispered, 'Ask Palmeira to stop clutching that note, would you, sir? Honestly, no one can do anything. There's absolutely nothing to be done.'

———

Back at the station, Twitten came face to face with Inspector Steine for the first time in about a week. It was quite a shock. He had just popped back to collect the holdall. It was like running into someone you assumed was dead.

'Gosh, sir. Good morning, sir. It's you.'

'Of course it's me. Where is everybody?' said Steine. 'Where's Mrs Groynes? I was hoping for a cup of tea.'

'I don't know, sir. She was here earlier.'

Twitten glanced at the holdall on the desk, next to the dossier. He was torn. Did he want to explain what was going on? No, he really didn't want to do that. But on the other hand, did he have a duty to explain it?

Luckily, there was something else he could say for the time being.

'Ooh, I have important news for you, sir,' he said. 'The Maison du Wax would like you to go and see your model this afternoon. They say their Inspector Steine figurine is a jolly triumph, sir. Although I have to say that Monsieur Tussard might not be the sternest judge of his own work, sir, even though he's probably only pretending to be blind.'

Twitten stood awkwardly. He was hoping Steine would say 'Well, carry on' – but something seemed to be stopping him. He was evidently in a pensive frame of mind.

'How good are you at making tea?' said the inspector, waving at the accoutrements in Mrs Groynes's corner of the office.

'Bally awful, sir. But I could pop downstairs and ask for instructions, if you like.'

'No, that's all right.'

Steine pulled out Brunswick's chair and sat in it, and waved to Twitten to sit down too. As he sat down at his own desk, he quickly moved the dossier and the holdall to the floor.

'So how's the delusion going?'

'Sorry, sir?'

'Oh, come on, Twitten. You know what I'm talking about. Do you still believe against all the evidence of your own eyes and ears that our uneducated cockney charwoman is an artful criminal? On a scale of one to ten?'

Twitten frowned. He couldn't help remembering that the whole *Argus* operation was the brainchild of Mrs G. And what was it Sergeant Brunswick had said? *You've got to get over this nonsense about Mrs Groynes. It will ruin your career if you don't.* On the other hand, honesty should always prevail.

'I'm afraid it's still ten, sir.'

Steine sighed a weary sigh. 'Oh, well. And how's the what-do-you-call-it – the *case*?'

'I have reason to believe we'll have cracked it by the end of the day, sir.'

'Oh, good. Good old Brunswick.'

This wasn't the time to tell Steine how useless his sergeant had been. Instead, Twitten decided to face the music regarding the *Argus* story. 'Sir, I have to tell you something. I'm afraid that *without your permission*, sir, I am using a slightly unconventional subterfuge to flush out the murderer—'

But Steine wasn't listening. 'Do you realise, Twitten, that if it weren't for that poor boy's death, I might never have met my niece, Miss Vine?'

Such an abrupt change of subject was slightly bewildering.

'Oh.' Twitten searched for something platitudinous to say. 'Well, I expect she'd have found her way to you sooner or later, sir.'

At this, Steine seemed satisfied, so it showed particularly bad judgement on Twitten's part to press on by saying, 'Sir, are you absolutely certain that Miss Vine *is* your niece?'

Steine eyed him steadily. 'Yes, thank you, Twitten. I am perfectly certain.'

'You don't think a little caution … ?'

'As it happens I met with her solicitor just this morning.'

'What, already?' Twitten could not disguise his alarm. 'Oh, cripes, sir!'

'What on earth do you mean?'

Twitten thought quickly. 'Nothing, sir.'

'You said *cripes*.'

'Did I?'

'Yes, you did. It was highly un-policemanlike.'

'Then I'm very sorry, sir. But I do hope you didn't sign anything, that's all!'

Steine frowned. 'Not that it's any of your business, Constable, but our meeting concerned matters of inheritance that are highly complicated. I have been informed that it was inconvenient for Miss Vine's prospects when I turned up in her life, so I needed to do the decent thing and – well, in fact, sign a few papers, yes. As I say, it's very complicated but at the same time beautifully simple.'

Twitten bit his lip. 'I'm sure it is, sir. And – and I apologise again for saying "cripes". It was both unprofessional and a tiny bit blasphemous. Perhaps I should just tell you my news and then go? You see, we've planted a story in the *Argus*—'

Steine accepted the apology with a wave of his hand, but was still not interested in what Twitten had to say. 'It's really knocked me for six, all this.'

'What has? Oh, are we still talking about Miss Vine?'

'It's made me think a lot about Mother.'

'Yes, sir.'

'And … Father.'

Twitten had now tried several times to deliver his confession to Inspector Steine. It was time to try a different approach.

'Look, sir,' he said, 'can I take it that you'd rather I *didn't tell you* about my slightly unconventional method for flushing out the murderer by planting a false story in the *Argus*?'

'Absolutely right, Twitten.'

'You don't want me to tell you anything?'

'Don't tell me anything.'

'Not even that it involves planting a story in a newspaper, which might constitute entrapment and thereby compromise any potential subsequent prosecution, sir?'

'Not even that.'

Twitten jumped up. 'In that case, may I borrow a few chaps to help with the arrest, sir?'

'You may.'

That was all Twitten needed to hear. He grabbed the hold-all, and started filling it with books to make up the right weight.

'Thank you, sir,' he said, cheerfully. 'And I jolly well hope Miss Vine *is* your niece and not some beautiful confidence trickster worming her way into your affections and making you sign away your rights to some huge inheritance or other, as would be the obvious supposition, sir, to anyone not acquainted with the parties concerned.'

'What?'

'But I did see something jolly interesting about her in the dossier Peter Dupont assembled. I meant to tell you, but it slipped my mind.'

'Something about Miss Vine?'

'Yes. Dupont was present, you see, at one of the meetings concerning the formation of the Brighton Belles, and advised on a grammatical point. Apparently it was *Adelaide Vine herself* who first proposed the idea of the Brighton Belles to the council! Wasn't that clever of her, sir? Part of the proceedings was to compose a letter of thanks, inviting her to be the first-ever Brighton Belle. That's interesting, isn't it, sir? Whether she's really your niece or not, she's definitely a very fine and upstanding young lady.'

Half an hour later, at the *Argus*, men in braces were busily ferrying page proofs in and out of the editor's office; Ben Oliver was having a cup of muddy tea at his desk; Twitten was poring over the copy Ben had written.

'This is perfect,' he said. 'Not a word untrue. It just omits to say that we know where the bag is, and have already digested its contents. It's very clever, Mr Oliver. And I particularly appreciate the way you've pluralised me as "the tireless men of the Brighton Constabulary".'

'Yes, I thought you'd like that.'

The telephone rang on Oliver's desk. The call was for Twitten.

'It's me, son,' said a familiar voice.

'Sergeant Brunswick?' Twitten felt both relief and utter fury. 'Where on earth have you been, sir?'

'Where have *I* been? Where the flaming heck have *you* been? I've telephoned you at the station a dozen times! I finally got the inspector just now, and he suggested you might be at the *Argus*. What the flip are you doing there?'

'Why didn't you just come to the station to report once in a while, sir?'

'Why didn't I just come to the *police station*? Because I'm undercover!'

'I have needed your bally help, sir!'

'Look, it's been frustrating for me too, Twitten. But as I am trying to explain—'

'Why couldn't you just change out of the disguise, sir? It's only a quiff and a pair of shoes!'

'Because I don't want the Bensons to suspect anything.'

'Well, if you'd communicated with me *at all*, I could have told you that the Bensons already do suspect you, sir.'

'What? Oh, no.'

'Yes, sir. But luckily they think you work for Terence Chambers.'

'*What?*'

'And, of course, they're working for him in some capacity themselves. It's likely that he killed Uncle Kenneth to keep them in line.'

Ben Oliver, who was pretending not to listen, doodled the word 'Chambers' on a piece of paper, added a series of exclamation marks and drew a circle round it. This did not escape Twitten.

'Look, I can't really speak here, sir,' he said. 'People might overhear. Can we meet?'

'All right. How about the wax museum? Twenty minutes. In the horrors bit. But who the heck told you that the Bensons think I work for Terence Chambers? And who told you Chambers killed Kenneth Benson?'

'I'm afraid I can't say, sir.'

Brunswick's money was running out, but Twitten shouted over the beeps, 'But I'm jolly glad to hear your voice, sir!'

The Brighton Belles had less to do when the weather turned misty like this. There was no point promenading in your smart uniforms and little pillbox hats when no one could see you coming. But the council had provided them with a small, gaily painted caravan near the entrance to the West Pier, to which members of the public could come with their enquiries. At ten-thirty a.m. Adelaide and Phyllis had already been on duty for two hours, and had so far directed one person to the post office, and another to the nearest set of public lavatories. Neither enquiry had, disappointingly, necessitated speaking in a language other than plain English.

'Phyllis, didn't you say you had some information for the police?' Adelaide said, suddenly.

'It's something I remembered from the day of the murder. I don't suppose it's important, but that sweet young constable did ask us to think about it.'

Adelaide narrowed her eyes and said, teasingly, 'And you'd like any excuse to see him again, am I right?'

'Addy, don't say that!' Phyllis reddened. (She couldn't deny it.)

'Well, I'm going in to see Uncle Geoffrey this afternoon. Why don't you come with me?'

'All right.'

'About three o'clock?'

'That's perfect.'

Meanwhile, Mrs Groynes and Lord Melamine sat together in the morning room of Colchester House. Hoagland was downstairs with the tearful Mrs Rogers, supervising removals.

'Look, this note,' Mrs Groynes whispered. 'It might not be as bad as we think. Hoagy is assuming the sender knows where Marriott is, knows all about what happened. Perhaps it's all baloney, though.'

'I'm afraid it might not be, my dear. Captain Hoagland didn't want to alarm you, but he spotted the woman the other day. Here in Brighton. The woman Vivienne. He was in J. Sainsbury's buying bacon and he spotted her in the mirror behind the counter.'

'Oh, no.'

'So it's likely that Marriott is nearby.'

'Why do you think they've asked for so much money? It's a ridiculous amount.'

'I expect, like everyone, they think I am rolling in cash! But in fact I'm not. I could certainly raise the sum – and I certainly *would*, to help Hoagy. He's one in a million. But within the day? Impossible. These people want the money in just a few hours' time. What does the note say again?'

From downstairs, they could hear the side door closing, and Captain Hoagland locking it from the inside. He would be back with them soon.

'It says to leave the readies in a suitcase in the alley at the back here by half-past two. Look, Melamine, just between us, what if I could get the money together?'

He laughed. 'Oh, my Lord, what a suggestion! I appreciate that you care for Captain Hoagland, but what are you going to do? Rob a bank?'

———

The *Argus* published a morning edition, but most people waited for the afternoon before they bought one. On a misty, nasty day like today, the sellers on the street corners had to work harder at shouting the headlines. The seller on the corner of Grenville Street was a man named Phil, who over the years had perfected his shout so that the original message, 'Get your *Evening Argus*', was now abbreviated to a singsong: 'GIT-your-own-ARSE!' In the early editions today the main story was about the upcoming beauty contest at the Black Rock swimming pool, to be judged by comedian Arthur Askey. 'Git your lully gels! Git your own arse! I thank you!'

Members of the Black Cat band passed this man every day, and all of them bought their papers from him. It was part of their cover, to show interest in local news. Only Tommy Drumsticks was a genuine avid reader of the paper. He had a particular interest in the disappearance of Humbug Hastings; since the killing of Dickie George, he had bought virtually every edition, hoping for follow-up news.

The assault had been a terrible thing – swift and brutal. Drumsticks had witnessed it himself, being in the crowd at the time, watching the humbug demonstration, as always. The shock when Dickie appeared behind Hastings's back, like an apparition! The way he stood there, blinking against the dazzling light of day, and then held out an accusing hand, as if to say, 'You! Drumsticks! Why did you do this to me?' And then – struck down, dead.

It was Dickie's own fault, of course. He had been about to help the girl get away.

I had to do something, Drumsticks told himself. *I had to stop her going away with that silly boy.*

He bought a paper from Phil, and riffled through it. There was nothing on Hastings. He glanced across the road to the rock shop, closed until further notice. The large roll of striped, malleable humbug mixture that had been abandoned by the master sweet-maker (when Hastings, seeing what he had done, dropped everything and fled the building), had quickly subsided and spread across the table, forming long drips and puddles on the floor. While other people called for the police, Drumsticks had stood there watching as the mixture sank and hardened, thinking it the saddest sight he had ever seen in his life.

As midday struck, many things were happening simultaneously (as they generally are). At the *Argus*, page proofs of the story were being checked by printers. At the railway station, Ben Oliver was briefing Ted. At the wax museum, Brunswick (minus quiff) was lurking behind an ill-lit and dusty display of the Princes in the Tower being strangled by professional murderers whose faces had (at a guess) originally been modelled to represent Henry Irving and Ellen Terry. In the fog, Henry Hastings hid, shivering, behind a pillar underneath the West Pier. At Colchester House, Captain Hoagland was securing shutters and patting Mrs Rogers on the shoulder. And at the police station, Mrs Groynes was unlocking her secret cupboard in the office, with the intention of removing cash to the value of thirty thousand pounds.

The telephone rang. It was Dupont's bothersome aunt, calling from Eastbourne. Could she please leave a message for Constable Twitten? It might have a bearing on poor Peter's death. With a sigh, Mrs Groynes picked up a pencil and asked her to proceed.

The meeting between Brunswick and Twitten was a trifle one-sided, when considered from the exchange-of-information point of view. Besides seeing Mrs Groynes enjoying a kiss with an unknown man in Grenville Street yesterday afternoon, Brunswick had virtually nothing to report. He had heard Frank Benson shout in a threatening manner at a few staff members, but by and large the fabulous vantage point he was supposed to have gained by being onstage at the Black Cat every night had benefited their investigations very little. He hadn't even known that Deirdre had run away. On the plus side, he was getting more solos than ever – but from the warning look in Twitten's eye, Brunswick thought this might not be the right time to dwell on his moments of transcendent performance.

'Look, sir. There is one thing you could do for me,' said Twitten. 'Dupont gave Deirdre one of those record-your-own-voice discs; he mentions in his notebooks that he wishes he'd done it better, but he was feeling scared; he was sure he was being followed. Now, what Mrs Groynes thinks—'

He stopped himself. What a slip!

'Sorry, what *I* think, rather, is that the killer is someone who was "soft" on Deirdre – jealous because Peter Dupont was taking her away. And it's my hope that this record might tell us something. Do you think you could search for it, sir? In Deirdre's room? It's possible she took it with her, of course; but it's also possible that she wouldn't know its significance, you see.'

As he meekly took these orders from Twitten (and saw the state he was in), the sergeant realised for the first time how totally and dismally worthless he had been to the investigation. He experienced a wave of shame. Leaving the whole case in the hands of a raw twenty-two-year-old constable? What had he been thinking?

'You've done very well, son,' he said, generously.

'Really, sir? That's very kind of you but I'm afraid I can't agree. I feel the whole thing has been completely out of my grasp! I had a complete breakdown this morning in the office. Mrs Groynes was very kind.'

'Well, good. I'm glad to hear you're getting on better with her. I suppose the inspector hasn't been much help?'

'Oh, he's too bally obsessed with the idea of Adelaide Vine being his niece.'

'What? Why should he think that?'

'Because—' Twitten paused. 'We really don't have time, sir.'

'Look, I can pull out of the Black Cat, son, if you like. It's not fair.'

'No. I think we've got enough chaps now for the stake-out at the railway station this afternoon. Do try to find that record, though, sir. I sometimes feel as if the identity of this killer is being shouted and shouted at me, but I just can't hear the name!'

———

An hour later, at the *Argus* office, the page proof containing Oliver's story was given its last reading in the newsroom, then a messenger boy carried it down the corridor towards the rackety, smelly realm of the compositors, known as the stone. Oliver and Twitten followed the boy until he reached the thick leather flaps that marked the transition from journalism to hot metal: there they stopped and watched the lad shoulder his way through. The page had gone to press. It could not be changed now. Within the hour the first copies would hit the streets of Brighton, and be read by thousands of people. But the gamble was that one man – one unknown murdering man, either a hardened criminal, or a man with commando-type training – would read the story, panic, and head for the railway station with his Left Luggage ticket clutched in his sweaty hand.

Twitten and Oliver went straight to Brighton Station. The 'chaps' Twitten had recruited were allocated their positions. The hands on the big station clock showed ten-past-one. But if you looked at them intently enough (as Twitten did), you could watch the minute slowly pass.

Captain Hoagland had a lot to say about Palmeira coming up with the money for the extortionists, but the main thing he said was an angry 'no'.

Meanwhile the main thing Lord Melamine said was an astonished, 'But I thought you had a job as a charwoman!'

'It's a long story, dear,' said Mrs G. 'I've got the money, that's the main thing.'

Together, they all looked at the wheelable trunk she had just breathlessly arrived with.

'But where … ?'

'Just don't ask. And don't tell that housekeeper of yours, either, for gawd's sake. You've let her get much too close, Lord M; you've both told her far too much about yourselves. Hasn't it occurred to you that she might have written that letter?'

'What, *Mrs Rogers*?' laughed Hoagland.

'Look, let me do this, Hoagy. I want to. I have to.'

'But you don't, my dear,' he argued, calmly. 'That's where you're wrong. You seem to be under some illusion that you owe me something, but it wasn't your fault I fell in with those awful people. It had nothing to do with you. It wasn't your fault that I failed to notice a bomb near London Bridge had started ticking again either.'

'We haven't got time for this, my darling,' she said. 'The money needs to be put in position, and soon.'

Hoagland shook his head.

'If you won't take it, I'll bleeding well go and put the money there myself.' She indicated the trunk that had, interestingly, been recently used for a very similar purpose – when the thirty thousand had been removed from the basement of a bank in North Street.

'No, you won't.'

'Just watch me.'

She started lugging it towards the stairs to the side door.

'Oh, please take it from her, Hoagy,' said Melamine. 'I don't quite understand what's going on here, but surely we should never knowingly let a woman put herself in the way of danger?'

Captain Hoagland shot her an accusing look.

'This really offends me, Palmeira,' he said, coolly.

'Oh, just take it,' said Melamine. 'Please.'

And so Captain Hoagland, furious, disappeared down the staircase, heaving the trunk behind him.

'I'll help,' called Melamine. Then he turned to Mrs Groynes and said, 'You wait there, promise me?'

'I promise.'

Mrs Groynes watched them both struggle with the trunk to the bottom of the short flight of stairs, where they opened the door and went outside.

'Take care, Hoagy!' she called. 'Please take care!'

And then she heard a car engine start, and two car doors slam, and a jubilant cry of 'We did it!' as the car drove quickly off.

———

Brunswick had rarely been inside the Black Cat during daylight hours, but Ma Benson accepted his story that he needed to get something from the dressing room; believing him to be an employee of Terence Chambers, she felt she'd better not stand in his way.

'The boys are out, Kevin,' she said. 'We've – we've had a bit of trouble. My daughter Deirdre seems to have run away.'

'So I heard,' said Brunswick. It was very strange to realise that Ma Benson was partly afraid of him. It was also very strange to look at her and see a woman worried out of her mind. She was puffing away on her churchwarden pipe like nobody's business.

'Look, Kevin. It's not you, is it, that took Deirdre? Do you know where she is?'

'No, I'm sorry. But I'll gladly help you find her.'

'Tell me what you're looking for.'

'A record,' he said. A few minutes ago, the idea of telling Ma Benson why he was here would have been unthinkable. But now it just seemed the quickest way to achieve results.

'Come with me,' she said, and led him up to Deirdre's bedroom. On the way, he explained that the record had been made by young Peter Dupont in the Voice-o-Graph on the Palace Pier.

'Really? In one of those machines?' She pulled a face. 'You'd think *Brighton Rock* would have put paid to those completely, wouldn't you?'

'I know,' laughed Brunswick. 'That's what I said.'

In the Lilley & Skinner shoebox under the bed, there it was.

'We'd better play it,' said Ma Benson. And downstairs to the club they went, record in hand.

———

At ten to three, Tommy Drumsticks bought the *Argus* and read the story about the missing dossier. So did Henry Hastings and Frank Benson, along with hundreds of holiday-makers and railway passengers alighting from the trains. From Twitten's hiding place behind the W. H. Smith bookstall, he watched as the paper dispersed in a hundred directions. It was like a News Cinema 'Look at Life' on how the newspaper industry worked. He signalled to Ben Oliver, who was leaning against the fruit stall, pretending to peel an orange. They grinned at each other. This really was thrilling. Every time a new person went into the Left Luggage office, they held their breath. Twitten had a moment of confusion when he thought he saw Mrs Groynes going in – but then he decided it must have been his own tiredness tricking him, as the woman didn't come out again.

Everyone had been briefed about the holdall. The moment they saw the man emerge with it, they were to pounce. More papers flowed from the news-stand in the station.

'Git yor own arse!' yelled vendors from street corners all over town. 'Git yor own arse!'

People were reading it in deck-chairs, in the library, in pubs, in Luigi's ice-cream parlour and at the police station. On their way to see Inspector Steine, Phyllis and Adelaide bought a copy, which made them quicken their step.

Brunswick and Ma Benson were listening together to Peter Dupont's record in the bar-room of the Black Cat. They were both in tears.

'What a sweet boy!' Ma Benson sobbed.

'He does sound very nice, yes!' sniffed Brunswick. 'And so scared!'

They had listened as Peter said how much he loved Deirdre and how he was anxious about whether he was old enough to cope with everything that was happening: the outrageous bribing of the council officials not to investigate problems with the drains (Ma Benson looked a bit worried that he knew about that), and prising Deirdre away from her scary relations (Ma Benson looked shifty). But then, when he started talking about how he'd been threatened and nearly run over, Ma Benson looked simply confused – and then Peter spotted the man in the crowd watching them both as he made the record.

There's a man watching us now, Deirdre, even as I'm saying this. He's been following us about. He's wearing dark glasses and a doorman's uniform with medals on, like you see on the men opening the door for people at the Grand and the Metropole. And he's a bit bent over. I keep thinking, it can't be Captain Hoagland, can it? But he walks like Captain Hoagland, he's got the same limp. But now the light's flashing and I have to stop—

'So who's this Hoagland?' said Ma. But Brunswick was already heading for the door.

'I have to be somewhere, I'm afraid,' he called back. 'But thank you.'

———

At the police station, Adelaide and Phyllis, clutching their *Argus*, ran up the stairs to Uncle Geoffrey's office.

'Phyllis has remembered something, Uncle Geoffrey,' panted Adelaide, as they burst in. 'Is your Constable Twitten here? She needs to tell him something.'

'Could she tell me instead?'

Phyllis, leaning against the wall while she got her breath back, was clearly disappointed to be dealing with the monkey instead of the organ-grinder.

'We thought Constable Twitten was in charge of the case,' explained Adelaide, confused.

'Look, young lady,' said Steine, 'if you've got information—'

'It was when we were going down the steps from the promenade!' panted Phyllis. 'A man pushed past me, and I didn't think anything of it at the time. It was a man in a doorman's uniform, and he had a very distinctive limp!'

———

At the railway station, Twitten watched as two businessmen, a secretary, a conscripted soldier and a limping hotel doorman entered the Left Luggage office together in a group. He had been in position for less than an hour but was already finding the tension unbearable. A dozen questions passed through his mind. Might the murderer not come in person? Might he send the doorman from his hotel? Might it be a woman, after all? The only thing they had to go on was the holdall. *Wait for that holdall! Wait for the holdall!*

And then Sergeant Brunswick appeared in view, evidently puffed out from running, and looking round for Twitten.

'Over here!' he called.

'It's someone called Hoagland,' panted Brunswick. 'The man who followed Dupont.'

'But why would Captain Hoagland—?'

Twitten never got to finish his question. From the Left Luggage office came the sound of a kerfuffle: raised voices, then a bang and a scream. The swing doors burst open with several women running out, shouting, 'A gun! A gun!' – among them the woman who reminded Twitten of Mrs Groynes. Staff and passengers on the concourse scattered and hid, and there was a further bang from outside the station, followed by more screams.

Immediately, all the chaps on lookout abandoned their positions and ran to the Left Luggage office where they found poor old Ted, pointing down to an unmoving figure on the ground. It was dressed as a doorman, and in its deathly grip was the canvas holdall. It was Captain Philip Hoagland, formerly of the 35th Bomb Disposal Company. And he was dead.

Eleven

Of all the *ersatz* musicians in the Black Cat band, it was the chap playing alto sax who was nearest to the end of his tether. John Bamford was his name, and he was the man from Interpol – an organisation which, thanks to a great deal of unfortunate disinformation spread by irresponsible post-war screenwriters, stood high in the popular imagination as the coolest of all the law-enforcement agencies of the world, not excluding MI5.

So here he was – this keen, fit young man licensed to carry a weapon in special circumstances; protected by diplomatic immunity in the event of excessive parking fines; capable of taking Monaco's tightest hairpin corners at *thirty-two* miles per hour; two clear points above average at downhill alpine skiing while carrying a hunting rifle – here he was, this veritable 007 of a man, playing a lame arrangement of 'My Blue Heaven' every night for a dance floor full of drunken, left-footed, over-dressed businessmen in a sordid little seaside town, in a venue reeking of Old Spice.

Unlike his more realistic fellow Interpol recruits, Bamford had never quite accepted the limitations of the job – which was why he had done the Monaco-bends and downhill skiing stuff on his own time without telling anyone. He had passed through the stolid Interpol training process in Paris – with its emphasis on conscientious desk-work, and a reliable, up-to-date knowledge of obscure extradition agreements – and he had done well. But still he harboured fantasies of chasing international playboy jewel thieves across the rooftops of Kowloon, or preventing the assassination of rich South American polo players in Gstaad.

So when the chance arose to help the Metropolitan Police in their investigations of the notorious Terence Chambers – whose suspected activities had started to extend to art theft in Madrid – Bamford was quick to say yes, imagining that the assignment held at least the potential for glamour.

'We have reason to believe that Chambers is using the Black Cat night club in Brighton as a front for criminal activity,' he was told at his briefing.

'I see, sir.'

'A considerable amount of money is paid to the Benson family for their co-operation, but it is unclear how far the Bensons are privy to the activity itself; very possibly they know nothing. The main things you need to know are these: *first*, at least one man has been killed on the orders of Terence Chambers for threatening to uncover the activity; *second*, officials have been systematically bribed so that the activity can continue undisturbed; *third*, Chambers is bound to have an inside man at the Black Cat, so trust no one; *fourth*, the Brighton Constabulary are utterly, shockingly obtuse, so expect no help there; *fifth*, we have absolutely no idea what the activity is, not a clue. All we know is that it happens *underground*.'

'Could it be a headquarters for the forging of high-denomination bank-notes, sir?'

'It could be, Bamford. According to information supplied by our British friends, a character known locally as Dave the Forger is often seen in the vicinity, but this could be mere coincidence. He is known to be a regular customer of a sweet shop on the corner.'

Bamford winced. 'Dave the Forger' was not a promising name for the sort of charming master-criminal he was prepared to engage with. He preferred something like 'Scaramouche'. The mention of the sweet shop on the corner didn't help much either.

'Perhaps it's a hoard of illicitly procured treasure, sir? Heaps of diamonds, gold and so on? The proceeds of the London Airport robbery? The stolen Goyas, perhaps?'

'I have to confess I lean towards the Aladdin's Cave theory, myself. It's very attractive. And it's true that the money from the London Airport robbery has never been traced. But not every criminal is in the Raffles mould, Bamford, as I've had reason to remind you before when we were discussing the illegal trade in bananas.'

'What if it's a torture chamber for disposing of enemies, sir?'

'As I say, we rule out no possibilities.'

'With the walls coated with blood—'

'Yes, yes. Let's not get carried away, Bamford. My advice would be, remember the motto of Interpol at all times.'

'Yes, sir.'

'Which is?'

A sigh. 'Connecting police for a safer world, sir.'

And so Bamford had joined the Black Cat band, where he had acquitted himself well – all the while entirely unaware he was playing alongside one man from MI5, one from Scotland Yard and a further one from the Brighton Constabulary; also one man who reported to a charwoman at the police station, and another (tickling the ivories) who had a couple of years ago murdered and sawn up Kenneth Benson for poking his nose in where it wasn't wanted.

'Watch and wait, Bamford,' they told him, each time he petulantly filed an uneventful report. But in his frustration, Bamford had started to haunt the club during the daylight hours – letting himself in through a door from the Maison du Wax. And this was how, on the afternoon that had seen Brighton disappear under a blanket of damp fog (and also Captain Hoagland shot dead at the railway station while in the act of retrieving an incriminating canvas bag), Bamford was present in the Black Cat, and heard the recorded voice of Peter Dupont, which suddenly – with an ear-splitting preliminary feedback shriek from a stylus making contact with wavy vinyl – boomed through the silence of the darkened, empty club.

Bamford, despite his training, jumped in the air.

Deirdre, I love you, said the voice.

'Oh my God!' gasped Bamford, clutching his chest.

Ma Benson had already heard the record once. Its contents had inexplicably sent trumpet-player Kevin racing out of the club. Now she was playing the record for a second time, on the gramophone inside her private office, with the door closed – forgetting that the gramophone was wired to powerful speakers outside, with the volume adjusted for night-time conditions, when it needed to be heard above the hubbub of a boisterous, well-oiled crowd.

I love you, Deirdre, and I wish I weren't so frightened. You are looking at me now with such a loving expression, and it makes me – oh, it makes me want so much to protect you.

'Peter?' whispered a voice behind Bamford. He swung round. It was Deirdre, the Benson girl. She looked weird and ethereal – but then, she always did. In contrast to most men, Bamford found this pallid, help-me quality in her quite annoying. It was as if she stood permanently under a glowing spotlight and was being filmed through gauze. At this moment, as her pale, anguished face loomed from the shadows, she was more ghostly than ever. It made him impatient.

'Deirdre, where have you been? People have been worried,' he said, reaching out to her.

But she didn't reply. She was swaying, with her eyes closed, humming 'The Man That Got Away' in a distracted fashion over the disembodied voice of her dead boyfriend. From beyond the grave, Peter was telling her that there was a man watching them: a man in a doorman's uniform.

'No, seriously, Deirdre. Look at me. Where have you been?'

'Down there,' she said, dreamily. She pointed to an open trapdoor at the front of the stage, where the piano stool normally sat. Why had he never noticed it? Surely not just because Gerry-on-the-ivories always sat on top of it?

'I've been down there,' the girl repeated, pitifully.

'What's down there, Deirdre?'

'Heads,' she said. 'Hundreds and hundreds of heads.'

———

In Inspector Steine's defence, the people who had set out to defraud him of his inheritance (and kill him in a faked accident at the Maison du Wax) were among the best in the business. They were a talented team of magsmen who had met in wartime and had now worked together for fifteen years. Collectively and individually, they were imbued with all the qualities required for the 'long con': they were thorough, hard-working, patient, attentive to detail and unhesitatingly ruthless.

One of the many mistakes the police had made in investigating (and prosecuting) the infamous unfinished-house scam in 1949 was to imagine that such an operation could be carried out by just two people, i.e. Joseph Marriott (Wall-Eye Joe) and Vivienne Alexander (The Skirt). It should have occurred to them that successfully gaining the trust of one's victims necessarily involves a small network of ostensibly independent 'convincers': in the case of the unfinished house, you would need, at least, a second man to back up the story about the enormous sum required for the unfinished building work; and ideally, also a second female person – a young girl, perhaps, with luxuriant brown pigtails – to accompany each fated woman in the car on their visit to the country. ('This is so exciting, Mrs Phillips! I can't wait to see if they've finished my room!')

Wall-Eye had been particularly proud of his pigtailed convincer. If awards were ever given in the world of cons, his schoolgirl would win 'Best Innovation'. Who would hesitate to get into a con-man's car with their life savings if an enthusiastic thirteen-year-old dressed in a gym slip and boater was already bouncing around inside?

No, Wall-Eye and The Skirt rarely worked alone. In their considerable experience, most cons required two or three men working efficiently together, along with Vivienne and her attractive daughter, sadly too old now to play the schoolgirl, though she was growing up to be the most accomplished of them all.

But sometimes, if the plans were neatly contiguous (as they had turned out to be in Brighton), they could split into teams. With Wall-Eye, the longer and more complex the con, the better he liked it, and the better he played. Thus, 'Angélique' and 'Monsieur Tussard' had been in place at the Maison du

Wax for more than four months (the real Angélique and her father had been smartly kidnapped and eliminated; the woman working at the ticket office was allowed to live, as she was half-blind and had never known the 'real' Tussards very well anyway). Meanwhile, the establishing of the Brighton Belles had been proposed a full year in advance (there were backup ideas if the council didn't go for it). What Wall-Eye loved about his job was this combination of deliberate long-term planning and fast reflexes: as when, out of the blue ('I've written to Mother in Kenya'), a London solicitor needed to be impersonated at just a half-hour's notice, and the whole scheme brought forward by a week.

Thus, by the time Inspector Steine was due to enter the Maison du Wax on the afternoon of his planned assassination, nothing would have been left to chance. He and Adelaide would be escorted into the so-called modelling room in the basement by Angélique and shown fascinating processes involving molten wax and naked flames – one of which would be casually dropped on to a pile of paraffin-soaked rags by Adelaide just before the only door to the room was shut and secured by her on the outside, and the building evacuated. Nothing would be explained to him. He would die believing that the whole thing was an unfortunate accident in a dry old building full of shockingly flammable materials, which, thinking about it, there really ought to be a law about.

And when his pathetic cries for help went unheard, he would resign himself to death never knowing that his estranged grandfather in Dorset had died a year ago, leaving a considerable fortune; and also never knowing that he had in turn just been tricked into bequeathing the whole lot to a young woman with eyes shaped like almonds, who was no relation to him whatsoever. By the time the flames were noticed by passers-by (and the fortuitous fog would delay this), his cold-blooded murderers would be clear of Brighton, driving up the London Road. Just before the turning to Hassocks, they would find waiting for them, in a designated lay-by, two other vehicles conveying not only their associates but also a fortune in gold bars and thirty thousand pounds in untraceable notes. After which, the entire happy crew would proceed London-wards in convoy.

How fortunate, then, that something interfered with their plans. How fortunate that the station charlady had smelled a rat when first informed about 'Miss so-called Adelaide so-called Vine', and taken the trouble to read the first chapters of Steine's memoir, and make enquiries concerning the true fate of the inspector's sister. Just a few hours ago, Mrs Groynes had intended to tell Twitten all about her initial findings. But she had been interrupted: events at Colchester House had understandably hijacked her attention; and since then, even by her own standards, she had been exceptionally busy.

It was only when she had returned to the police station, hung up her coat, donned her patterned overall, lit a calming cigarette and locked her revolver away (still warm and missing two bullets) on a shelf in the weapons-and-loot-stashing cupboard, that she realised Inspector Steine was missing.

'Afternoon, dear! Cup of tea?' she said, opening his office door. And then, seeing his abandoned desk, 'Oh, bleeding hell, not already?'

On Twitten's desk was a note from Steine.

Twitten – the girl Phyllis was here. She said that she saw a DOORMAN at the scene of the crime. A doorman with a LIMP. He appeared to be in a hurry.

Does this help? Aren't there limping doormen everywhere in this town? And aren't they always in a hurry? I'm sure I see a dozen every day, lurching along the pavements, performing their many errands. So in my opinion, if the murderer assumed this disguise, it wasn't very clever of him.

But the girl was very keen that you should know, so now you do.

And now for the real news. My wax model is ready; my niece Adelaide and I are to be given a 'preview' this afternoon ahead of the official unveiling. Please meet us there if possible at 4 p.m.

By the way, Twitten, perhaps later you will explain to me more fully the tactic you mentioned about placing a false story in the evening paper to entrap the murderer of Peter Dupont. I've been thinking about this, and I believe I should have forbidden it, so if it's not too late TAKE NO FURTHER ACTION UNTIL WE HAVE DISCUSSED THIS.

And can you remind me where Brunswick is, please? Adelaide keeps asking me what you're all investigating and also WHERE MRS GROYNES IS (!!) but I can never remember.

Mrs Groynes grimly stubbed out the cigarette, and unlocked the cupboard again. She reloaded the two empty chambers of the gun, put it in her handbag, patted her hair and reached her coat down again from the coat stand. What a day. But before she left, she picked up the telephone receiver and asked to be put through to the Metropole, where she gave the number for the penthouse suite.

'Tony,' she said, calmly. 'You wouldn't be a diamond for me, would you, love?'

———

Twitten, when he later pieced all the events of the day together, calculated that at the moment Mrs Groynes was calling Diamond Tony, and Deirdre was making her dramatic reappearance in the Black Cat, he was sprinting towards a car in the station approach – a car around which a small crowd of agitated onlookers had gathered.

The most notable features of this open-topped car (whose engine was still running) were the elaborate family crest painted on the driver's door, a large wheelable trunk on the back seat and the corpse of Lord Melamine slumped at the wheel. On the passenger seat beside him was a copy of the *Argus*, with the story of the missing dossier prominent on its front page. It was soaked – like everything else in the car – in blood.

'Oh, crikey! Oh, flipping, flipping crikey!' yelled Twitten – in an unprofessional outburst that he later publicly apologised for. (He even, in his understandable anguish, struck the side of the car with the flat of his hand, which caused the crowd to make disapproving 'tsk' noises.)

Oliver and Sergeant Brunswick caught up with him – Brunswick still panting heavily from the run uphill to the station.

'Oh, no!' said Oliver. 'Is this man dead, too? Who is he?'

'Blimey, Twitten!' panted Brunswick, accusingly. 'What have you done now?'

'I don't understand,' wailed Twitten.

'Who is it?' asked people in the crowd, jostling for position.

It was at this point – when Brunswick informed the public that there was nothing to see; and they replied hotly that of course there was something to see, they had already seen it, thank you very much, they'd seen a man with his brains blown out – that things threatened to turn ugly.

'Look, just stand *back*!' Brunswick said, repeatedly. 'I am asking you nicely. Stand *back*! And stop mentioning the flaming brains!'

And in the end, with the help of some railway employees blowing whistles and waving flags in people's faces, the sergeant got his way, and the crowd reluctantly dispersed – but not without grumblings and narky parting shots in which the defiant word 'brains' was audible, prominently and often.

When the crowd had gone, Twitten leaned into the vehicle and switched off the engine. He felt bewildered, terrible. Meanwhile Oliver's face had drained of colour.

'Did we do this, Constable? Are we responsible?' he said, quietly. 'Who is he?'

'I'm not sure,' said Twitten.

'Well, I am,' said Brunswick. 'I saw him sitting here with the engine running as I arrived to tell you about Hoagland. It's the bloke I followed to Colchester House the other day. It's Wall-Eye Joe, I'd bet my life on it.'

'Wall-Eye Joe?' repeated Oliver.

'Famous con man,' explained Brunswick. 'Joseph Marriott. Notorious case a few years back. Acquitted.'

'What did he do?'

'Look, please, both of you,' said Twitten, 'I think we're getting ahead of ourselves. I'm still trying to imagine why Captain Hoagland would have murdered Peter Dupont.'

'So how does Wall-Eye Joe fit in, then?' said Brunswick, confused.

'Look, I don't think he does, sir!' Twitten took a deep breath. 'Captain Hoagland worked for Lord Melamine. I have it on very good authority that this poor man was not Wall-Eye Joe but Lord Melamine – as you would know, sir, if you hadn't abandoned the investigation at the very start to devote valuable police time to playing the flipping trumpet!'

Brunswick pulled a face, and shrugged. 'All right,' he said. 'So you're saying this *isn't* Wall-Eye Joe?'

'Yes!'

All the time, Twitten's mind was racing – and its destination, every time, was sickeningly the same: it was always Mrs Groynes.

'No one but us knew about the Left Luggage stake-out,' said Oliver, reasonably. *No, they didn't, except of course for Mrs Groynes, who gave me the idea in the first place.*

'It's no one local who's done this, son,' said Brunswick. 'We don't have villains in this town who shoot people in the head.' *No, except for Mrs Groynes, who shot dead a theatre critic in the stalls of the Theatre Royal in precisely the same manner just last month, but no one would believe me.*

It was clear enough. Whoever had shot Captain Hoagland had evidently shot Lord Melamine as well – presumably for the same reason – and disappeared into the fog. The only upside was that the unknown assassin hadn't also shot Sergeant Brunswick in the leg for good measure, as had so often been the case in the past.

But why would Mrs Groynes have done it? Didn't she have feelings for Captain Hoagland? Hadn't Twitten heard her say on the telephone, 'I can't lose you again, Hoagy. I'll help you, whatever it takes'? In his own pocket was the handkerchief she had lent him earlier in the day: the one with the initials 'PH' embroidered in the corner.

Ambulances and police vehicles were arriving.

'I was only trying to catch the man who killed Dupont,' Twitten said quietly to Brunswick. 'I didn't intend all this. Not two more brutal murders in a public place! It was supposed to be a glorious arrest, not a bloodbath.'

Brunswick put a hand on his shoulder. 'You've got nothing to reproach yourself for, I'm sure, son. And I'm not saying this *is* Wall-Eye Joe, because it makes you angry for some reason;

but if it *was* Wall-Eye Joe, son – just for the sake of argument – we both know he flaming well deserved it.'

Twitten didn't have the strength to argue. 'Yes, sir,' he said.

'But for now, son, we need to pull ourselves together and get on. We have to report what's happened. We need to tell Inspector Steine.'

———

'Well, I have to admit, I don't feel very happy about this little private expedition of ours, my dear,' said Steine. Having parted from Phyllis outside the police station, he and Adelaide were now making their way along the eerily shrouded seafront towards Russell Place and the Maison du Wax. It was not an easy stroll. Due to the prevailing conditions, they had to keep dodging other pedestrians who periodically loomed into view at unusually short notice, and Steine was tired of saying, 'Excuse me', and 'I do beg your pardon', and 'No, no, my fault entirely'.

'Really, Uncle Geoffrey? I didn't realise. I thought you'd be pleased.'

'Well, I am, of course. But it's a shame none of my colleagues were free to come along. And a shame about this awful sea fret, too, of course. I feel quite chilled by it – chilled and damp. Don't you?'

'Won't they come to the official unveiling next week, Uncle Geoffrey? Your colleagues?'

'Yes, of course they will. You're right. Yes, yes. But seeing it like this in advance of everyone else seems wrong.'

'Well, if you ask me, this chance is a godsend, Uncle Geoffrey. What if the waxwork isn't very good? It would be better to know now. Between you and me, as a Brighton Belle

I'm afraid I've always had to be quite diplomatic about the standard of the modelling at the Maison du Wax. After all, it does cost tuppence to go in, and we have our good name to protect!'

Steine smiled, nervously. There was evidently something on his mind, something he needed to share with her. And it wasn't about waxworks or tuppenny entrance fees.

'Look, Adelaide,' he said. He stopped walking. 'Sorry!' he said to a man who immediately crashed into him.

'Yes, Uncle Geoffrey? I hope there's nothing wrong?'

'Look, my dear. Come over here, out of the way.'

He led her to the sea-green iron railings. Below, they could faintly hear the sound of lapping waves and shifting shingle, and a few echoing shouts from children obscured from view. It amazed Inspector Steine sometimes, how many obstacles to enjoying himself the British holiday-maker was prepared to contend with.

'Look, something has come to my attention, that's all, regarding the formation of the Brighton Belles.'

This sounded serious.

'What is it, Uncle?' Steine observed the faintest of sea breezes lifting Adelaide Vine's beautiful chestnut hair. The almond-shaped eyes were wide.

'Well, it might be nothing,' he said, 'but I need to ask you about it, because I – well, because I'm a policeman, you see; and when something comes to my attention like this, I have to act. I have no choice. Duty and instinct come together to create what you might describe as an unstoppable force.'

'You're worrying me, Uncle.'

'Look, it's this. I remember you told me, while we were on the train to London, that you were the last recruit to hear about the formation of the Brighton Belles.'

'Yes. That's right.'

Adelaide smiled – innocently, expectantly. A more observant person than Inspector Steine would have noticed that she kept casting her eyes away from his face and up to the right.

'Well, the thing that has come to my attention is that it was *you* – Miss Adelaide Vine – who came up with the idea for the Belles in the first place. My constable has seen the minutes of a council meeting last year in which your proposal was discussed. He told me because he assumed I would be proud.'

Adelaide blinked a few times as she took this in. 'So?' she said.

'So there's a discrepancy, my dear. You didn't tell me the whole truth of the matter, and I'm sorry to say it pains me.'

Adelaide's eyes quickly looked right, looked left, then right again (as if preparing to cross the road), and then she gushed, 'Oh, Uncle Geoffrey, there's no discrepancy at all!'

'Yes, there is. I just explained it.'

'No. I mean, I *did* propose the scheme to the council, that's true.'

'I see. But why didn't you mention that?'

'Because I also proposed it in Bournemouth, and Southend, and – oh, ever so many other places. Blackpool, even! And no one replied. That's what happened, you see: no one replied, so I thought no one had picked up my clever idea.'

'You must have been very disappointed.'

'I was. But then, you see – this is what happened. And it absolutely explains the apparent "discrepancy", as you call it. At the last minute, you see, I found out that Brighton had been advertising for Belles, and had all but filled the posts, without telling me. They'd been advertising, you see, not realising that the young woman who'd written to them in the first place actually wanted to be a Brighton Belle herself. Which is how I came to apply at the last minute, just as I told you. So both things are true: I did propose the scheme, and I also nearly missed out on joining it! Do you see? It makes me so unhappy that you doubted me, dear uncle. You have to believe that finding you has been the best thing that's ever happened to me!'

A tear rolled down Adelaide's lovely cheek. But truthfully, she looked more relieved than reproachful.

'You do believe me?' she said.

'Of course. Why wouldn't I?'

'Thank God. I mean, oh, good.'

'And I apologise I put you through all that unpleasantness, my dear,' said Steine, happy to resume their walk along the front. 'I'm sorry I was so relentless in my questioning. I suppose I just can't help being a policeman on whom nothing is lost.'

'I forgive you, Uncle. And I'm sorry I didn't tell you the whole story before. The thing is, since we discovered we're related, I've been so desperate for you to like me, you see, and it's off-putting to men sometimes when they find out a young woman is ambitious.'

'Surely not,' said Steine, reassuringly, but on consideration it gave him pause. The notion of an ambitious young woman was indeed *very* off-putting. Even hearing the words 'ambitious' and 'woman' together in the same sentence made his nose wrinkle.

'Well, I've discovered that it's quite common for men to be horrified by the idea of a woman wanting any sort of influence in the world,' continued Adelaide, as she put her arm through his. 'Between you and me, Phyllis told her father last week that she wants to join the police, and he shouted at her that she could do so over his dead body. She was very upset.'

'Oh, dear,' Steine said, supportively. But then – he couldn't help himself – he started smiling at the idea of the lovely Phyllis joining the police, and broke into hearty laughter. Adelaide was shocked.

'It's not funny, Uncle Geoffrey. There's no reason why she shouldn't—'

'But it *is* funny, my dear. It's hilarious. Oh, my goodness, imagine *Phyllis* hitting someone over the head with a truncheon; imagine her being able to repeat the relevant clause of the Offences Against the Person Act of 1861! Oh, Adelaide, my dear, be reasonable. How can she ever be a policeman? Phyllis is a woman!'

———

Anyone who has seen the film *House of Wax* starring Vincent Price will remember its outstanding fire scene. On its release in 1953, the impressionable Sergeant Brunswick had gone back to the Savoy in East Street to watch the whole programme through again several times, just to re-experience that fire – even though the famous three-dimensional effects elsewhere in the film started to make him feel a bit sick on repeated exposure. The images of those wax figures melting in a Technicolor inferno were so sensational that Brunswick had even tried to persuade Inspector Steine that he 'hadn't lived' until he had seen them. But Steine had counter-argued, reasonably enough, that here he was: living proof that the reverse of this cliché was true.

In the film, wax-artiste Price tries to save his 'children', as he whimsically calls them: he wrestles with his dastardly (and strictly one-dimensional) business partner as the flames spread, while bits of the building crash ominously down. But his unhurried efforts with shallow pans of water are predictably ineffectual, given the abysmal flammability of the dry old building and everything it contains. As the fire builds quickly to a roar, Price's treasured mannequins – his Joan of Arc, his Marie Antoinette, all his historic tableaux – catch flame, scorch, blacken and melt. Faces dissolve and drip to the floor; eyeballs tumble out; heads fall off; Joan of Arc's body curls forward pathetically as she collapses into ash. And in the end, overcome by the heat and fumes, Price himself drops to the floor, and is left for dead (except that he survives, and is next seen a few years later as an embittered wraith with disfiguring scars, who purloins dead bodies and coats them in wax to achieve suspiciously lifelike results).

At the Maison du Wax in Russell Place, a similarly gruesome scene had been due to take place. Old 'Monsieur Tussard' and his daughter 'Angélique' had spent the morning of the great day liberally slopping paraffin over Max Miller, Tinkerbell and William Ewart Gladstone. And while this was technically an act of vandalism, it's fair to say that it was also an act of mercy. Adelaide herself had arranged the heap of oily rags in the modelling room, before heading out to complete the last phase of the oh-so-perfect plan.

So it was a considerable surprise for Adelaide Vine when the door to the Maison du Wax was opened, not by a silly, wittering, *faux*-French Angélique in a frilly gown, begging her guests to 'On-tray! On-tray!', but by the more solid figure of the charwoman from the police station, holding a mop and with her hair tied up in a turban. She was looking a tiny bit tired (which was understandable in the circumstances). In every direction, the floor was wet.

'Mrs Groynes, what on earth are you doing here?' asked Steine, delightedly.

'What am I doing here?' she laughed. 'What does it look like? I'm mopping, dear! What are *you* doing here, that's what I'd like to know!'

Steine and Adelaide stepped into the museum. And if Mrs Groynes savoured the moment, no one could blame her. It was beautiful to observe the confusion on Adelaide's face. What had gone wrong? Where were her confederates? What had happened to the foolproof plan?

'We've, um – we've come to see the inspector's wax model,' Adelaide said, carefully. 'But perhaps we came at the wrong time.'

'Well, I wouldn't know about that, dear. All I know is, it seems they had a bit of a spillage with some paraffin, and I happen to know the regular cleaner here and she cried out: "Palmeira, we need you! This place could go up like a box of Brock's Fireworks on Guy Fawkes Night, and we don't want that!" So I've been here for the past little while, dear, haven't I – *cleaning things up a bit.*'

As she said the last five words, she looked straight at Adelaide and smiled, just as a tall, smartly dressed man with shiny shoes came upstairs from the area of the 'Dungeon of Horror' exhibits. He was wiping his hands on a large handkerchief, cleaning an antique gold ring before placing it on his little finger and admiring the effect. Adelaide blenched. She knew that ring. It was her mother's.

'That'll be Tony,' said Mrs Groynes cheerfully, looking round at him. 'He came to help. All done down there, love? That was fast work. You're a diamond.'

'My pleasure, Mrs G,' he said, tipping his hat to the others. 'Is this the lovely young lady you told me about?'

'It is, yes. By lucky chance.'

'I should take a good look,' he said. 'For future reference.'

Steine swelled with pride to hear his niece referred to as a lovely young lady, although he wasn't entirely happy about the intense way Tony stared at her, as if committing her face to memory.

'This is Miss Adelaide Vine,' Steine said. 'And you are … ?'

'Tony. Just Tony.'

'Well, it's always nice to meet a friend of Mrs Groynes.'

'Ta,' said Tony, then leaned over to her and said in a low, conspiratorial tone – but loud enough to be heard by the others – 'I'll be off now, Mrs G. And I hope you're happy with the job. I tried to be artistic-like.'

'Cheers, Tony!' Mrs Groynes called after him, as he let himself out.

'Yes, goodbye, Tony,' added Steine, because he felt it was called for.

He grinned at Adelaide and shrugged. He had no idea what all this charmingly incomprehensible gorblimey chit-chat was about, but he knew he enjoyed being part of it. Oddly, Adelaide didn't grin back.

Mrs Groynes leaned on her mop. 'Look, I don't know about you two, but I could murder a cup of tea. Ooh, but speaking of *murder*—' She laughed at the little unintentional joke. 'Speaking of *murder*, who wants to see the fantastic new tableau downstairs in the Dungeon of Whatsits?'

Steine wrinkled his nose. 'Not particularly,' he said. 'I'd rather have the cup of tea you mentioned. What about you, my dear?'

Adelaide said nothing. She was behaving very strangely, he thought. He wondered if she was uncomfortable in the company of this honest-to-goodness cockney woman. In which case, this was something they would need to talk about. Snobbery was something he couldn't abide.

'What's the tableau meant to be?' Adelaide asked, in a small voice.

Mrs Groynes rubbed her hands in relish. 'Well, it's only a double hanging, dear. Man and a woman. A pair of criminal lovebirds.'

'Oh, my God.'

'Let's say it's Sweeney Todd and Mrs Lovett, dear, freshly executed for all them murders they done. That's it. Sweeney Todd and Mrs Lovett. Ooh, it'll make your flesh creep, dear. They look so real, it's as if they were alive just an hour ago.'

'Well, we certainly don't want to see *that*,' shuddered Steine. 'My niece and I came here for one reason only—'

But when he put out his hand to take Adelaide's arm, he found she was backing away from him, in an unaccountable state of alarm, and (suddenly) flourishing a small gun.

It was just then that Brunswick and Twitten burst through the door, having come directly from the police station.

'Sir, I got your note, sir,' said Twitten, all in one breath. 'I'm afraid I've got rather a lot to tell you about two men shot dead at the railway station which might be all my fault but crikey is that Mrs Groynes what on earth are you doing here Mrs G and where's Angélique and why is Miss Vine pointing a pearl-handled revolver at Inspector Steine?'

It was indeed a confusing scene, especially for the inspector. He'd been expecting such a placid – one might almost say static – afternoon.

'Adelaide?' he demanded. 'Now, this strange behaviour of yours has gone far enough. Where did that gun come from? Is this a joke?'

Adelaide gave him a steely look he had never seen on her face before. It left him more bewildered than ever.

'I don't want to shoot you, Inspector,' she said. 'But, believe me, I won't hesitate for a second if anyone tries to stop me leaving.'

Twitten and Brunswick exchanged glances, both knowing that they had no plan whatsoever for dealing with such a delicate situation. Should one of them attempt to snatch the gun? Steine made a small whimpering noise. It was terribly unsettling to have a gun pointed directly at you. What if it went off by mistake?

Luckily, Mrs Groynes knew what to do.

'Oh, sod this for a game of soldiers,' she huffed, and struck out at Adelaide's wrist with the handle of the mop so smartly that she dropped the gun, which fired on impact with the ground.

'Ow!' yelped Adelaide.

'Ow!' said Brunswick, falling to the floor.

'Go after her, men!' the inspector yelled, as the disarmed Adelaide fled into the open air, and disappeared into the convenient fog. Twitten, his heart pumping, obediently raced outside, saying, 'You go that way, sir!' But then he realised not only that he could hardly see the hand in front of his face, but that he was, worryingly, alone.

'Sir?' he said, anxious. 'Sergeant Brunswick, sir?'

He heard a call from the inspector. 'Come back, Twitten. It's pointless. She's gone.' And then he heard Steine add, 'And stop groaning, Brunswick, there's a good man. It's not as if it's never happened to you before.'

When Twitten re-entered the Maison du Wax, he discovered an interesting tableau. One male figure lay prone on the marble tiles, a woman beside him leaned exhausted on a mop, and another man (in uniform) was standing with his head in his hands. This last figure looked up at him.

'Would you believe it, Twitten? Sergeant Brunswick has allowed himself to be shot in the leg – *again.*'

Twelve

It was a week later, and all the violent deaths were safely in the past tense. The eventual body count didn't bear thinking about, but only two of the dead deserved to be grieved over: Peter Dupont and Dickie George. Peter had indeed been killed for being the man who bally well knew too much (but not in the way anyone had suspected); Dickie George had been a victim of sheer bad luck. If Dickie's death illustrated anything, it was the general principle that you should never sneak up on a pumped-up former member of the Special Boat Service, especially when he has easy access to heavy, pointy lumps of peppermint-flavoured confectionery.

No one will ever know precisely what Dickie George suffered during the days he was missing. All that is clear is that Tommy Drumsticks – madly possessive of Deirdre and angry because she had asked Dickie for help in getting away – coshed him and dragged him next door to the wax museum, leaving him in a basement room containing gruesome (but waxen) spare body parts. Drumsticks had gone back later to collect him and found him mysteriously missing. Why had he gone? Because in this room Dickie unfortunately spotted the real severed head of Uncle Kenneth, secretly stashed there previously by the frightened Bensons after a henchman of Terence Chambers delivered it to them. (Its miraculous state of preservation, two years after death, was thanks to a typical Chambers flourish – he'd given orders to have it specially embalmed, to make it a proper Benson family memento.)

Understandably scared for his life, Dickie must have opened a random door and found himself lost in the network of tunnels that were formerly part of the delights of the Colchester House garden – and then somehow, by awful chance, he found his way into the actual (unmaintained) sewers and up into the sweet shop. His last, croaked words were indeed, 'Help me.'

Had he been able to report for crooner duty at the Black Cat this week, however, he would have found it dark and deserted. The very day of Deirdre's reappearance, the building was closed up and the entire family left town. What Deirdre had found in the underground room (as Uncle Kenneth had found it before her, and paid the fateful price) was indeed shocking: knowledge of it marked the family as enemies of Terence Chambers in perpetuity. For years, Ma and the boys had managed not to know the secret they were protecting, and their ignorance had, in turn, protected them. So what was down there? Well, it was not – as previously supposed by everyone – a bloody torture chamber, a gothic ossuary or even a sparkling Aladdin's cave. The fact that Dave the Forger was the sole person authorised to come and go was a bit of a clue. In the underground room of the Black Cat was housed Terence Chambers's extensive and beautifully curated stamp collection.

Thus, when Deirdre had talked brokenly of 'hundreds and hundreds of heads', she had spoken truly while at the same time giving a seriously misleading impression. But, as Ma Benson reflected afterwards (while Frank, grim-faced, drove the northwards-speeding car past the small and – until recently – relatively unknown village of Gatwick), the reality of the stamp collection represented a far greater danger to them than anything they had imagined. Given how Chambers traded on his reputation for madness and violence, the sort of secret he would kill for was precisely what they had uncovered: that he was actually an ardent and lifelong philatelist specialising in stamps from Commonwealth dominions.

And was his secret safe, now? Well, the Bensons certainly weren't going to tell anyone – and, oddly, nor was John Bamford, the only member of a law-enforcement organisation present when the secret was unearthed. He wasn't going to tell anyone because he was, simply, excruciatingly embarrassed. From the law-and-order point of view, this was a tragic missed opportunity. Tell the world about (say) the entire album (in a glass-topped display case) devoted to ninepenny Australian stamps from 1910 to 1914, and Chambers would become a laughing-stock throughout the criminal fraternity. But Bamford was vain and young, and concerned far more with his own reputation; he was guided purely by the fear of becoming a laughing-stock himself. And so he returned to Interpol in Paris and he lied. He said there had been nothing in the infamous subterranean room after all, and that he resented being sent on a fool's errand, and that in future he'd prefer the desk-job option, please, with additional extradition duties, if possible.

Mrs Groynes sat with her feet up on Twitten's desk, and blew a thoughtful smoke ring. Beside her was the copy of Nancy Mitford's *Noblesse Oblige* that she had picked up at Colchester House the last time she was there – the one from which

Wall-Eye Joe had evidently learned how to sound so perfectly Non-U. Many parts of it were underlined. Looking back, she remembered how 'Lord Melamine' was forever turning the subject to lounges and radios and cruets and mirrors, and exclaiming 'Lovely to meet you!' He had evidently got it all from this annoyingly useful book.

Blimey, he'd been a clever operator, that man; she had believed in him until (almost) the very end. Whenever she happened nowadays to glance at her secret weapons-and-loot-stashing cupboard, she felt her heart stop as she remembered *actually starting to remove the cash*. Because, yes, she had been prepared to stump up thirty thousand pounds to secure Captain Hoagland's safety – until, in the nick of time, Dupont's aunt in Eastbourne had called to speak to Twitten, and blown the entire scam wide open. It wasn't going to be easy for the next few weeks, having to admit to two hundred individual informants, 'I'm sorry, you were right, he *was* Wall-Eye Joe. Yes, I know I told you he wasn't. Yes, I know I threatened to shoot the next person who told me that he was.'

By now, Twitten had called on Miss Stanford in Eastbourne himself, and was beginning to grasp what had compelled Captain Hoagland – of all people – to murder Peter Dupont. In Peter's notebooks, it merely said that when they met, they talked easily about a number of things, including the fact that Peter's father had likewise served in the Bomb Disposal service and had been killed in a blast in 1941. Peter also noted that he had shown Captain Hoagland a blurry black-and-white close-up snapshot of his father, with three other lowly sappers, taken a week or so before he died.

On his return to the office, Twitten had compared notes with Mrs G. He felt she had a right to know what he had learned. To accompany their cups of tea, they had Dundee cake, which Twitten had recently (after too little consideration) nominated as his favourite, forgetting how dry it could be. He was wondering if it was now too late to change.

'So, what Peter's aunt said, Mrs G,' he began, carefully, with his notebook open on his knee, and a slight obstruction in his throat from a sugary Dundee crumb, 'was that when Peter met Captain Hoagland, he was thrilled to meet a bomb-disposal man because his own father had been in the Engineers, and had been killed by a UXB.'

'Right, dear.'

'And he showed Captain Hoagland the picture of his father that he kept in his wallet – a group photo of four fellow sappers, all smiling. And of course Hoagland recognised everyone in the picture: one of them was actually him, and the other three had been killed in that explosion. And I suppose he was very worried, because the picture showed he was just a sapper in the Engineers, not a captain at all.'

Twitten paused, then added, 'I'm sorry. I know Hoagland was your friend. I wish you would tell me, Mrs G, about how you knew him and why you trusted him.'

So she had told him as much as she could bear to disclose – about giving him up years before because she wanted to protect him; about feeling she didn't deserve someone so *good*; about believing later that he'd been killed at the unfinished house. What she most hated to admit, however, was that she had spotted Hoagland's doorman uniform hanging in the wardrobe in his room, and had not thought anything about it. For a man of Hoagland's age, dressing as a hotel doorman in Brighton was a brilliant disguise for someone up to no good. No one looked at you. They saw the limp, perhaps, and the medals on the chest. You were just another injured veteran washed up by the war.

'No, he was never an officer,' she said. 'I checked, dear. All that stuff about his "men" calling him Hoagy. I bet it was his own captain who called him that.'

She sighed. 'Look, all you really need to know is, I thought he was a ruddy hero, dear, and I was sure he was a toff. That's what I can't get over: I believed he was above me in every way; that he was noble and selfless and *not like me*. He had it all down pat: the modesty, the selflessness, all the after-you-Claude-after-you-Cecil. He never said he loved me, you know. That was clever. Made me say I loved him, and then didn't say it back. And you wouldn't believe the show he put on, when I was begging him to let me supply the extortion money, about how when a man has seen death so many times, he greets it like an old friend – I was in bleeding tears, dear! Me! And of course Wall-Eye Joe was sobbing away too. How they stitched me up, dear – how the pair of them stitched me up. I can hardly stand to think about it. I even believed in the ostriches.'

'Ostriches?'

'Yes, dear! Bleeding ostriches!' she said, thumping the desk – and it was clear that the shame of this particular aspect of the grand deception was so very great that she could bear to elaborate no further.

'And so, just to be clear, you killed them both?'

'Well, yes.' She smiled. 'The gun's in that cupboard, as it happens. What am I like, eh? You don't get many of me for ninepence.'

'I ought to arrest you, of course.'

'I know, dear.' She reached and patted his hand. 'That's your burden.'

'You must have been very angry with them both, then?'

'Oh, don't misunderstand me, dear. I didn't kill them for the con they pulled on me.'

'No?'

'No! I would never kill just for money, dear! Or even out of wounded pride. No, once I'd realised Hoagy was the one who killed that boy, and why he'd done it, *because he was a bleeding great fraud, dear*; and once I knew for sure that his lordship *was* Wall-Eye Joe after all, and they were therefore in cahoots when they told their fantastical story about Hoagy escaping from that unfinished house, I knew what I had to do.

'I left that copy of the *Argus* in their car and then went directly to the station to see if they turned up. Because I'd decided: if they did turn up, I would kill them. If they didn't turn up, I would – for the time being, anyway – chalk it up to experience. They were welcome to a trunk full of torn-up *Police Gazette*s. I would have loved to see their faces when they opened it, but sadly it never came to that.'

'Because they did turn up at the station.'

'Yes, they did.'

'It was you who came up with that "missing dossier" plan, Mrs G. Is it hard for you to think of that? That if you hadn't come up with the scheme, Captain Hoagland would still be alive?'

'Well, that's very sensitive of you to ask, dear. Because, on the one hand, it was a good plan. But on the other, I thought it would catch some brutal, unstable idiot who was soppy about Deirdre Benson. I hardly expected it to catch the only man I ever bleeding loved.'

Twitten had never had such a grown-up conversation before. Hearing of Mrs Groynes's heartache, it was as if he had waded a small way into the sea and then suddenly found the water was up to his chest and sploshing up his nose, while his feet had lifted off the bottom. He was also, to be honest, finding the Dundee cake completely unpalatable, but sensed that this was not the right moment to mention it. But mostly, he couldn't get out of his mind the fact that, in order for Mrs Groynes to open the wardrobe in Captain Hoagland's bedroom in the morning, *she must have spent the night there.*

But still, his zeal for clarification drove him on.

'Dupont's aunt said that the main thing about this Hoagy in the war – she said he was a secret looter, Mrs G.'

'I know, dear,' said Mrs Groynes, sorrowfully. 'She told me that, too.'

'I'm sorry. She said he'd been seen stealing from evacuated buildings. He even took jewellery from bodies.'

'Yes. Well, people just had to clear out, didn't they, when there was an unexploded bomb? Abandon all their world-lies. There's a lot of scope for opportunism in wartime, dear; making hay out of other people's distress. Looting wasn't uncommon, exactly, but it still makes me sick to think of my Hoagy doing it.'

'But the main thing was, he might have engineered Peter's father's death,' said Twitten.

Mrs Groynes closed her eyes. 'That's right.'

'Peter didn't know any of this, of course – but Hoagland couldn't risk exposure just when he was engaged on such a huge job with Mr Marriott and all the others. Back in 1941, Peter's father confronted Hoagland about the looting and recorded their argument in his diary. Dupont Senior said he was going to report Hoagland; Hoagland, in turn, threatened him. And it was the last entry in the diary, because the next day Peter's father was conveniently killed in the blast at Borough High Street, while Captain Hoagland – I mean *Private* Hoagland, presumably – was injured but survived.

'The family asked for an inquiry, because onlookers at the end of the street behind the sandbags said they saw the bomb being hoisted, and Hoagland starting to run for cover *a full five seconds before the explosion*. But at the court martial, he came up with a convincing story for the whole thing, swore blind there was no ticking when he'd listened to the bomb, played up the extent of his own injuries – and got away with it. It was only afterwards that the diary was found, and the family suspected Hoagland of actually orchestrating an explosion that killed three people.'

Mrs Groynes listened to all this with a look of utter misery on her face. All the time she had loved Hoagland, he had been this callous fraud. He had never cared about her: to him she represented unfinished business, nothing more. She couldn't even take comfort from the lengths he had gone to in conning her. Clearly, the main (double) purpose of Wall-Eye's Brighton operation had been to purloin the Penrose inheritance from Inspector Steine and nick the gold from the safe in Colchester House, where the 4th Marquess ('Lord Loopy') had indeed left it twelve years ago and forgotten it. It was quite likely that relieving Palmeira Groynes of a few thousand while conveniently operating in the area was a mere afterthought.

'And to think I laughed at the inspector falling for that harmless spaghetti hoax,' she said.

'Oh, Mrs Groynes. I'm very sorry.'

'Well, that's good of you, dear,' she said, wiping a tear from her face and sniffing. 'It doesn't help, but it's good of you.'

In hospital, they had given Sergeant Brunswick his usual bed. When Twitten visited, he was surprised and gratified to find his superior officer reading *Noblesse Oblige* by Nancy Mitford.

'This is fascinating, son,' said Brunswick, proudly indicating the book. 'You ought to read it.'

'I have already, sir,' said Twitten.

'It turns out that posh people have a flaming code for recognising each other.'

'I know, sir. Do you remember we talked about mirrors the other day, and you got quite upset?'

'Mirrors? Was that because of this book? Well, I never. You should have explained it better, Twitten. I didn't understand.'

'No, sir. I rather guessed that you didn't.'

Brunswick put down the book.

'You've heard that the Bensons have scarpered, son, and that there was nothing in that underground room by the time our boys broke in? It had all been cleared out.'

'I went to look myself, actually, sir.'

'Did you? Knowing there was nothing there?'

'Well, I have to confess, I was interested just to see the room itself. Dupont's dossier led me to an account of the garden of Colchester House in the old days, you see, and I liked the description of the polygonal underground chamber, curtained in red and white and carpeted with golden sheepskins. It turned out to be just a small and oddly shaped room – but dry and well insulated, a good place for a bunker, or an archive. You could see marks on the floor where a number of items of furniture had stood, and there was an interesting smell that I found quite nostalgic.'

'What sort of smell?'

'I'm still trying to put my finger on it, but it reminded me of dark Saturday afternoons in front of the fire – Father reading a learned journal, Mother knitting, and me with my little magnifying glass and tweezers, carefully sorting my latest acquisitions from Stanley Gibbons, while the man on the wireless announced the football results. I wonder if I'll ever get to the bottom of that powerful association.'

'So you called it a wireless in your house?'

'Yes, sir. I'm afraid we did.'

Brunswick pursed his lips. He had suspected as much.

'The inspector sends his regards, by the way, sir.'

'Oh, good.'

'He's still reeling a bit, as you can imagine, from Miss Vine turning out to be *just pretending*, as he puts it. He has periods when he looks very confused, but then he says, "So it was *Captain Hoagland* who killed young Dupont, and then someone shot him in the head, so we don't need to prosecute?" And I say, "Yes, sir. It's jolly convenient, sir." And that seems to reassure him. I think the worst aspect of the whole thing for the inspector is that there won't be a waxwork model of him at the museum. He had really set his heart on that.'

———

As he walked back to the station from the hospital, it occurred to Twitten that he wasn't angry with Mrs Groynes. This was both interesting and surprising. It was like realising that a chronic pain had gone.

Standing at the clifftop railings overlooking the sea, he pondered. Had Mrs Groynes tricked him in some way? Was that why he felt differently about her? Not so long ago, he had been determined never to be alone with her in the same room, whereas nowadays, he had to confess, a tête-à-tête with Mrs G was something he positively looked forward to. The thing was, it was only in her company that he could expect a friendly and professional interest in the matters that interested him. And hadn't she, in turn, confided in him about Captain Hoagland, almost as if she regarded him as a friend?

So, while part of him wanted to scream, 'She shot two people in the head! She uses everyday baked products as a smokescreen! She's bally despicable!', another part simply didn't, and he genuinely detested the horrible con practised on her by Hoagland and Marriott. From what she had reluctantly told him, they had not only targeted her, but played a very sophisticated hand. The way Marriott had drawn attention to himself with that inept con-man business! It had been masterly. And from whom had the police first heard about the terrible con man? From Adelaide Vine, of course.

Although it pained him, Twitten was obliged to acknowledge that it was Mrs Groynes who had explained to him every single puzzling aspect of the case. *Were the two scams connected, then?* Yes, of course they were, dear. Five people in total were involved: Hoagland, Marriott, plus the third, unknown male who impersonated both Monsieur Tussard and the so-called London solicitor; then Vivienne ('Angélique') and her daughter Adelaide Vine. They had all worked together on the unfinished-house scam; all were responsible for disgusting murders in cold blood. All but one were now disposed of. *What did they hope to gain from these cons?* Mainly, an enormous amount of money. Thirty thousand in notes from Mrs Groynes; then at least a million from the Penrose estate, on the tragic 'accidental' death of Inspector Steine; plus at least fifty thousand in gold. But the Mrs Groynes ploy had presumably contained a personal element, too: Hoagland having been furious when she dumped him (mid-con) all those years before. *Did the others in the gang know about Hoagland murdering Peter Dupont to protect himself?* Probably not. He no doubt realised quite quickly that he'd made a big mistake opening up to the seemingly harmless Peter. If Adelaide Vine had known about the murder, she would hardly have encouraged Phyllis to come forward to the police with her memory of the doorman with his parcel.

But how had Adelaide known the story of Inspector Steine's parents? Because, as a juvenile accomplice in the unfinished-house scam, she had travelled in the car with the victims, chit-chatting with them to set any doubts to rest. And one of the victims was Gillian, Inspector Steine's sister. *Oh, no. That's horrible.* Yes, it is bleeding horrible. Gillian must have told the eager little girl the story of that romantic meeting in Bloomsbury; and also told her that because old Penrose would never forgive his daughter for what she'd done, one day the estate would be left to the grandchildren – meaning herself and the inspector, who as yet knew nothing about it, because of the grandfather's irrational loathing for the police. *Are you absolutely sure, Mrs G, that the inspector's sister was one of the victims?* Well, yes, dear. I checked and she went missing at just this time. She withdrew her life savings. She told friends she had found a wonderful man through a dating agency. She even mentioned the unfinished house. And when Vivienne was arrested, she was wearing a brooch with the Penrose coat of arms on it – you could see it in the news pictures of her. But, of course, no one at the time put two and two together.

Twitten sighed. Would he (or could he) have worked out everything on his own? Perhaps he could, given time. But he was beginning to think that, quick as he was, his own imagination had limits – too many of the crimes in the background to this story were virtually unimaginable to him. While Mrs G saw the world of crime in all its venal reality, his own mind

269

rebelled at the idea of people like Joseph Marriott and Captain Hoagland, who would scheme and lie like this – and actually murder fellow human beings – just for pecuniary ends. And as for the beautiful Adelaide (who had got away in the fog), she was almost the worst of the bunch. To think of that little girl riding in a car with Inspector Steine's sister, sweetly begging for more family stories – while knowing full well that when the car arrived at its destination, the nice lady would be instantly killed and her body disposed of. He couldn't get it out of his head. It made him want to cry.

Best not to explain this to Inspector Steine, Mrs G? That his sister was murdered? Absolutely. He must never know.

'And looking on the bright side, dear,' she had added, 'we can safely assume he'll never work it out for himself. He would never work it out in a million bleeding years.'

———

On Brunswick's first day back at the office, Inspector Steine burst out of his room, carrying a letter and beaming.

'Great news,' he said. 'According to this, I have inherited an estate in the West Country!'

'Blimey,' marvelled Mrs Groynes, convincingly. 'Good for you, dear.'

Brunswick and Twitten offered their congratulations.

'What a bally surprise, sir,' said Twitten – which gained a nod of approval from Mrs Groynes.

'And I don't know how this happened,' Steine continued, 'but there were some papers I signed concerning Miss Vine, and I've been a bit worried about what had happened to them, but here they are!'

He held up some legal-looking documents.

'They turned up on my desk this morning, along with my original will, which I'd lent to her solicitor. I suppose he returned them all to me.'

Twitten raised an eyebrow at Mrs Groynes. He would never dare to ask what had been done with 'Angélique' and 'Monsieur Tussard' at the wax museum by the terrifying-sounding Diamond Tony, but presumably Mrs G had retrieved these documents before their bodies were dumped off the West Pier. He didn't ask what had happened to the missing gold, either – but he felt sure he could guess the answer to that one. (Incidentally, with her excellent instinct for tying up loose ends, Mrs Groynes would also intercept the return letter from Steine's mother in Africa when it turned up a few days later. 'Whatever it says, it will only confuse him, poor thing,' she said to herself, as she dropped it in the bin.)

'Oh, my goodness, it's just occurred to me,' said Steine. 'What if that man was just pretending, too, and wasn't a real solicitor?'

'Oh, I'm sure he was,' said Mrs G, laughing. 'You've got a suspicious mind, Inspector.'

'Well, I suppose I do, that's true. It comes with the job, unfortunately!'

'But about the estate, sir?' said Twitten.

'Well, I now discover that my grandfather died around a year ago. To be honest, I hadn't expected anyone to tell me when he died, as I assumed I'd never inherit anything. He wasn't at all happy at the match my mother made, you see; and he particularly hated the fact she'd married into the police. They've been looking for my sister, because she was the first-named sole beneficiary.'

'I didn't even know you *had* a sister, dear,' said Mrs Groynes, straight-faced.

'Oh, I suppose not. I hadn't seen her since I was fourteen, I'm afraid. It was a great sadness to Mother when Gillian cut herself off from us all. Now that I think about it, someone did ask me last year whether I knew her whereabouts, and they mentioned something about her having lived in Newmarket, but they didn't say why they were looking.'

'And they found her?'

'No. Sadly, they drew a blank. That awful Miss Vine woman told me Gillian had died, of course, and now I must accept that it's probably true.'

Steine's face clouded over. Mrs Groynes and Twitten were both careful not to look at each other.

'But it seems that after such a search proves fruitless,' said Steine, brightening, 'the law allows them to turn to the next option. So they did, and the second option was me! Apparently they have a small test for me (set by Grandfather) but, assuming I pass it, I will acquire a large country house and at least a million pounds!'

———

Colchester House had been boarded up. The real Lord Melamine (at home in Herefordshire, as he had always been throughout these weeks, if anyone had bothered to check) had been contacted by the new planning committee of the council in Brighton, to check his wishes concerning its future, and he told them they had his blessing to knock it down. Lord Loopy's famous dislike for Brighton had been passed on to his eccentric son, and when he was informed that the whole site belonged to him, including the (former, now evacuated) wax museum and the (former, now evacuated) Black Cat, he said he'd be happy for them to raze the whole lot and build either a nice modern car park or a box-like conference centre, whichever was the less aesthetically in tune with the surrounding architecture.

At the railway station, Old Ted in the Left Luggage office was informed he would receive a small medal for bravery from the *Evening Argus*, which was the paper's way of acknowledging it had put him through yet another nightmare experience (and please don't sue). The ruse worked: he was thrilled to bits. A medal was really something, and the ceremony was recorded on the front page of the paper. His wife cheered up for the first time since 1939.

Meanwhile Ben Oliver (who had been anxious about his future, given how badly the operation at the station turned out) was surprised to find himself lauded as a hero by the editor, and given a pay rise. His grisly first-hand accounts of the two Mafia-style executions at the station sent circulation figures through the roof. It transpired that the more Oliver warned the people of Brighton that cold-blooded killers stalked their streets, the more they lapped it up. It was decided *not* to credit Inspector Steine with the whole idea of the 'missing dossier' story, however. Given the way things had gone, he would not have been pleased with this honour. Instead, Oliver gave the impression it had mostly been his own idea. For this, Twitten was very grateful, and a kind of friendship was forged.

'So who do you think was responsible for those shootings, Constable?' Oliver asked him one day.

'Oh, you know what I think, Mr Oliver. Mrs Groynes is usually responsible for everything.'

At which Oliver had pulled an amusing face and said, 'Ah. And one day *I and everyone else will think it too*?'

And Twitten said, 'You will, Mr Oliver. You will.'

Meanwhile, what else had happened? Henry Hastings gave himself up for the accidental killing of Dickie George, but luckily for him, no one was remotely interested, so he went back to the sweet shop to clear up the mess left by molten humbug (it involved using a pneumatic drill). A small crowd watched him do it. It turns out that people will gather to watch anything whatsoever when they're on holiday, especially when it's free.

Tommy Drumsticks, finding himself without a band to play for – and guessing correctly that Mrs Groynes was not particularly impressed by his record at the Black Cat – sensibly skipped town and got a job (briefly) backing the eminent skiffle star Lonnie Donegan.

Mr Reinhardt, in France, gave way to regrets of various kinds: for his career, for his good name, for the way he'd allowed wicked criminals to corrupt him. He also regretted that there were uncashed cheques to the value of seven thousand pounds in his safe when it was cleared out by Peter Dupont.

At the council offices, Lillian the disillusioned secretary applied for the job left open by Dupont's death. But at the interview she was told that, even if she got it, she would be paid nothing like as much as the teenaged Peter had been. She resigned.

Phyllis, disenchanted with the Brighton Belles, began the process for enrolment with the police.

Mrs Rogers received a confusingly businesslike letter from the real Lord Melamine, informing her that Colchester House was to be emptied of its contents and then demolished, and that she should vacate as soon as convenient. She never discussed those short, happy weeks at Colchester House with anyone. Thus, she never found out that the two posh men who had shared such thrilling confidences with her were actually unscrupulous villains and liars, who had met violent deaths within minutes of leaving the house. Years later, she still regarded Captain Hoagland as the nicest and most decent man she had ever met.

As for young Shorty, he was finally able to catch up with his reading. In fact, it was rather lovely. He arrived at his usual leaning-spot one morning to find a string bag tied to the lamp-post stuffed with fresh copies of the *Dandy*, *Beano*, *Topper*, *Wizard*, *Beezer* and *Chips* (which featured a dog detective). He couldn't believe it. '*Well done, love. I couldn't have managed without you*,' said an accompanying note from Mrs Groynes. He felt so proud, he thought he would burst.

———

'I've been thinking, Mrs Groynes,' said Twitten, one day when they were alone.

'About what, dear?'

'I've been thinking that I don't seem to be as angry with you as I was before.'

'Really, dear?'

'Yes. I've got used to it – that you are what you are, and that the others don't have a bally clue. I used to find it hard to grasp, for some reason, but I don't any more. I even quite enjoy it.'

'Well, well.'

'I mean, this morning, when Sergeant Brunswick came in and said that on the Palace Pier last night a large hole had been sawn in the planks just below the accounts office and their safe had gone through it, I didn't even have to look at you. I knew you'd done it. I just said, "Oh, who would do such a bally thing? I expect we'll never know", and got on with eating my lovely sugary Dundee cake.'

'I saw you, dear. Cool as a cucumber.'

'And I expect you'd been planning it for weeks, Mrs G?'

'Try years, dear.'

'Really? Well, in that case, jolly well done.'

'Thank you, dear. It means a lot. I'd thought about postponing it, but in the end I told the boys to go ahead. They'd been learning underwater safe-cracking techniques and what not; hired all the equipment. The trick, as you can imagine, was to deal with the obvious problem of the safe dropping straight to the seabed, on account of being so heavy. But you don't want to hear about my problems with anti-gravitational magnetic pull, now do you, dear?'

'No, indeed. Although a huge electromagnet was stolen not long ago from the Royal Observatory, I believe. But I expect that was a coincidence.'

She came and sat beside him.

'What I said to the lads, dear, was that I needed something to cheer me up right now. I know I don't show it, but I do have feelings, you know.'

Twitten bit his lip. He wasn't sure what he was expected to say.

'Are you perhaps still upset about Captain Hoagland, Mrs G?'

'Of course I'm still bleeding upset about Captain Hoagland!'

Twitten hesitated.

'Look, this might not be the right time to mention it, but about the Dundee cake, which is absolutely super—'

But Mrs Groynes signalled to him to stop talking. To his alarm, she went to the door and locked it. She evidently wanted another serious talk.

'Look, it's nice what you said just now, dear. About not being angry any more. But it's not enough. What I'm wondering is, have you reconsidered my offer, dear? Because I'm serious. We really could help each other out.'

'I wouldn't say I had reconsidered it, exactly.'

'I mean, I did help you, didn't I, with your Dupont thing? I don't like to blow my own trumpet, but it was me that had the idea about the "missing dossier" story that flushed out the murderer – even if I wasn't ecstatic with *who* it flushed out. It was me that explained to you that people like the Bensons don't go around slicing people's throats in broad daylight, and helped you get off the wrong track. The thing is, dear, I'm very interested in helping you; I almost can't stop myself. Crime is my life, you see, and it always has been. So what do you say?'

'What I mainly say is, could you unlock the door, please, Mrs Groynes?'

'Oh. All right.'

She did so.

'Thank you,' he said.

'And what do you say now, dear?'

'I'm thinking, Mrs Groynes. I'm thinking.'

———

The following day, a strange, hushed atmosphere greeted Sergeant Brunswick as he limped into the station with his walking stick. Beyond the door to Inspector Steine's room could be heard odd noises of furniture being moved about and moaning noises that sounded animal – rather than human – in origin.

'What's happened?' he hissed.

'We don't know,' whispered Twitten. 'But we're guessing it's bad news about the money.'

Mrs Groynes knocked softly on the door.

There was no answer. She knocked again.

'What is it?' came a small voice.

'Bit of lovely Dundee cake, dear?'

The door opened, and Steine stood before them all. He looked bug-eyed and distraught. While arguably the other people in the room had been through more than he had recently – getting shot, for example, or having their hearts broken by the only man they ever bleeding loved – this had been a terrible period for him. It had been up and down, up and down. First he had a lovely niece, but then he *didn't* have a lovely niece. Then he had a fortune, but then he *didn't* have a fortune. And to top it all, a heavy safe on the Palace Pier had apparently fallen through the boards into the sea, and the pier's owners were insisting it was a police matter, when it might equally be a case of woodworm.

Distractedly, he sat in Twitten's chair and started to drink Twitten's cup of tea. The others discreetly looked away.

'What happened, sir?' asked the sergeant, politely. 'You look flaming fed up, if you don't mind my saying so.'

Steine steadied himself.

'Look, Brunswick, I don't suppose you've heard of a book called *Noblesse Oblige*?'

'But I have, sir.'

Steine looked outraged. 'Have you?'

'Yes. I read it the other day. I found it very interesting.'

This was not the answer Steine had hoped for.

'I've read it, too, dear,' volunteered Mrs Groynes. 'In fact, I got everyone down the Princess Alice to read it, too, and blow me, we've talked of little else in the evenings these past weeks.

Phone for the fish-knives, Norman! It was a real eye-opener, that's what we all thought. Looking-glass, indeed!'

Steine groaned. 'And Twitten? Need I ask?'

'Well, I don't know what to say, sir. *Noblesse Oblige* was the book I was telling you about when we first visited the Maison du Wax. When I asked you about mirrors and so on, and you got so upset.'

Steine narrowed his eyes. 'So you're telling me you've *all* read this blasted book?'

'Seems like we have,' said Mrs Groynes. 'But as Miss Mitford would probably never find herself saying, dear, *what's that got to do with the price of fish?*'

'Well, everything, unfortunately. As you may remember, my grandfather had left one small stipulation in his will.'

'The test you mentioned?' said Twitten.

'Yes, the test I mentioned. Having read this blasted book when it was published last year, just before he died, my grandfather saw a perfect way of determining whether his socially contaminated descendants were up to snuff – by testing their vocabulary!'

'But we can all help you with that, sir,' said Twitten, delighted. 'If he wanted to check that you knew the U words and not the Non-U words, we could all help. Because, as we've already established, we've all read the book.'

'Too late, I'm afraid, Twitten. There was just one question, and it was this: did I own a cruet set?'

'Ouch,' said Brunswick.

'Oh, no!' gasped Mrs G.

'And what did you say, sir?' asked Twitten, anxiously.

'Naturally, I answered yes, thank you, I owned two cruet sets, as it happened. I had a very nice home.'

The others recoiled in horror.

'Oh, sir. I'm so sorry,' said Twitten.

'And as a consequence, I will continue to live in my nice home with my two cruet sets, and not own Penrose House with its legendary knot garden, grotto, polo ponies and extensive private beach!'

He looked so sorry for himself that they all felt sorry for him, too – but only up to a point.

'The constable did keep telling you to read that bleeding book, dear,' said Mrs Groynes. She turned to Twitten, who was trying to remonstrate with her. 'Well, you did!'

They all sat in silence for a moment – Brunswick in pain from multiple injuries; Twitten experiencing the mixed delights of being proved right; Mrs Groynes enjoying the discomfort of everyone else; and Inspector Steine wishing he had never heard of the Maison du Wax, or Adelaide Vine, or Penrose House, or (come to that) the Brighton Constabulary.

'Can anyone say anything to cheer me up?' he said, at last.

'Yes, sir,' volunteered Twitten. 'I believe I can.'

They all looked at him.

'How?' said Steine.

'Ask me about Mrs Groynes, sir. Do the question-and-response thing.'

Steine narrowed his eyes. 'This isn't a trap?' he said.

'No, sir.'

'Should I ask her to leave the room?'

'No, sir.'

'All right.' He cleared his throat. 'Constable Twitten, tell me your thoughts concerning Mrs Groynes, our lovable cockney charlady.'

'I believe she is a wicked criminal capable of cold-blooded murder, sir.'

There was a general 'tsk' and groan of disappointment from the other three, but Steine continued.

'And on a scale of one to ten, how convinced are you of this?'

Twitten took a deep breath. It was his big moment.

'Nine,' he said.

And while the others said, 'Well done, Twitten' and 'Good lad', Mrs Groynes came over and hugged him, and actually burst into tears.

Acknowledgements

Huge thanks are due again to my editor Alison Hennessey at Raven Books, and to my agent Anthony Goff at David Higham Associates. I have never felt less alone in the enterprise of writing books. Thanks also to Marigold Atkey for her eagle eye.

As with the previous book in this series, I am indebted to my own radio comedy *Inspector Steine* – but have been far from constrained by it. However, the voices of the regular radio cast who helped me create these characters will never desert me, and I will thank those clever actors for ever.

In *The Man That Got Away*, the immediate inspiration for the terrible wax museum came from a 1951 film *Penny Points to Paradise* (starring members of The Goons, before they were famous). It is a rightly obscure film, but it contains excellent location shots of Brighton's traffic-free seafront (the museum interior scenes are clearly done in a studio). It is possible that I visited Brighton's own Louis Tussaud's on King's Road in the 1970s (I definitely remember a prone Sleeping Beauty with the chest wheezily going up and down) but by the time I came to live on the coast the wax museum had long gone (it closed in 1981). The grand regency abode Colchester House is a complete invention, as are the streets to either side, but

Brighton *aficionados* are welcome to imagine it roughly on the site of the present-day Brighton Centre

The highly unpleasant 'unfinished house' scam I did not invent. It was a 'true' crime from the early 1950s that I found dramatically recreated in the B-feature series *Scotland Yard* (presented by Edgar Lustgarten). In the real case of the unfinished house, the perpetrators disposed of the body parts in barrels of tar, and sent postcards from the victims ostensibly on holiday in Switzerland. Thinking about this now, I have to admit I didn't check whether 'The Unfinished House' was a true-life case or not. The less heinous 'gold-brick scam' was certainly a reality, however: I found it described in Sir Harold Scott's very readable Penguin original about Scotland Yard first published in 1954. (He also mentions the Black Museum containing the enormous socks worn by the super-quiet burglar christened 'Flannelfoot' by the Metropolitan Police.)

Nancy Mitford's *Noblesse Oblige* was very much a talking-point of 1956–7, and I felt it was a book that any clever policeman would lap up. After writing *The Man That Got Away*, however, I watched the US series *Manhunt* (about the search for the Unabomber) and discovered that even as late as *the 1980s* the FBI had little faith in linguistic analysis as a means of identifying criminals. Yet again, I'm pleased to say, Constable Clever-Clogs Twitten was brilliantly ahead of his time.

A Note on the Author

Lynne Truss is a columnist, writer and broadcaster whose book on punctuation *Eats, Shoots & Leaves* was an international bestseller. She has written extensively for radio, and is the author of six previous novels, as well as a non-fiction account (*Get Her Off the Pitch!*) of her four years as a novice sportswriter for *The Times*. On radio, she is currently engaged in writing a continuing sequence of short stories for Radio 4 entitled *Life at Absolute Zero*. Her columns have appeared in the *Listener, The Times*, the *Sunday Telegraph* and *Saga*. She lives in Sussex and London with two dogs.

A Note on the Type

The text of this book is set Adobe Garamond. It is one of several versions of Garamond based on the designs of Claude Garamond. It is thought that Garamond based his font on Bembo, cut in 1495 by Francesco Griffo in collaboration with the Italian printer Aldus Manutius. Garamond types were first used in books printed in Paris around 1532. Many of the present-day versions of this type are based on the *Typi Academiae* of Jean Jannon cut in Sedan in 1615.

Claude Garamond was born in Paris in 1480. He learned how to cut type from his father and by the age of fifteen he was able to fashion steel punches the size of a pica with great precision. At the age of sixty he was commissioned by King Francis I to design a Greek alphabet, and for this he was given the honourable title of royal type founder. He died in 1561.